... it is good to see a publisher investing in fresh work that, although definitely contemporary in mood and content, falls four-square within the genre's traditions.
- Martin Edwards, author of the highly acclaimed Harry Devlin Mysteries

Creme de la Crime... so far have not put a foot wrong.
- Reviewing the Evidence

First published in 2007
by Crème de la Crime
P O Box 523, Chesterfield, S40 9AT

Typesetting by Yvette Warren
Cover design by Yvette Warren
Front cover image by Peter Roman

Printed and bound in Great Britain by
Cox & Wyman Ltd, Reading, Berkshire

ISBN 978-0-9551589-3-3
A CIP catalogue reference for this book is available from the British Library

www.cremedelacrime.com

About the author:
Roz Southey is a musicologist and historian, and lives in the North East of England.

My thanks …

… to Lynne Patrick and Crème de la Crime for allowing me to achieve a lifelong ambition, and to my editor, Douglas Hill, for his insightful and patient advice, and unfailing encouragement.

… to Jackie, Jenny, Laura, Anuradha and Sandra for their support during rejections and disappointments. Without their insistence, I would never have dusted off the manuscript of *Broken Harmony* and put it in the post.

… to all the staff of many libraries who over the years have hunted out old newspapers, diaries, tradesmen's accounts and music manuscripts for me, particularly the staff of Newcastle Central Library's Local Studies Department.

… and to all my family, especially my husband Chris who has listened to the same stories again and again without complaint, and brewed untold cups of Yellow Label tea …

For Chris

Wind sweeps across the fell, shivering the reeds and cotton grass at the pond's edge. The water is misty in the early morning light. Cold drills into my bones; a thin drizzle chills my face. I am talking to a dead man, trying to persuade him to give up the name of his murderer. Trying to persuade him that justice is more than private vengeance. And getting nowhere.

His spirit is as secretive as the man himself ever was. It is infuriating, especially when spirits, as everyone knows, are generally eager to tell the whole world exactly how they died.

I have never even liked the fellow. Over these past few months he has done everything he can to drive me out of the town. He has been rude to my face and disparaging behind my back. He has belittled my abilities and looked down that long nose of his as if he smelt something unpleasant every time he looked at me. Why should I care who killed him?

Because, of course, there is more at stake here than 'mere' justice. Because there has been more than one attack already, and who knows who may be the next victim? It may be me. Or someone close to me.

The cold air chills my bones. A sheen lies upon the water.

"Tell me," I say again to the spirit.

He is silent.

1
OVERTURE

The harpsichord is a reticent instrument, chiming delicately in the background of the music. For an audience (at the rehearsal in which we were engaged, for instance) the sound would be as variable as the candlelight flickering among the cobwebby roof timbers of the ancient ale-house that sheltered us, the Turk's Head. Among the violins and basses the harpsichord could no doubt be heard only as a hint of sound – a metallic ping-ping – and perhaps even that would be suggested more by the energetic movement of my hands than by any actual sound. If the instrument was heard clearly, it would be because the band had faltered or lost its place. (Which with this band happened all too frequently.)

I am not fond of playing the harpsichord. I am not a reticent man. Give me a church organ any day, filling the stone vaults with a thunder of noise.

But there were no vacancies for a church organist in the town, so I was forced to be content with my engagement in the Concerts. And I did not take kindly to sitting at the back of the band rather than in the harpsichord's usual place at the front. I had been relegated to that position by the enmity of, as the papers say, *a certain person.* So there I was, sitting in semi-darkness even in the light of midday, gazing between the bobbing figures of my excellent-hearted but musically deficient gentlemen employers and the all-too-few professional players they employed to keep them in time and tune, biting my tongue and restraining an impulse to lean forward and whisper in a few ears. (I am not a silent man, either.) The ear of Mr Ord in the second violins, for instance, who persisted in trilling every held note and looking about him with a sly smile as if for compliments. Or the ear of young Henry Wright, our only player of the tenor violin, who bit his lip in concentration as he carefully played every note just fractionally flat. No, I knew my place – though *a certain person* would allege otherwise.

As the harpsichordist to the Concerts, I was charged with ensuring that, no matter what happened among the gentlemen amateurs who sawed away at their violins, the harmony would continue. I must bring down the chords decisively so that every man could pick up his place again when he lost it. Should the violins, playing an air, collapse completely, I must play the tune – and smile when an elegant gentleman murmured, with raised eyebrows, "I didn't know the harpsichord part had that melody, Patterson." I must not say, "Only since you have given up playing it for its difficulty, sir." Not if I wanted to keep my wages.

Of course there was one gentleman who might be able to say such things. That *certain person*, the leader of the band, ought to have been using the rehearsal to say – diplomatically – certain things that needed to be said. Why did he not turn to the enthusiastic gentlemen on the cellos and murmur, as I would, that he admired them most when they played their most delicate *pianissimo*? (To put it in other words, would they please, sirs, play more quietly!). Why did he not make it clear to Mr Ord that the only player who may ornament the melody is the leader of the band?

Ladies and Gentlemen of Newcastle upon Tyne and its Environs in this year of our Lord 1735, behold our leader, our adored, exquisite, posturing leader, that damned black violin in his hand, waving his bow-stick as enthusiastically as sly Mr Ord, then plunging into a morass of passage-work of the sort that gentlemen amateurs love to gape at. Trills here, mordents there, a cascade of notes from top to bottom of the strings, a sawing away in alt like a pig squealing at slaughter. I once heard Mr Ord say admiringly that if our esteemed leader played any higher, he would be off the strings altogether. But, damn it, *what was it for*? Did such scraping engage our passions? Our pity? Our piety? Not at all. It engaged only, as it intended, our admiration.

Monsieur Henri Le Sac's playing succeeded, of course, in quietening the music lovers who had come to gossip knowledgeably over our scratchings. (Those who attended rehearsals were generally those who did not choose to mix with the common sort at concerts, or who liked to know the pieces in advance so that they could talk learnedly of them later.) In the front, Lady Anne, elegant as always despite her plainness, had naturally been silent all along; she could hardly chatter while her protégé displayed his skills. Her cousin too, by her side, had been coolly restrained throughout; she looked so bored I wondered why she had come at all. Others were more animated. The ladies Brown, coming out of duty to papa on the cello, fluttered their fans to cool their flushed and adoring faces; and Fleming the stationer, in his massive old-fashioned periwig, listened attentively to the sound of the fiddle strings he supplied at cost price. My friend Demsey at the back scowled through the entire rehearsal; he of course had had a prejudice against Le Sac and his cronies ever since that unfortunate contretemps over the newspaper advertisement.

In truth (and it is a truth that made me sigh heavily) our esteemed leader was an excellent technician. Somewhere in his youth in Switzerland, Le Sac had an careful master who trained his nimble fingers and taught him to draw an excellent tone from his violin. A pity he did not also teach him manners. Or morals.

Of course, from where I sat, I could only see his back. A dark-coated back – dark blue, I fancied. Le Sac had excellent taste in clothes and, for all his squat, stocky figure, set them off well. I sighed over that further injustice. I am not a plain man, but no matter how hard I tried I never quite seemed to be in fashion. I did not have the money for it. Le Sac's hair was dark and his own – wigs are the very devil to wear when you bob about as much as he does in performance. Occasionally, as he dipped into a phrase, I could see his profile, the sharp nose, the distant gaze, the high forehead. Some even called him handsome. *I* did not think so, but then I daresay I was prejudiced.

A final flurry of notes and we were set at liberty for a few minutes while Le Sac received the tribute of his patroness. I slipped out of the room and rattled down the back stairs into the tavern yard. The sunlight startled me – I am always so wrapt up in the music that I forget the time. An ostler led a horse clip-clop across the yard and nodded at me as I pissed against the wall. A voice behind me said: "Bloody ale. Lousy stuff."

The spirit of old Hoult, the former landlord, inhabits the scene of his death as all spirits must do. One dark night five or six years ago, Hoult crept out to add a few coins to his secret hoard and was found dead in the frost the next morning. Mrs Hoult, his unbeloved wife, went some while later to look for the hiding place, argued with the spirit of her husband (who refused to give up his treasure), and dropped down dead on almost the same spot. They bicker in death as they did in life.

I laced myself up again. "Lousy ale? I thought *you* passed the recipe on to your son."

Hoult's spirit had lodged itself temporarily in the wall by the door. "He's never had the knack, Mr Patterson, sir. Always messes things up. Why d'you think I never let him touch the business while I lived?"

His wife cackled from the lamp-bracket. "And you were better?"

Demsey clattered out to me, grabbed my coat sleeve. "Charles! That damned fellow – looked straight through me!" His round face was red with fury. "Pretended he knew nothing about it."

"About what?"

"That latest advertisement," Hoult said. He had moved to a stray shaft of sunshine on the wall and added apologetically, "One of the maids overheard you talking about it. The gossipy maid – the one that died two years back." The communication of spirits is legendary; it is said they can pass a message from one end of the town to the other before a man can draw a breath.

"Oh, shut up, Hoult!" Demsey cried. "Go and intrude on someone else's private conversation!"

Old Hoult sniffed, and the stones in the wall lost a certain sheen just as young Hoult emerged and blinked at the sunlit yard in happy complacence, as his late father did many a time before him.

"What has Le Sac to do with the advertisement?" I said tolerantly and prepared myself to pretend to listen.

"Le Sac? Not him. You have the fellow on the brain!" Demsey was beside himself. I've seen him work himself into a frenzy this way and young Hoult must have too; he was looking our way in some concern.

"Not Le Sac," Demsey repeated. "That crony of his who has the nerve to call himself a dancing master."

"Ah," I said. "Nichols." It was the same old story, the one

we have all heard a dozen times these past three years. Demsey, like the assiduous businessman he is, goes off to London every summer to learn the latest dances so he may bring them back to the eager young ladies and gentlemen of this town. Nichols, who is not so handsome nor so young and much more disapproving in his manner to his pupils, sees an opportunity to increase his meagre practice and sets in the paper an announcement, something of this sort:

We hear from London, that a certain Mr D----y, dancing master in this Town, is not to return but has set up a School in Clerkenwell, where he teaches the Sons and Daughters of Lord A---- and Lady Y----.

Some years Demsey is said to remain elsewhere (Bath last year, if I recall correctly) but the general purport of the announcement is the same. And every year Demsey must tour every rich house in the town to leave his card and say, yes, he is returned and yes, he will open School again next week.

Demsey had stopped speaking and was glowering at the stairwell. The man himself stood there, staring at us over the bridge of his nose, imitating the haughty mien of the worst kind of gentleman. He kept his distance from young Hoult, I noticed.

"Ah, Mr Light-Heels," I said, then covered my mouth as if stricken by my *faux-pas*. "Forgive me, I cannot imagine what I was thinking. Mr *Nichols*. Am I wanted? Do we begin again?"

"If you can tear yourself away from such riff-raff company," he said. He has a voice like a turkey. Young Hoult smirked in my direction.

So it was back to the shadows at the back of the band where I must know the music by rote for all the light there was to read it. Light-Heels Nichols stood where I could see his disdainful profile as he cradled his violin in his arm. Le Sac regretfully took his leave of his patroness and strode to the pile of music books at a side table. What were we to play now? Some concerto violino by Corelli, perhaps, or Geminiani? Or one of Le Sac's own works, so that he could show off his skill in the solo passages?

One thing was for certain; it would not be *my* music. I had the audacity to give him a piece for violins when I first came back from London, when I did not know him. He has not yet finished tearing it to pieces.

The wainscoting to my left acquired a sudden sheen. "You know," old Hoult said conversationally, "I never did like music. Or musicians. But I except you."

"Most generous."

"No airs about you," he said. "Never look down on folk." The room was full of murmuring; Le Sac was still searching through his books. He straightened with a face like fury. Old Hoult said, "O – ho," and disappeared.

The music, it seemed, had been stolen.

2
CONCERTO FOR SOLO HARPSICHORD
Movement I

It was midnight when I came at last to Mrs Hill's in the Fleshmarket. When I pushed into the ale-room, it was almost deserted except for a few glum miners hunched over their tankards, listening unwillingly to the raucous singing (a bawdy song I had not heard before, strophic with a distinctive Scotch snap). The spirits singing the tune were an oily patina across a table in a dark corner of the room and sounded drunk. Everyone who departs this life in an inn is drunk, except perhaps for the landlord. But I never encountered Mr Hill; he was killed, I understand, in a brawl among Scotch keelmen on the Key.

Demsey glowered from a far corner, his eyes as bright as the brass buttons on his immaculate coat. His hands cupped a full tankard; another was set beside it for me.

"Damn Light-Heels," he said as I sat down. "Five pupils, damn it, five!" He added sourly, "What kept you? The concert must have been over hours ago."

"Not what, who." I sighed. The memory was not one I wanted to dwell upon. We had filled in the gap in the concert with one of Mr Handel's overtures (a fine piece of work for once) but our esteemed leader had not been inclined to let the matter of the missing music rest. He had steered clear of accusing me directly, but had indulged in many loud comments about his 'enemies' while casting significant glances at the harpsichord. I gulped down Mrs Hill's excellent ale.

"How in heaven's name does he suppose I made off with his precious band-parts? Am I supposed to have tucked them beneath my coat-tails and smuggled them into some secret cache? I was never out of sight of half a dozen people!"

Demsey was plainly having trouble thinking. "Why?" he managed at last.

"The missing work is one of his own compositions. His favourite, he swears."

"No, no." Demsey shook his head. "Why *you*?"

"Oh, I am violently jealous of him, he supposes, and will seize every opportunity to do him down." My face had burned at that hint, as it burned now. And Le Sac's wide dark eyes had gleamed at me; he had known, oh yes, he'd known, how much I envied him his pre-eminence in the Concerts. I took up Mrs Hill's ale again. "It is not important. Le Sac will have reached home and no doubt found the books still sitting on his table. Or his apprentice will say he took them to read upon his sickbed."

"And there is another thing," Demsey said violently. "His so-called phil –philanthropy towards his apprentice makes me sick."

"You cannot condemn a man for his kindness to an injured boy."

But Demsey was right. Any sensible man would have sent the boy back to his parents until his broken arm healed and it was seen whether he would play again. Le Sac, however, made pious noises about his duty as a Christian loudly enough for everyone – everyone of consequence, at least – to hear.

Demsey banged down his ale and roared at the spirits on the other side of the room to be quiet. They did not even hesitate in their rollicking rhythms. "Le Sac – Nichols –

they're both the same. One thing on the surface, another below it. I'm off home. Sleep off this damned ale."

A hazy recollection of Demsey's routine prodded at me. "Don't you teach in Durham tomorrow? Damn it, Hugh, you will have to be up before dawn to get there."

"Sleep on the horse," he said thickly.

We parted at the inn door, shivering in the chill night air. I offered to see him to his lodgings, but he shook me off and staggered away, mumbling. I had seen him worse, much worse, yet still get home safely, but I would have been glad to accompany him. I was wide awake and not pleased with my own company. Le Sac's face kept rising before me; I saw constantly those gleaming eyes and too-knowledgeable smile. Truth to tell, what I really envied him was his facility in composition. Vapid though those rants of his were, with their cascades of notes and meaningless extravagances, they were still ten times better than the pretty tunes I turned out. Which was why I had not set quill to manuscript paper for months.

In the wider spaces of the Bigg Market, I drew breath and slowed. The bright shining of the moon lit the dark corners and doorways where thieves generally linger, and gleamed on a faint glittering of frost, the first harbinger of winter. I heard the distant call of a drunk and a raucous laugh. My mind was dulled, cut off, curiously detached. I felt despondent; it is unpalatable to know that your dearest wish in life is beyond your capabilities.

So I wandered I don't know where until I found myself in Caroline Square, that newly built monument to our beloved Queen. As I stood beneath one of the trees of the central gardens, the elegant facades of the houses seemed to lean mockingly over me, the new white stone gleaming in the moonlight, darkened windows reflecting back the crisp night sky with its speckle of bright stars. Only two of the householders had hung out their lanterns, so the place was nearly dark, although lights flickered behind two or three of the uppermost windows.

The house directly ahead of me belonged to Lady Anne, Le Sac's patroness. Lights still showed on the first floor. Perhaps the lady lingered awake after the stimulation of the concert; perhaps she had brought Le Sac back here to bestow on him the honour of a glass of wine and the illusion, for a short while, of being an equal. Le Sac was too intelligent to mistake such patronage for genuine friendship, but he was a businessman and would accept the benefits it brought.

Approaching the house, I stumbled on a stone and caught at the railings to prevent myself falling. For a moment the world tilted oddly, seemed to blur. Perhaps I was more drunk than I had thought. A sudden chill made me shiver, a deeper darkness suddenly descended. I panicked, grabbed at the railing, found nothing.

The flickering lantern light returned.

I was no longer in Caroline Square. I was standing on an ordinary street, hemmed in by houses of the sort wealthy tradesmen or the gentry occupy, old but well-kept for the most part. A few lanterns burned over the doors; raindrops touched softly and damply against my hands.

The house immediately in front of me was well-lit; lamps hung over the door, candles guttered behind curtains on the upper storeys. From one of the rooms at the front, just behind the railings, bright light fell across the street like a pool of water. I walked forward in a daze and looked through the window. Inside was a scene of revelry; eight or ten ladies and gentlemen sat at a table that was laden with food. Footmen were reaching to remove the soup tureen, replacing it with a platter of fish wrapped in pastry. Guests were laughing; one gentleman was whispering to his pretty young neighbour.

I looked from one figure to another. A stout, red-faced man of middle age sat at the head of the table; the lady at his right looked very like the wife of the mayor. I shifted to see the other end of the table. There was Lady Anne, in full rig with satins rippling, one ringlet falling across her shoulder, bending to listen to the elderly gentleman on her left.

I strained my ears but could hear nothing. It was a dumb show in front of me. Perhaps the thickness of the glass muffled the sound. The pretty girl looked straight at me, looked away. She had plainly not seen me.

Cold was in my bones, like the worst ice of winter. My foot slipped, I pitched forward...

And found myself once again gripping the railings in Caroline Square.

The moon was extinguished behind a cloud; huge cold drops of rain slapped against my face. I ran. I am not ashamed to admit it. I ran through the near-deserted streets, ignoring the jibes of drunks and whores, ignoring the dirt and the dark corners, the curious spirits and the excited dogs. I was drunk, yes, I was drunk. I kept repeating that litany to myself – it had all been an ale-induced delusion. What else *could* it have been?

By the time I turned into my own street, I was almost calm again.

And there, at my door, was a posse of people: three or four neighbours, a woman of the streets, and lanky Thomas Bedwalters, the parish constable. And, of course, Le Sac.

3
CONCERTO FOR SOLO HARPSICHORD
Movement II

I wished them all at the very devil and tried to brush past them to the door. But Bedwalters turned on me a weary gaze.

"Mr Patterson, sir," he said. "We have been waiting to see you for some time."

Somehow I found myself apologising to him. Bedwalters is the kind of man everyone apologises to. "I trust you are not cold."

"No, sir. I had a pint of ale before I came out, expressly for the purpose of fortifying myself against the chill air."

"I require my music!" Le Sac cried. "Patterson, return to me my music!"

He was wrapped in a heavy greatcoat that made him seem squatter than usual and his cheeks were so red that it would have been easy not to take him seriously. Yet, staring at his flushed face, I had the impression that he sincerely believed I had his music.

My landlady's spirit gleamed brightly on the door knocker. "I have been explaining to these gentlemen," Mrs Foxton said, "that I cannot allow them into your room without your permission."

Her words caused an outburst from the posse gathered around Bedwalters. Phillips the brewer cried out that women had no business obstructing the law, especially not *dead* women. Monro the cheesemonger sniffed and said that private concerns must inevitably give way to public matters for the sake of society. Shivering and feeling sick, longing only for my own company, I waited for Bedwalters to restore order.

"It is, I understand," he said, "within my powers to request that those persons not directly concerned with this matter should retire to their homes."

No one questioned whether it was indeed within his powers. No one ever questioned Bedwalters. I once ventured into the room of his writing school and spied two very small scholars laboriously but industriously inscribing letters in fearful silence; in equal silence, the neighbours withdrew, putting on an air of dignity that suggested they followed Bedwalters's instructions only because they chose to. Only the street-walker remained; she closed up behind Bedwalters, setting her head against the back of his shoulder and stroking his arm.

"I must regain my music," Le Sac said. "I *will* regain it."

"Mr Patterson," Bedwalters began again, apparently oblivious to the street girl. "It is my understanding that you were present when certain books of music were abstracted from the Long Room in Hoult's tonight."

"I was present when their loss was announced," I said carefully. I was still trembling. I made an effort to be calm and pay attention to the matter in hand.

"I trust you are examining the rooms of everyone so present," Mrs Foxton said sharply.

"If it is necessary, I will," Bedwalters agreed.

Silence. Bedwalters regarded the doorknocker steadfastly; Le Sac glared at me. The street walker traced imaginary patterns on Bedwalters' shoulder.

"I believe it is your decision, Mr Patterson," said Mrs Foxton. "Will you let them up?"

"Oh – yes, certainly." No other course of action seemed

possible. After all, what harm could it do? The book of music was not in my room. The sooner they looked, the sooner they would be gone and leave me to my aching head.

Mrs Foxton swung the door open. We all trooped in, Le Sac treading upon my heels and the girl entwining herself with Bedwalters. (Did Mrs Bedwalters know of the girl, I wondered?) The hallway was dark and empty; when Mrs Foxton swung the door shut again, we were in blackness like a coalpit.

Bedwalters's voice floated out of the darkness. "Are there no other tenants in the house?"

"Miners," I said.

"Ah," he said. (The irregularity of such men's lives is known to all.)

"This is a reputable house," Mrs Foxton snapped. "And will be as long as I own it."

"Dead persons can own nothing!" Le Sac scoffed.

A light flared in the darkness. The street girl held up a candle and slipped a tinder box back into the recesses of her clothing. Bedwalters was blinking. Mrs Foxton lay like condensation across the glass of a picture on the stairway. "Until my heir is discovered, this house is mine," she said firmly.

Mrs Foxton's 'heir' – a brother of a pious bent – sailed for Philadelphia some years before his sister's death and has not yet been made aware of that event. I explained as much to Bedwalters, glad to have something to distract my mind, although I made no mention of the popular belief that the brother is long dead without issue. Mrs Foxton had once, in a rare incautious moment, referred to the fever that was prevalent on board ships bound for the colonies. She was a shrewd woman and had no doubt always intended to retain possession of her own affairs, both before and after death.

We climbed the stairs, the street girl leading the way with her hand cupped about the candle to protect the flame. A thin grey twist of smoke drifted upwards into the darkness. My room is on the third floor; in front of the door I set my body between the lock and my guests so I could palm the wedge that kept it closed without their noticing I had no key. As I released the wedge Le Sac swept past me, heading straightway for the table upon which I customarily write.

"Mr Sac!" Bedwalters protested, shocked. But for once he did not get the obedience to which he was accustomed. Le Sac was apparently beyond reason. He leant upon the table to seize up the nearest books (Corelli's concertos). But the broken leg of the table gave way and threw all the papers and books into his lap; he toppled backwards, grabbed at the nearest support – Bedwalters – and dragged him down too. They sat upon the floor, as the volumes slid one by one to the floor around them with great crashes. I started to laugh; they looked at me with astonishment.

"I did remind you to repair that, Mr Patterson," Mrs Foxton said from the door-hinge.

Le Sac rifled my books and papers, impatiently muttering over Bedwalters' more sedate and polite searching. He even tore open my fiddle case – not, I believe, to see if I had hidden anything there but to snort at the poor quality of the instrument. As it happens, it is a violin by Agutter, once of London before – alas! – he came home to this town to die; it is a fine instrument, although mild in its manner of speaking. It does not, however, look very distinguished, and Le Sac had his snort.

He did not, however, have his music. He glared over Bedwalters' shoulder into my cupboards, at my meagre stocks of food, of raven quills and of ruled paper. He flicked through my letters – including the last letter from my mother (at which I nearly set upon him) – and insisted on Bedwalters turning over my mattress. When he was for pulling up the floorboards, however, Bedwalters stopped him.

"I do not imagine any benefit from the exercise, sir. I have tramped upon all the boards and there are none loose."

And down the stairs they went, one by one, the girl leading the way with her candle, Le Sac huddled in his greatcoat and muttering some nonsense in French, and Bedwalters bringing up the rear.

"I shall see the visitors out," Mrs Foxton said loudly – and then softly, so only I might hear, "while you get the boy out of the attic cupboard."

4
CONCERTO FOR SOLO HARPSICHORD
Movement III

The boy was very ugly. He looked at me pleadingly from a face covered in red scabs that he had scratched; some were bleeding still. In the dim light of a candle, I could see that he hugged a violin case to his thin chest and over the case, like some hairy animal, an old tow wig. His own hair was as threadbare as a child's toy, stringy dark strands barely covering his reddened scalp. And he smelt rancid.

"What are you doing here?" I demanded. My head was pounding; I really did not wish to deal with Le Sac's apprentice or any such matters now. What was the boy's name? Wilson, Wilkinson...no, Williams. "If you have run away from your master, you must know I cannot shelter you."

"Turned off," he said and burst into tears.

So much for my commendation of Le Sac's generosity. I dragged the boy down the creaking stairs into my room, and told him to sit on the bed while I lit a branch of candles. By the time I could pay attention to him again, he had stopped snivelling and was holding out a letter to me. I turned the crackling paper over – it was addressed to Jas. Williams on the Key. A chandler, evidently. The seal that held the paper's edges together was already broken.

It is, we are taught, impolite to read letters addressed to other people. There are times, however, when temptation overwhelms good principles, and I had been tried much that night. I unfolded the stiff paper and read.

Sir,

I return with this letter your Boy. He is no longer able to fulfil his Duties as Apprentice since his Arm is broke. I hereby acquit him of all Obligations to me.

Your Obt. Servt, Henri Le Sac.

I glanced up at the boy. "I don't suppose he gave you your premium back?"

"Him?" the boy said scornfully. "Give money away? Never!" I liked him better for that flash of spirit, but there was no doubt that his situation was unhappy. His father had probably saved for years to pay his son's apprentice premium. If Le Sac did not return the money, he might well be unable to find the sum a second time.

"Well," Mrs Foxton said from the latch. "Hear the boy play."

The boy jumped up eagerly and turned his back to open his violin case upon the bed. "What are you doing?" I whispered to the gleam on the tarnished metal. "I can't afford to take on an apprentice without a premium."

"Hear him play," she said again, then more loudly to the boy, "Come on, hurry up!"

I thought her sharpness might overset him again but he turned, face glowing, with his violin in hand – a small one as befitted his age (twelve? thirteen?). I saw the injury the accident had caused; it had been the left arm broken and it had healed with an odd kind of twist; when he lifted his violin to his shoulder, it seemed to stick out from his body at an impractical angle.

Presumably Le Sac felt that this would always prevent him from playing well. But I disagreed; he played very tolerably. There was something to be desired in the expression of the slow melodies and a great deal too much flamboyance in the fast passages – a certain carelessness, even – as might be expected from a pupil of Le Sac. But nothing that might not be mended.

"You could do very well with an apprentice," Mrs Foxton murmured in my ear as I leant against the door jamb. "Three shillings and sixpence every time he plays in the band. Train him up a bit and he might be fit enough for a solo – that would be five shillings a night. Then there are the dancing assemblies – three shillings sixpence a week in winter. He could increase your present income by, oh, a third."

Old habits die hard, or, in Mrs Foxton's case, do not die at all. She had always been an excellent businesswoman. And she was right – even without a premium, the boy could prove profitable. But what would Le Sac say? He had already accused me of stealing his books; would he not also accuse me of stealing his apprentice?

"Anyway," Mrs Foxton said, "the boy's father might well be able to afford a second premium. He's a chandler, isn't he? He'll be coining money. Ships' merchants are all rogues."

The late Mr Foxton had allegedly been a chandler, I recalled, in Sunderland-by-the-Sea. I say allegedly, because no one had ever proved there had been a late Mr Foxton, though no one had ever said as much to his widow, alive or dead. But what really decided me was that vicious snort of Le Sac's as he had looked upon my Agutter violin. I could not compete with him in the Concerts, and even his nonsensical compositions were better than mine; but I could in this one thing do him a bad turn by doing someone else a good turn. Ignoble of me to think in such a way, I know, but Le Sac irresistibly invited such thoughts.

So I agreed. I bedded the boy down on the floor with a blanket and next morning went down with him to his father's shop. The Key was crowded with sailors, hauling coals on board the keels anchored there, smoking vile-smelling tobacco and spitting into the water that slapped up against the river walls. In the chandler's shop coils of rope and unlabelled sacks were piled high, a dog panted from a heap of nets. I gagged, the moment I walked in, at the stink of tar and soap and piss.

The boy's father was a good bargainer but he was anxious to be rid of a runt of a son who started heaving and wheezing when he came too close to the clouds of flour in the store. In the end, I took a guinea from the fellow and he promised me five shillings every week for the boy's food. I bore George (for that was his name) off to the nearest breeches shop and used part of the guinea to buy him clothes decent enough to play in at the Concerts.

If I had known what would happen, I wouldn't have looked at the boy twice.

5
SONG FOR THREE VOICES

Sly Mr Ord was the first to remark on the matter, pouncing on me the moment I set foot in his house the next day (to instruct his grandson upon the harpsichord). I was feeling somewhat better; I had decided that the strange events in Caroline Square the previous night had been a drunken delusion and determined not to think of the matter again. (What else *could* it have been?)

Mr Ord's fingers pinched my arm. "Naughty boy," he scolded with the cosiest of chuckles, and wagged a finger. "Causing such uproar!"

"I, sir?"

He drew me to one side of the hall to prevent his footman hearing our conversation. "I've just come from *his* house. For my lesson, you know. Of course it would be more proper if he came here but one must make allowances for Genius."

"Of course," I agreed, perfectly aware that Genius would unhesitatingly run to the house of the titled. Sly Mr Ord, unfortunately for his dignity, had made his money in trade. "I take it, sir, that you refer to Monsieur le Sac?"

"Who else, who else? He has taken it very ill, you know."

I thought of the boy I had left at home, assiduously copying music. My heart sank.

"He says you have stolen the boy."

I looked into those sly eyes and understood – gratefully – that Mr Ord had made his money not by chance, but from shrewdness.

"Of course," he said with a dismissive wave of his hand.

"That is mere wild talk. But we must make allowances for the continental temperament. The French, you know."

"Swiss," I said before I could stop myself.

"Besides, the lad's father says that Le Sac wrote him a letter repudiating the boy. And between you and me –" he prodded my arm with a plump finger – "the father called the letter *disrespectful.* Of course one must also make allowances for the language problem, though why foreigners can never speak English when it's so easy, I cannot fathom." He sighed. "Well, even Genius has its weaknesses. And Le Sac can hardly say you stole the boy when he had cast him off."

"So I judged."

"But I thought you would want to know the state of affairs," said sly Mr Ord. In truth, he did not seem sly any longer. "You can be sure I have told my friends there is no truth in the accusations. But…" He sighed again. "You had better not have done it, sir."

I was concerned by the hints in his words that accusations had spread widely, but I murmured, "You are very kind, sir."

Mr Ord shook his head so vehemently the flaps of his wig flew up and down. "I like you, Patterson. I would hire you myself, you know, to learn me my violin, for Le Sac gets a little impatient from time to time. But, as I say, we have to make allowances for Genius."

And, thanking heaven for the small mercy that I had not to struggle day upon day with Mr Ord's propensity towards shakes and other ornaments, and feeling a twinge (but no more) of sympathy for Le Sac who did, I proceeded to *shrewd* Mr Ord's library and his eager, but heavy-handed, grandson.

Demsey caught me near mid-day at the door of Nellie's coffee-house in the Sandhill, as I was about to step inside for a pie. He slapped me on the back and shouted for the entire town to hear. "Well done, man. Well done!"

"Demsey –"

"I've not known a better trick!"

"I would not call it –"

"Think me up a similar game to play with Light-Heels!"

A pair of Scotch sailors went past, cackling in their unintelligible patois. I bundled Demsey into the coffee-house. "In heaven's name, keep your congratulations close, man. It was not as you think."

"Of course not." He grinned and tossed back a stray lock of black hair. Demsey keeps that irritating lock for show; his mere flick of it makes all the young ladies swoon. It is the oddest thing; Demsey in his street clothes looks but a lout, noisy and argumentative; but put him on a polished floor, in evening dress and a pair of dancing slippers, with a kit-fiddle in his hands, and he is the lightest, most elegant man you ever saw. Which is why all the young ladies long for his classes, and all the young ladies' mamas seriously consider sending them to Light-Heels Nichols.

The noise from the crowd in the coffee-house was fearsome. We raised our voices to shout at each other as we stumbled over legs and tripped over sleeping dogs. The acrid stink of the brew pervaded every corner, combined with the delicious savoury aroma of Nellie's famous meat pies; a rustle of papers accompanied the clink of dishes and the scrape of knives upon plates.

A cat scampered across my path; I stumbled and trod on a shoe. Or rather a pale blue slipper encasing a slender foot. A newspaper was drawn down and green eyes looked coolly over its folds.

"Lady Anne," I said, bowing. "Forgive my clumsiness."

She regarded me for a moment, her delicate lips pursed in thought. "Perhaps," she said and drew up the paper again.

Demsey pulled me to a table deep in the back corner of the room. "Damn women. Shouldn't allow them in here."

Lady Anne, in her blue and pink satin splendour, was the only female apart from the serving girls. "Lady Anne goes where she chooses." It crossed my mind to talk to her of what had happened in Caroline Square – but admit my drunken state to a woman? No, it would be halfway round the town within hours and in the ears of concerned mamas who would talk to fond papas. The result would be lessons cancelled and pupils taken elsewhere. A teacher, particularly one allowed into family homes, must be of a saintly disposition, or at the very least discreet.

We ordered game pie and broke our fast hungrily. Demsey pulled a bedraggled letter from his pocket and made me read it. It was a fulsome encomium from M Bagieu of Paris, extolling the dancing prowess of M Hugo Demsey and detailing his proficiency in this dance and that dance and all the other dances that were the present rage in the French court.

"*Hugo*," I remarked, handing the paper back. "Are you turning Italian, my dear *Hugh*?"

He waved pastry at me on the end of his knife. "If I did, it would be sound commercial sense. The Italians are all the rage now."

"I like Italian music," I said. "Corelli, Geminiani –"

"Vivaldi?" he suggested, as slyly as Mr Ord.

"Fit only for children," I said severely. "As you well know. Come to think if it, not even fit for them if you want them to grow up with decent musical taste. Defective in harmony and no idea of how to write a decent melody. In fact –"

But I was interrupted by a swirl of blue satin and the heavy thump of a chair. Lady Anne sat down.

"Mr Patterson."

"Lady Anne."

"My lady," Demsey said. The lady took no notice of him.

"I hear you have clashed with Monsieur le Sac."

"Then you have heard incorrectly, madam."

"The matter of a boy." She raised thin eyebrows. "A boy who was his apprentice and is now yours."

"He got the better bargain," I said. "He got – and kept – the premium."

She threw back her head and laughed as freely as any man. The gesture exposed even more – if such a thing was possible – of her chest. I say *chest* for Lady Anne was not the most well-endowed of women; her figure was scrawny although her skin was soft and fair. Her arms were her best feature and she knew it, taking care to display and use them obtrusively. Her hair, uncovered, was a brownish shade. One does not pry into such matters as age but I fancied she was thirty-seven or thirty-eight years old – perhaps a decade older than myself.

"If you do not make a profit from the boy," she pointed out, "what other reason can you have for taking him on other than to spite Monsieur le Sac?"

"But I will make a profit, Lady Anne. Three shillings and sixpence for every concert he plays."

"That seems a paltry return."

"You were born the possessor of a fortune, madam."

"True," she said curtly. I fancy she was offended. "But there are more creditable ways of making a living than exhibiting yourself on a public stage. Even to be a tradesman is more respectable."

"What about being a dancing master?" Demsey said

sourly. He had been reddening with anger throughout our conversation, chiefly I believe at being so contemptuously ignored.

I nudged my foot warningly against his under the table. "I assume you have said the same to Monsieur le Sac, my lady?" Did my anger show in my voice? I think not.

The lady shrugged. "He is a foreigner. They have lower standards. I am told that in France they even tolerate musicians socially."

"How unfortunate," Demsey said savagely.

I indicated the crowded coffee-house. "Is this not a social occasion?"

"One cannot govern whom one meets in public," she said disdainfully. "One can, on the other hand, pick and choose who sits at one's own dinner-table. No musician will join me there, I assure you." She leant forward. "I have an investment in Monsieur le Sac, sir, and I do not desire to see that investment threatened by a young man of little talent who chooses to indulge in petty enmities out of envy and jealousy."

"That is a comprehensive assessment of my character, madam," I said as coolly as I could. "And I would let no *man* utter it unchallenged. You take advantage of your sex."

"So I do," she agreed, rising. "And you can be sure I do it deliberately. Be warned, Mr Patterson."

And she swept from the room in a flurry of satin and lace.

6
BATTLE PIECE
Movement I

I left Demsey to finish another slice of pie and strolled out upon the Key. A fitful sun shone, although there was little warmth in it; nonetheless the sailors on the Key were sweating as they heaved cargo across the cobbles and hung it on pulleys to haul it on deck. There was a smell everywhere of fish and of coal. Downriver, a great plume of smoke billowed into the air from the saltworks at Shields, close upon the sea. Today the smoke was almost pleasurable to look at, a thing of odd beauty; but I have known days – and many of them – when it comes rolling up over the town and lies heavy and stinking in the hollows, setting everyone who ventures out of doors coughing. Demsey jokes that the smoke is the reason that we have no singers of note in the town but must send south to the cathedral at Durham for them. We should banish the smoke by the erection of windmills surrounding the town, he says, and the man who builds the mills will earn a great reward from the Corporation, for the clear air will encourage native singers and so spare us the airs and graces of their lordships from the sacred precincts.

My mind was not at ease. It seemed that everyone was intent upon thrusting me into conflict with Le Sac. First Mrs Foxton with her urgings to accept the boy, then Mr Ord with his glee – and Demsey likewise – and Lady Anne who took offence at my interfering with her investment. Demsey's pleasure in the affair was nothing, merely a delight at seeing a crony of his enemy discomfited. But the others... I was uncomfortably suspicious that Lady Anne at least, and Mr Ord too perhaps, had games afoot in which I was a mere pawn.

I walked down the Key towards the Printing Office, wending my way between coils of rope and heaps of stone with the lady's voice, murmuring of *investment*, accompanying me. I found the term an odd one to apply to a man rather than a cargo of wood or coal. It is not uncommon for a wealthy benefactor to patronise a musician but it is generally from a love of the Divine Art itself, or from a desire to be in the fashion.

I glanced at two gentlemen, plainly merchants, in conversation at the side of a keel – and stopped. One of the gentlemen, the younger – was he not the fellow who had whispered to the pretty young girl at the dinner table, in that strange vision when I had seemed to have been transported from Caroline Square?

He saw me staring at him, gave me a chill look. I walked on. Clearly it had been nothing unusual after all. Lady Anne had been entertaining, I had glimpsed the party in a drunken stupor and imagined the rest, the impossible alteration of the surroundings.

And yet – who had been the middle-aged man I had seen at the head of the table? And why had not Lady Anne's cousin been present?

The Printing Office was at the far end of the Key; I dodged barrels and piles of shit and roaming dogs. This matter of Lady Anne and Le Sac was more to the point. The gentry were notoriously fickle; if Lady Anne had taken against me it might rebound greatly to my disadvantage. Might the lady and Le Sac be conducting a discreet affair of love? A man of Le Sac's stamp might enter such an affair cynically, for mercenary reasons. And they say the French – damn it! Ord's mistake was infectious. The French may be amorously inclined but the Swiss, for all I know, may be as frigid as the tops of their mountains. And I would swear the lady had not an ounce of the softer passions in her.

The Printing Office was a scurrying melee of men, running backwards and forwards with fragments of paper or staggering off with heaps of parcels. Clearly it was printing day. I made my way to the house behind the office, standing back from the Key down a narrow alley. An ugly old house, but as solid and well-built as I have seen in a long time, with thick walls that kept sounds from straying from one room to the next.

The old uncle's spirit swung the door open for me. "Master Patterson!" he said jubilantly. "Come ye in, come ye in."

The spirit clung to the door jamb as I entered the dark chill hall. He always calls me master, for he knew me when I was in frocks, and he knew my dead father and all my dead baby brothers and sisters too. He himself died three years since, in this very hallway, in the breath between one step and another. I was there and caught him as he fell lifeless and laid him down gently, and he has never forgotten that service.

"My niece has been practising," he said. "I've seen to that."

Elizabeth practises without being told, like many of my female pupils. She knows it will increase her chances in the marriage mart. She has always been a sensible, practical child.

"That piece you left her last time," the uncle said. "You wrote something like it for me, I recall, years back, before you went off to London. You never did tell me how you did there."

"I held a concert," I said.

"Just one?"

"Just one. At Hickford's Rooms."

He oohed in appreciation. "I've heard of them. Where the lords and ladies go."

"Not many came when I played," I said ruefully.

"Too many fish in the sea, eh?"

"Too many musicians in the capital, certainly. And I am not Italian enough."

He cackled. "Change your name. Call yourself Carlo something or other and you will make your fortune."

Teaching can be tedious and it can be exhilarating. With pupils like Elizabeth Saint, it is merely a tolerable way to earn a living. She is assiduous, listens carefully to what I say and executes everything exactly as I require. The sun through the garden window was warm on my back, and roses bloomed on bushes that autumn had almost stripped bare of leaves. From time to time I put my hand on the wood of the new harpsichord to assure myself it was not too warm in the sunshine. We were chaperoned, of course. Her older, widowed sister yawned in a corner; the governess sat at the table and copied out sums for her pupil's later solving. And I murmured and encouraged and corrected while my mind puzzled over the merchant I had recognised on the Key and the events of the previous evening. I came to no conclusions.

It was dark when I came to the front door again and looked out on the evening. The chill in the air nipped at my nose and hands, and I pulled my coat close and shivered. Suddenly the air tingled and the maid that had opened the door for me yelped and jerked back.

"Go, go, shoo, shoo," said the uncle, and the girl fled indignantly. "Master Patterson, don't go yet. Stay awhile."

"I have another lesson to give at the other end of town."

"Then go out through the garden."

"And clamber the hill past Butcher Bank? I would come to my pupils stinking of offal!"

"I warn you, Master Patterson," he said. "Do not go yet."

Perhaps I was influenced by his tone of voice – the same tone he had used when I was five years old and intent upon escaping my father's instruction. (Papa was not a good teacher.) I was tired, weary with teaching and with constant speculation on that other matter. "I must go," I said and stepped out into the alley.

I regretted my impulsiveness almost as soon as I reached the Key. In darkness, the Key has a different character, a reeling and rolling and dancing character, a singing and shouting and whistling nature, all accompanied by the loud good humour that can change to violence in an instant. I remembered that so-effective message system the spirits use and wondered if the old uncle had heard something that had alarmed him. Just like him not to tell me, to expect me to do as I was told as if I were still a child. But then, I had not given him much time to explain.

I hurried along, seeing my way by lanterns that guttered at the doors of brothels and taverns, dodging the sailors that leant towards me with breath stinking of sour ale. The wind had changed and was bringing the smoke of the coal-pits and the salt works in billowing clouds stinking with sulphur that clung in my throat and made me cough. The smoke collected here along the river; higher up in the town, in the gardens of Westgate and of Northumberland Street where the richer sort live, there would be hardly a trace of it. And Caroline Square would surely hold no whiff of corruption at all.

I turned to climb the Side, that narrow winding street

that leads up to Amen Corner and the church of St Nicholas. The organist there is half-dead and half-drunk and so deeply in debt he will never be able to recover. I have long hoped for his dismissal and the ensuing election for the post. I flatter myself that no one in this town can match me on the keyboard and the forty pounds per annum paid by the Town Corporation would allow me to rent a larger room. Except that the organist, Mr Nichols – for he is elder brother to a certain dancing master – lingers and lingers beyond reason. I was feeling angry, resentful, ungenerous.

The Side, like all streets, should have lanterns outside every private establishment; but many men are careless of civic duties, others have no money and, here at least, one or two have gone out of business and removed themselves, leaving houses empty. The Side therefore was lit by a single lantern outside a house about halfway up and I trod carefully, conscious of the shadows reaching out to me from alleys and doorways. Only a fool walks about the town on his own after dark (only a fool and a man with a living to earn), and even then he keeps to ways that are well-lit. But to retrace my steps and go by Butcher Bank after all would make me late, so I went on, nerves prickling with apprehension.

I failed to hear them, even then. Something slammed into my back, hurling me forward to crash into a wall. Hearing shouts behind me, I found myself on my knees, my hand slapping into a dog turd. Heart beating fast, breath in a flurry, I scrambled up, ready to defend myself.

But I was an unintended victim. Someone had hurtled out of an alley and knocked me flying as he passed. I could see him stumbling desperately down the Side, panting, only yards in advance of the two men pursuing him.

And even as I saw the cudgels hanging from the beefy hands of the assailants, I recognised their quarry.

Light-Heels Nichols, the dancing master.

7
BATTLE PIECE
Movement II

God help me, I almost turned and ran. Not out of cowardice but from the motive of self-preservation. In affairs like this ribs get cracked and heads get bloodied but, worse, hands get trodden upon and broken – an eventuality no musician can regard with equanimity. But Christian feeling took over and I stepped into the fray, roaring. One of my father's favourite maxims: "Charles," he would say, "make as much noise in the world as you can." No doubt he had not had a brawl in mind.

I grabbed the collar of the nearest villain, lugged him backwards. His hands flew up; I plucked the cudgel out of his grasp, and swung it at his head. He went down with a gasp. I rounded on the other fellow. Nichols was down on the ground, curled up as the remaining villain kicked at his most private possessions. I swung the cudgel. At the last moment, the ruffian realised his danger and ducked. He slipped and I thought I had him, then he lunged away and was off down the street.

Poor Nichols was writhing and groaning on the cobbles. The dark street was still deserted. No one had come out to see what was happening. Wise souls; I have bolted my own door against brawls before now, particularly in London.

"Guggle, guggle," said Nichols and spewed up his last meal at my feet. I leapt back and avoided the worst of it but the stench almost turned my stomach. He crouched against the wall, clutching his groin and making noises like a man about to expire.

"You are most fortunate, Mr Nichols," I said, "that I was about when those villains tried to rob you."

"Rob!" His voice ended on a squeak. "Why should they rob me? What do *I* have?"

"A watch," I pointed out. "And a ring upon your finger. Perhaps a guinea or two in your pockets. Ruffians have killed for less."

"Nonsense!" He straightened. I saw an idea dawn in his face. "I have been set upon deliberately! By that fellow Demsey!"

"Now, sir," I said soothingly. "You are confused." Damn him for getting that idea – but I won't deny it had been the first in my mind.

"And you're a crony of his!" Nichols drew back in alarm. "You're in league with him! You knew he'd set those fellows on me and came to watch the fun!"

"If I were in league with Demsey," I pointed out, "I would not have intervened to save you. But if it will reassure you, I will leave you and let you find your own way home."

Fear crossed his face. The moon, though still full, was half-hidden by clouds, and the head of the Side, rising above us, was in darkness. I did not much like the look of it myself but I flattered myself I was not a coward, or a dancing master.

"You may take this cudgel, sir, to guard you," said I. And I held up the stick I had taken from the first ruffian.

My luck was still running foul. As I raised the cudgel, we heard the clatter of hooves. A shadow moved in the darkness at the foot of the Side, then a black horse came up the narrow hill into the light of a torch and out again. Its rider was dressed in black to match; at first he was merely a pale shape of face in the night. Then a voice called out:

"Nichols, *c'est vous*?" and I recognised the abrupt tones of Henri Le Sac.

He reined in the horse beside us so sharply that the animal's head jerked up. Metal gleamed in a flicker of moonlight. I found myself looking into the muzzle of a pistol.

"Monsieur Patterson," said Le Sac. "I trust you have good reason to be attacking my friend Nichols."

"I can probably invent one," I said in the most affable tone I could contrive. "But you misjudge the situation. I was helping him fight off two ruffians."

"But how philanthropic!" he said, almost as cordially. "And I suppose these ruffians are now run off?"

"As a matter of fact..." But of course, when I looked round, I saw that the ruffian I had laid flat had taken advantage of our attention being elsewhere to make his escape.

"It's that fellow Demsey," Nichols cried. "He set the rogues on me and this one came to watch."

"Nonsense," I said briskly – for I fancied I had seen the pistol rise. "I was on my way to a lesson, which I may say I am now missing. I was just setting Mr Nichols back on his feet."

"He was in league with them!"

But Le Sac was lowering his pistol. The moonlight glinted off his horse's harness and revealed the dark shapes of a violin case and a bag of clothes slung behind. He must be on his way back from a lesson in the country. "My dear Nichols," he said with a sigh. "You do not understand people. Monsieur Patterson is not a fool. And," he added, turning his attention to me, "neither am I, sir. I know it is not poor Nichols who engages your attention." He leant forward confidentially. "I tell you frankly, Monsieur

Patterson, there is not room for both of us in this town!"

And as I stared at him in astonishment, he jerked on the horse's reins and the animal clattered past me, so close that I felt the warmth of the sweat on its flanks. Nichols stumbled after them.

"A real pair of fancy men," said a female voice from the wall behind my shoulder. The spirit sniffed, then added coyly, "Give me someone plain and honest any day, I say."

If the words were meant for me, I did not regard them as a compliment. And an invitation from a spirit is of little use to a man.

"We did try to warn you," she said, "since the old uncle takes such an interest in you. I could see those rogues were up to no good, hiding in the alley. And knowing you came this way every week..."

She seemed on the verge of coyness again. I said sharply, "Do you know where Hugh Demsey is?"

"The other tip-toeing gent? Now there's a handsome fellow. Wait on." Did I hear a murmur of voices? A moment later, she resumed. "Never could get the hang of those fancy dance steps, you know. And gentlemen did like it if you could tread a measure or two. What? Oh, much obliged. He's in his school room. Down Westgate."

I was angry as I started off towards Westgate and in a very short time I was cold as well. The clouds began to deposit a chill rain upon me, whitish drops like sleet splattering on my face and darkening my greatcoat. Around St John's Church I almost lost my way in the darkness and stumbled into a horse trough, splashing myself with water. On, up past the vicarage, past the trees of the vicarage garden and on to the street of tall narrow houses this side of the West Gate itself. This is a part of the town where people of the genteel sort live, so lamps are more conscientiously placed above house doors. Past the impassive face of the Assembly Rooms on the left, where old Mr Thompson was causing such havoc since he died in the middle of a country dance. Past Bedwalters's writing school on the second floor of a neat but shabby house.

And then the more welcoming facade of the clockmaker's with the clocks nodding behind the glass window. An archway leads back to the clockmaker's workshop behind and a side door, usually unlocked, gives access to a narrow flight of stairs to the floors above. On the first floor is Demsey's school room; on the second lives a widow who supports her children by painting delicate miniatures; and in the attic is Demsey's own lodging. This was old Harris's dancing school, bequeathed five years since to his last and favourite apprentice. He had the consideration to die at home so Demsey is spared the trial of his old master muttering instructions and admonitions over his shoulder, as he did in life.

I climbed the stairs. They creaked and gave advertisement of my coming so that when I pushed at the half-open door of the school room, Demsey was already looking towards me. He stood in the middle of the long narrow room, surrounded by brilliant branches of candles. The chairs had been stood in line around the walls and Demsey had evidently been gathering up orange peel abandoned by his scholars. Scuff marks in the polish of the floor gave the room an abandoned forlorn air.

I trod carefully across the polished boards towards him, knowing from experience how easy it was to slip when not wearing dancing slippers. Demsey – silently waiting my approach – was in his formal best, all peacock blue in his coat and a darker turquoise in his knee breeches that fitted as snugly as any mama might fear. He watched me coolly.

"Is it raining, Charles?"

Looking down, I saw that my boots were leaving a muddy trail. That and his cool manner, so unlike his normal mien, disconcerted me. "I am missing a lesson because of you," I snapped. "I can ill afford to lose that money!"

I saw a frown between his brows; I went on without pause. "I have faced down two ruffians with cudgels and I have been threatened with a pistol. I have been accused of complicity in an assault and informed that sooner or later I must leave this town and find another place. And all because of *your* schemes!"

He tossed the orange peel into a basket laden with such rubbish.

"Did you tangle with my surprise for Nichols, then?" he said with a frankness that took my breath away. "I'm sorry if you were inconvenienced."

"Inconvenienced!"

"But he cannot think you have any quarrel with him."

"He knows me to be a friend of yours. That is cause enough."

"As for the other matter..." He frowned again. "I did not think him man enough to own a weapon."

"Not him! His crony, Le Sac, came upon us, all eager to defend his bosom friend and to find reason to discredit me and run me out of town. God knows why he dislikes me so!"

"I daresay it is because you have more true musicianship in your little finger than he has in his entire body."

He spoke in such a casual manner that I hardly took his words in at first. He gave me a sideways glance as he straightened the last of the chairs.

"I do not flatter you, Charles. I save that for my pupils. If I may give you one piece of advice, it is to abandon those abominable compositions and to concentrate upon what you do best – managing people. If Le Sac was not here, the gentlemen would all be running to you to direct the Concerts and to tell them what to do in that charming manner of yours." I fancied I saw the trace of a smile. "Your greatest asset is tact, Charles. Le Sac is totally devoid of that admirable virtue but he contrives to escape condemnation because he is a *Genius*."

Astonished that he should speak to me in such a manner, I flung at him: "I do not need advice from you! And as for my compositions, I have had many compliments paid to them. I am thinking of putting forth proposals for publication."

"No, no, don't!" he said with a return of his usual impulsive manner, the first heat of emotion I had seen upon him. "The gentlemen would buy, certainly – they always buy the latest novelties – but they would laugh at you in private. And the writers in London..."

The mention of London stung. I saw he knew it as soon as he uttered the word. Try as I do, I cannot forgive the ignorant lords and ladies who give acclaim to the worst of the musicians there, providing they be foreigners. To their own, they give nothing but indifference.

"I believe I am capable of judging my own work with some discernment," I said. "You will see the notice in the paper when I do choose to publish. Damn it, Hugh, do you not even consider what this affair tonight will do to my reputation if it gets about?"

"*Your* reputation?" he repeated.

"If Nichols or Le Sac should spread the tale... No one wants a drunkard and a brawler to teach his children!"

"I see," he said, then lost his temper and roared at me. "*Your* reputation, *your* pupils!" I tried to interrupt; he raised his voice louder. "And you lecture *me* on selfishness?"

"I won't lose my livelihood because of your stupid pranks!"

"What about *my* livelihood?"

"To the devil with your livelihood," I said recklessly.

"I see," he said frostily. "In that case, there's nothing more to be said."

"No, there is not," I said and slammed the door behind me.

8
BATTLE PIECE
Movement III

Someone was talking to me from a great distance. I mumbled and turned over, not wanting to wake, or to leave the bed. Oh God, that argument with Demsey, that ridiculous scheme of his! The encounter with Le Sac, Nichols's accusations – it all returned to me with force.

"Master!"

Groaning, I struggled up. My head ached. How long had it been before I slept, turning over and over and listening to George's snores? Now George's poxed face hung over me, bleeding from the middle of his cheek; I must somehow persuade him not to scratch. His breath was sour too; ale, I fancied, and rather stronger than one normally allows youngsters. He was holding out a letter, and I took it without knowing what I did. "What time is it?"

"Nearly nine, master."

"What!" I struggled from my bedclothes. "Bring me water. Quickly!" I started hunting under the mattress for my clothes. "I'm late." I had lost a lesson the previous night and now I was late for another. And for Master Thomas Heron too! "Did you take those messages?"

"Yes, master." He was scratching at his neck now.

"Stop that! And get that water." At least the fond parents would have received my excuses for not turning up last night and perhaps they would not be too offended. I found myself still holding on to the letter. "Who is this from?"

"Mr Heron's servant left it, sir."

George scuttled out of the room as, with foreboding, I broke the letter's seal. The elegant lines of copperplate were brief and to the point. Mr Heron was always careful to regulate the persons who came into positions of influence with his son and did not choose to allow him to associate with those who had connections with ruffians, &c, &c. I crumpled the note and tossed it down upon the table. Claudius Heron was a fastidious man and where he led, others would no doubt follow. Damn Demsey.

George came back into the room with a ewer of water. I splashed it on to my face and aching eyes, dragged on my clothes. Should I see Le Sac and ask him to correct the impression that had got about? There was no point in seeing Nichols; the man would simply gloat over me.

"Will it do, sir?" George asked anxiously.

I realised that I had been unwittingly staring at the table and a neat pile of manuscript paper. George had evidently been assiduous in his work the previous day; four or five sheets were copied out with painstaking neatness – one of my concerti for violins.

George was nervously shrinking back. I wondered if Le Sac had been generous with blows. "It is very neat," I said. He still looked uncertain; I tried for a lighter tone – no point in frightening the boy. "And what do you think of the music itself?"

The boy's eyes flicked to mine, then away again. "It's very nice, sir."

Nice. Such a useful word; it may mean anything you choose or nothing at all. I had rather he had condemned it outright.

A chill in the air greeted me as I hesitated on the doorstep. Perhaps Heron would be the only one to credit the rumours? I could but hope, and seek ways to repair the damage his dismissal of me would cause to my income. I must begin to make use of George. I turned for the Assembly Rooms in Westgate, low in spirits but determined.

I was lucky enough to find the Steward of the Rooms drinking a morning bowl of coffee and inclined to be talkative. He has a partiality for scientific instruments and a yearning for good listeners, and bore me off to an inner room to show me his latest acquisition – a finely wrought orrery. I did my best to admire its workings, and allowed its owner to explain in detail the movements of the planets before dropping into the conversation the information that I had acquired something new myself – a young but excellent apprentice who might be of use to the dancing assemblies. The Steward's face brightened.

"Indeed?" he exclaimed. "I can be rid of that drunkard Ross at last! Bring the boy to play to me tomorrow. If he's fit, I'll take him on."

His eagerness for George's services was the one brightness in the following days. I took George to play for him and the boy was promised a part in the Assembly band. But upon that day and upon the next but one (the intervening day being the Sunday), I had three more letters in imitation of Mr Heron. I slept but little, lying in bed working through in my mind how much money I had lost, brooding over how to recoup the loss and pay the next quarter's rent. On the Monday, I rode out to Shields for a concert given for the benefit of an actress in the theatre company, and was promised more work by Mr Kerr of the Beehive Inn, who hires his room there for concerts. But I have had past experience of Mr Kerr's good intentions and knew better than to rely on them.

Having arrived home late on the Monday evening, I slept later than usual upon the Tuesday and spent the morning teaching the daughters of Forster the carriage-maker. Forster himself, a lean man with flaming hair and cheeks, met me at the door of the house and slapped me on the back. "Never mind, Patterson, I know better than to believe such tales." He meant to reassure me, I know, but he did not.

Around lunchtime, I walked down to the Key for a bite at Nellie's coffee-house, looking about me as I went in, looking for Demsey or any of the gentlemen who had dispensed with my services, to avoid the embarrassment of having to pass the time of day. I encountered only Lady Anne's cool gaze as I made my way to a corner and called for a serving maid. Lady Anne returned her gaze to her paper.

I drank ale, ate a chop and walked out again upon the Key in a thin chill sunshine that was tempered by a river breeze. As I reached the first of the coal barges bobbing at anchor, a merchant walked past me; I started, half-thinking I recognised him but no – it was not the fellow from the party I had seen. In heaven's name, could I not get that incident out of my head? I had been drunk, that was all...

"Mr Patterson!"

Turning, I saw Lady Anne striding towards me with a masculine gait. The river breeze whipped her skirts about her legs and tangled her ringlets. As ever, she was unaccompanied by maid or footman, and had no hesitation in raising her voice in an unladylike manner.

"Mr Patterson," she said again as she came up to me. She was breathing heavily with exertion and her thin chest rose and fell quickly. Her cheeks were becomingly pink.

"I have heard, sir, that you are accused of an assault last Thursday night upon Monsieur le Sac and his friend the dancing master."

"There is no truth in that accusation, my lady," I said stiffly.

She nodded. "So Monsieur le Sac has informed me."

"Le Sac?" I echoed incredulously.

"He tells me that you came upon the brawl by chance, as indeed did he. These rumours are all the fault of that prancing peacock Nichols." She looked at me shrewdly. "Mr Patterson, I have the greatest admiration for Monsieur le Sac's musical gifts – he is, as you must know, my protégé. He is also, I assure you, an honest man, if somewhat vain and arrogant. He has," she said, forestalling me as I would speak, "many amiable qualities."

I thought I detected a note of irony in her voice and did not know quite how to reply. "He has conceived a dislike for me."

"No less, I warrant, than you have for him. You are, after all, rivals."

"I had rather not be," I said wearily. We shifted to allow a cart to pass. The wind blew the dry stink of coal towards us, and I thought I heard a spirit call from the water. "If we are talking of professional matters, my lady," I said, "there can be no argument in the matter. Monsieur le Sac is a better performer than myself, although I flatter myself that I am the better composer."

She shrugged, the folds of her cloak whispering against the silk of her gown. "I can say nothing in favour of his compositions, certainly. They are meant to show off his gifts, nothing more." To my astonishment she took my arm and leant upon it. "Come, Mr Patterson, let us walk and you may tell me exactly what occurred."

I hesitated but she was insistent, so as we strolled along towards the Printing Office I recounted my encounter with Nichols. Lady Anne was an excellent listener and I found myself oddly enjoying the tale. She laughed heartily when I hinted at Nichols's injuries. "And Le Sac?"

I told her of Le Sac's arrival. "A pistol," she pondered. "I suppose he bought it for his travels in the country. A post-boy was robbed on Gateshead Fell a week or so back."

"I heard the story."

"Well," she said with greater decision in her voice. "I cannot allow you to be blamed so unjustly, Mr Patterson. Do you have any idea who was behind the attack? Was it merely thievery, or was there some deeper purpose?"

"I cannot say, madam," I said carefully. I turned to face her. "Forgive me, Lady Anne, but the last time we spoke on the subject of Monsieur le Sac you gave me to understand, in no uncertain terms –"

She laughed; the wind caught her hair and drifted it back from her face. "Give it its true name, Mr Patterson. I was abominably rude to you, for which I apologise. I was in a foul temper that day. Can you forgive me?"

I regarded her with some reserve. Her contrition seemed genuine, yet so had her animosity that day in Nellie's coffee-house. Still, she appeared to be in earnest in wishing to help me and I would have been a fool to refuse her.

"We must save your reputation at any rate," she said, tapping me on the arm and sending me a darting, sparkling glance. "Come, Mr Patterson, let us turn about and take ourselves out of this cold gale. Walk me back to the coffee-house and I will see what I can do for you. I am a woman who likes to see justice done."

And all the way back to the coffee-house she kept me amused with outrageous tales of her late father, who had been a Justice of the Peace and prone to making distinctive judgments. Some of the stories carried with them a certain oddity, although in what respect I could not quite define;

I took it she was merely spinning tales to cheer me.

We parted outside the coffee-house; Lady Anne turned and drew her billowing cloak about her. The sunlight gleamed on the ringlets that fell across her shoulder.

"You must drink tea with me, Mr Patterson. I have some new scores from… from a friend, and I think you would enjoy seeing them. The style is somewhat similar to your own work."

"I am most flattered, my lady."

"Tomorrow, then," she said. "At four."

She was swift to keep her word. When I returned home a few hours later, I found another note awaiting me from Mr Heron. He had, he said, sent me word a few days ago under a misapprehension – had been grievously misinformed – offered regrets – hoped that Master Thomas would see me the following day. I was pleased both by the purport of the letter and by its manner of expressing its message; Claudius Heron was generous in the matter of admitting his fault. Which is more than one expects from most gentlemen.

So I went to bed in a better frame of mind than when I got up, looking forward both to professional duties and a little social entertainment.

9
TRIO
for two sopranos and a tenor

Unlike Lady Anne's other visitors, I came to her house in Caroline Square on foot. The early evening light was sufficient to show me the way to the shelter of the trees opposite the house. There I paused, enjoying the fragrance of the last roses and the freshness of damp earth. The air held a hint of rain; looking up, I saw darkening clouds to the east. I had not been in the square since that unsettling night of the concert; looking around now, I thought how ordinary it appeared. It had been night, of course, when I was last here, and uncertain lamplight and deep shadows can make a place seem threatening when in reality there is nothing to fear. Yet I still hesitated to cross that last stretch of road to the door of the house.

"Good day to you, sir," said a voice from the bushes. The voice sounded tipsy and, for a moment, I even fancied I smelt a whiff of ale. Then I realised I was hearing a spirit, speaking with the extreme politeness of the very drunk. "Can you tell me how I came here? For I do not have the least idea."

"Do you remember a carriage, perhaps?" I suggested, thinking he might have been the victim of an accident. I had no wish to linger but it is good policy to be polite to spirits. They have great power of doing harm if they choose, by the whispering of secrets. And, conversely, they have an equal power of doing good, as I had learnt the night of the attack upon Nichols.

"Carriage? I wonder." He hummed and hawed. "I remember the church. That's it, 'twas Sunday and I remember the ladies and gents coming out of church. The big church."

"St Nicholas."

"That's it! And there was that organist fellow, what's his name?"

It was hardly difficult to remember, I thought gloomily. Nichols at St Nicholas – the name had a depressing appropriateness. A drop of rain fell warm and fat upon my hand. "Nichols," I said, tasting annoyance. "His brother's a dancing master."

"No, no, that's not the name." He hiccupped. "Patterson! That's it! Father was a town musician."

"You are quite mistaken," I said. "Charles Patterson is no organist. Yet."

"Wrong, sir!" he cried in good humour. "Wrong, wrong, wrong!"

"I would be the first to know if it was true," I pointed out. "I *am* Patterson."

"Nay, sir, he's a gentleman. He dresses well. Um…" He sounded doubtful now. "Yet when I look closer…"

More drops of rain. I began to be afraid that my dress, whether it was that of a gentleman or not, would be ruined before I came to my engagement. "I assure you I know my own name."

"Got a brother," he said with an air of triumph. "Makes stays."

I burst out laughing. "All my brothers and sisters died in their infancy, sir, and none of us were acquainted with any staymaker!"

"I am right," he said obstinately. "And then I turned to walk down this street and there was a cart and I stumbled and – and –" He started to sob; maudlin drunk, God help us, as well as dead. I bade him a polite goodbye and hurried through the thickening rain to the door.

At the railings, the feelings took me again.

I felt a shock like the buffeting of an icy gale, stumbled, flung out my hands. But they met only empty air. Daylight snapped into darkness. I fell, felt stone bruise my hands. *Not again, please God, not again.* Another scene was already forming in front of me – tall houses on an elegant street as before. But this time they did not stay in place; they were overlaid by the trees of the square. Darkness and light flared in my eyes as the two settings flickered and mingled, houses, trees, houses…

I lay on my back, staring up at the trees of the gardens as, at last, the surroundings settled firmly into the reality of the square. Voices were shouting. Hands took hold of my shoulders. A footman stared at me from the house steps with amused contempt. Closer, a woman's voice said, "Are you unwell, sir?"

I looked into cool grey eyes. They belonged to a woman of perhaps forty, very finely but plainly dressed. Lady Anne's cousin. Her dark blonde hair was dressed high upon her head; one gleaming ringlet hung down against the white skin of her neck.

"Are you ill, sir?" she repeated.

"A – a little dizzy."

"Come into the house."

So I made my entrance into the house where I had hoped to come so elegantly, on the arm of a supporting woman, attended by a knowing look from a footman who plainly thought me as drunk as the spirit in the gardens. He took my coat away to be brushed and brought it back a few minutes later together with a brandy requested by the lady. We sat in a withdrawing room, the lady looking on as I wretchedly shivered and trembled. Staring down at my hands, I saw a fine embedding of stones in the heel of my right hand.

I struggled to be calm. The lady had no qualms about remaining alone with me, I noted, which made her as careless of convention as Lady Anne. She addressed me in matter-of-fact tones, as if nothing untoward had happened, although her gaze was steady and watchful. She was, I realised, allowing me time to gather my wits and compose myself.

"We have not been introduced," she said as I sipped the unwonted luxury of fine brandy. "I am Esther Jerdoun, Lady Anne's cousin. And you are Mr Charles Patterson, music teacher."

She could not have summed up our social positions more nicely. Reddening, I sat on the edge of my chair and attempted an apology. She shook her head – a fine head with a clear profile outlined against the red-and-white-striped satin of her chair.

"I am grateful for your help, Mrs Jerdoun," I said, carefully according her the courtesy of the title as convention requires, though I did not know if she was married or no.

She waved away my gratitude. "Lady Anne, I believe, invited you to look at some scores she has acquired. She has an extensive collection of music, although I am afraid I do not know the precise score to which she alluded. She is still at dinner with her friends."

I remembered that other dinner party I had glimpsed through the window, days before. "You do not eat with her, madam?"

"I had a headache earlier in the evening and preferred to dine alone. If you are feeling recovered, Mr Patterson, perhaps you would care to see the library?"

I was hardly certain I could stand, but I knew she was still pursuing her aim of putting me at my ease, and followed her from the room. She talked on quietly, pointing out the attractions of the house, not waiting for responses, not asking for any. I was grateful for her consideration and did my best to be interested.

It was a very splendid house, decorated in the most fashionable (and no doubt expensive) style. Cherubs cavorted on plaster ceilings among swags of leaves and fruit, and looked down on cream wallpaper thinly striped with blue; chairs almost too delicate to sit upon stood beneath portraits of high-nosed ancestors; porcelain vases and vast bowls of fragrant potpourri stood upon marble tables. In the hall, a staircase swept up to the floors above; from a distant room came the sound of laughter.

Mrs Jerdoun led me to the rear of the house, opening doors on to an echoing chill space. The walls were lined with bookcases; the polished wooden floor gleamed in the light of many candles. The only furniture – positioned under a tall window – was a closed harpsichord and its stool. I ran my fingers over the elegant beading along the lid's edge.

"I would open the instrument for you," Mrs Jerdoun said apologetically, "but my cousin keeps the key. We found the servants would toy with it while we were out, and it goes out of tune so easily."

I nodded. "Do you play?"

"Not at all. I have no patience for it. Nor for singing. I find such amusements trivial."

So much for music. Perhaps Mrs Jerdoun thought from my silence that she had offended me. "Forgive me for plain speaking but I am impatient with the hypocrisy indulged in by most women. Their great interest in music lasts only to the end of the marriage ceremony."

"I wonder anyone ever plays music," I said with some asperity. "Ladies regard it as a means to show off their charms and catch a husband while gentlemen consider serious practice requires too much exertion and is therefore unbecoming."

"It is," she said decisively. "It is a craft, and no gentleman should involve himself in anything so beneath his station."

"There is an element of *craft* in it, certainly – although a better word would be *science*. But it is also surely an *Art*."

"Certainly not."

"Is it not Art, madam, to convey in one's compositions the passions of the human soul – joy, grief, exaltation?"

"Do you speak of Monsieur le Sac's works?" she said dryly.

"Hardly. But consider the acknowledged masters..."

"I would prefer not to," she said, moving away to snuff a candle that was guttering wildly. "Besides, I can acknowledge a man expert in his work without considering him an artist. The man who made these candles, for instance. He has produced an object that is of excellent quality, admirably suited for its purpose. But that is merely to say that he has learnt well when he was an apprentice and knows how to apply the techniques of his craft. It is the same with music."

I was intrigued and admiring. It is not usual to find a lady with such strong and well-expressed views. But this was an unusual household altogether; her cousin was not conventional in her manners, and as for the house itself...

My hand trembled on the lid of the harpsichord. I cleared my throat, determined to banish thoughts of what had happened on my arrival. "But consider the music used in divine worship."

"A mere tool to sharpen our awareness of the words

of the gospels. Though even there – " She frowned in contemplation of the drift of smoke from the extinguished candle. "Even there, it is fit only for the generality of people. Any man or woman of common sense can judge the truth or otherwise of God's word without such aids."

The truth or otherwise. Did that suggest she doubted the word of God? We were approaching dangerous ground. I pointed out a second dying candle and we moved naturally on to consider the books around us. Mrs Jerdoun was proficient in both French and Italian, which I much envied her, my Italian being merely tolerable and my French greatly deficient. She seemed surprised that I knew any.

She took down a book of engravings, of the ancient ruins in Rome, and in speculating upon the purpose of the remains I contrived to lay aside the remembrance of my unorthodox arrival. Mrs Jerdoun had visited the ruins and had interesting tales to tell; she was describing an ancient pillar when the doors were thrown open. In swept Lady Anne, in yellow satin and old gold lace, fanning herself and laughing at something one of her guests was saying. Ladies and gentlemen both together, elegant in bright colours, indolent in manner and tinkling in laughter. Even Mr Claudius Heron, a gentleman of about forty, in a light-buff-coloured suit which complemented his pale colouring (he too wears his own hair in defiance of fashion) raised a faint smile at the sally of a young lady. And from her privileged position at the head of the throng, her expression visible only to Mrs Jerdoun and myself, Lady Anne raised her eyebrows to the ceiling as if to say 'Heaven help me!'

She introduced me to her guests, an honour I had not anticipated. Mr Heron cast me a frowning look but acknowledged me civilly, if curtly. Upon Mrs Jerdoun remarking that we had been looking at the engravings of Rome, a general conversation began in which I was kindly included. Her ladyship's guests were prepared, it was clear, to follow her lead and accept me, if not as an equal, at least as tolerably worthy of notice. Heron particularly was generous enough to convey his personal apologies for his misunderstanding of my encounter with Nichols.

But my attention was distracted by the servants bringing in chairs for the company and tea tables with all the necessary paraphernalia. All the chairs, I noted, were being placed at one end of the room as if to leave the other end, around the harpsichord, free.

A servant came in with a music stand.

I flushed, answered one lady's questions at random. Could Lady Anne have brought me here merely to afford her guests after-dinner entertainment? But if so, what an invidious position she had put me in by introducing me to them as an equal. There is always a clear division between the entertainer, who is paid, and the entertained, who pay.

But no, Lady Anne was indicating a chair, and praying me to sit down and tell her how I preferred my tea. I was to listen. Perhaps one of the younger ladies was to entertain us upon her harp; that would be unexceptional, if trying to the musical connoisseur. One of the footmen was unlocking the harpsichord and propping up its lid, revealing gorgeous paintings of dancing nymphs. A few songs from the young lady, then? But from the hall came the sound of a footman greeting a newcomer and a scuffle of preparation. Footsteps approached the door. I was seized with a hot premonition of disaster.

The doors were opened. In the space, pausing for a moment so that we might appreciate his elegance, was Henri Le Sac. *He* was to entertain; Lady Anne's behaviour clearly indicated that *I* was to be entertained. She could not have prepared a greater insult.

10
DUET FOR HARPSICHORD AND VIOLIN

What was I to do? The moment Le Sac set eyes on me he would take offence, and indeed I would not blame him. Here was I, greatly his inferior in performance, set to lord it over him as if I was one of the gentry. How could he tolerate that? Yet if I offered to play, which might satisfy Le Sac (particularly as I would be at the lowly accompanying instrument), I would set Lady Anne's guests against her for having the audacity to introduce them to a mere performer.

And while I delayed and hoped to fathom Lady Anne's motives for playing such games, Le Sac glanced round and saw me.

For a moment he was blank-faced, then drew back in disdain. "Milady," he said, "you desire *this* person to accompany me?"

Nothing, his tone said, could possibly be less welcome. All eyes turned to me; with a frown, Claudius Heron said, "Do you play tonight, Patterson?"

Silence. Then Esther Jerdoun said, "Mr Patterson is *my* guest. He came to examine some music books in my possession."

There was a collective sigh of relief, as if the company regarded Mrs Jerdoun as some eccentric whose will must be humoured. Only Claudius Heron continued to frown, and to look from myself to Le Sac to smiling Lady Anne in turn. Not a man to be fooled easily and his previous mistake over the brawl must have made him wary.

I hurried into speech. "But I would be honoured if Monsieur le Sac would consent to my accompanying him. Though I cannot of course hope to do the pieces justice."

So the proprieties were preserved. Lady Anne was considered to have been most kind to her eccentric cousin; I was most obliging in helping to retrieve the situation. And, as I was clearly not being paid to play, it was possible to regard me (for this night at least) as a gentleman amateur. My dish of tea cooled on the table as I disposed myself on the harpsichord stool, and Le Sac bent to fetch out his music. He swung with a flourish and a smile for his audience, and presented me with the harpsichord part; his eyes met mine and I saw by their glitter that there was one person in the room who was not appeased.

I say one, but there was another also. As I glanced across at Esther Jerdoun, I saw her cast her cousin a look of annoyance and reproof. Lady Anne lounged in her chair, one leg crossed mannishly over the other, swinging a slippered foot and smiling a smile of triumph. I had seen that look before, on a dozen of my older pupils; it was the enjoyment of a chance to cause consternation.

It was not an evening I care to remember, although the harpsichord was excellent. Le Sac was determined to make life as difficult as possible for me. He speeded up and slowed down outrageously, drew out melodic phrases to a perfectly ridiculous extent then unexpectedly galloped away at top speed. He cut sections out of the music and repeated others that were not meant to be repeated so that I constantly appeared to be unsure of my place. In short, he was every accompanist's nightmare.

But his audience – with the exception of Mr Heron, who sat stony-faced throughout – loved every moment. They gasped at every rapid dash of notes, every dramatic flourish, no matter how coarse and meaningless. In truth, there was nothing of worth in the entire piece – it being one of Le Sac's own compositions – and my only consolation was that the harpsichord part had been copied out by George and was therefore eminently readable. Unlike Le Sac's part which, I saw over his shoulder, was an illegible scrawl.

He came at last to the end and enjoyed the applause with great flourishing bows in the continental style. I did not share the applause; not only would it not have pleased Le Sac but it would have underlined my status as a performer and I was still trying to walk that fine line between guest and hired help. But as Le Sac turned to his music case for another solo, Esther Jerdoun stood up and spoke in a voice that cut through the conversation.

"Monsieur le Sac, I am sorry to inconvenience you but I must reclaim my guest. We have not yet concluded our business."

Le Sac looked outraged but he was powerless to object. I was tempted, as I bowed to him, to point out that he should have brought his own accompanist. But he was as much a victim of Lady Anne's playfulness as I was; I kept silent.

So Mrs Jerdoun and I withdrew to the far end of the library where we conducted our conversation in low voices while Le Sac fiddled away unaccompanied, with renewed energy. As she lifted down a music book from the shelves, she said, "Forgive me if I seem abrupt. But my cousin's habit of setting people at each other's throats annoys me greatly."

I opened the book – Geminiani's Opus 8 – to give credence to our conversing. "It sometimes seems –" I hesitated for fear of offending her – "that Lady Anne enjoys an uproar."

She shook her head. "It is something more than that, I think. I have been in France and Italy for some years, you know, and when I returned, a twelvemonth ago, I found Anne greatly changed. Of course, she was a girl of only ten when I saw her last, so perhaps I should not be surprised. Here, sir, is another book of Italian violin pieces. What do you think of Signor Vivaldi?"

I winced. "You wish the truth?"

She smiled. "Indeed, sir."

"Defective in harmony and poor in melody."

"Alas." She sighed. "I have always found him a pleasant diversion."

"Did you not say you found music trivial?"

"I do indeed, but it has some useful effects. It is particularly good for easing social relations. One may talk to all the world at a concert and see one's neighbours in a congenial setting, and that must be of benefit to society."

One could say the same of the horse races, I reflected. "Then far from being a trivial occupation, madam," I said, "music and its practitioners –" I bowed – "are performing a great service to the world."

She laughed. Heads turned; Le Sac played more loudly. I did not care; I found the lady's company most agreeable.

"I must allow you the final word, sir," she said, reaching for another book. "You argue excellently. Let me show you another volume. This was obtained recently by my cousin. She thinks most highly of these concerti."

It was a handwritten volume, but most unfortunately the first page, with the author's name upon it, had been torn out. I hummed a few bars of the first tune and found myself agreeably taken by it. The accompanying parts were simple but that is not a bad fault; perhaps the players for whom the composer wrote were not expert. Rather like the gentlemen in our own concert band.

"Indeed, I like these very much," I said and then gave way as the lady's cousin beckoned to her. Mrs Jerdoun went to Lady Anne and I leafed through the volume. Oddly, the handwriting was not dissimilar to my own neatest hand.

Esther Jerdoun returned to me. "My cousin says that if you wish to borrow that volume, you are most welcome."

I could hardly refuse; I bowed and Lady Anne inclined her head. Mrs Jerdoun beckoned to a servant and he took the book away to wrap it against the weather. As we waited at the back of the room I said, somewhat hesitantly, "Was your husband French, madam?"

"I am not married. My mother's second husband was French and I adopted his name as my own. He was an official of their government."

Unmarried. Ridiculous to take such pleasure in the thought; there was a great gulf between us, both in station and fortune.

The servant returned with the book; I took it, kissed the lady's hand, then took my leave of Lady Anne in the same manner. Claudius Heron nodded to me civilly. In the hall, the servant returned my greatcoat; clasping the book in my arms, I stepped out into a heavy drizzle, breathing a sigh of relief for my escape.

But I knew it would not be for long. Le Sac was not a man to forgive slights. My safe, dull life was beginning to collapse about me. I had earned Nichols's enmity (through no fault of my own) and Le Sac's (for no reason at all – or rather an imagined rivalry) and I had quarrelled with Demsey. I was somehow a pawn in a game Lady Anne was playing, though what that game was, or what purpose it had, I could not tell. And I was in danger of losing my living, or would be, if Le Sac had his way.

And more than that, there was that other puzzle which I could not fathom. I hurried for the shelter of the gardens, passing that place where I had twice fallen, as quickly as I could. Nothing happened. Had I imagined it after all?

More than my living, I began to fear for my sanity.

11
FULL PIECE

Halfway home the heavens opened and spat all the venom they possessed at me. A vicious wind seized my tricorne from my head and drove a deluge of rain on to my hair, plastering it to my face. It lifted the tails of my coat and splattered my breeches and stockings with mud; passing carts splashed puddles over my shoes. I tucked the book under my coat and ran the last streets. In the dryness of my own room, George was curled into a ball on the floor, snoring noisily into his blanket. I stripped off my wet clothing, hung it over the chair to dry, and slipped silently into bed, falling asleep at once.

Rain was still falling when I woke in the morning, pattering against the window and obscuring my view of the sodden street below. I rose with some weariness. It was the day of the weekly concert – the worst day to rain, for only the most ardent music-lovers turn out in such weather. And I would have to face Le Sac once more. Well, I would not be blamed for what had happened; it was Lady Anne's doing. She had been generous to me but for all that she was a shallow frivolous woman, as Le Sac must already know.

I prepared myself with my usual care as was my wont on concert days, calling up the fellow on the floor below – apprentice to a barber – to shave me. He came with such speed and readiness that it was obvious he knew the day as well as I and was ready to earn his fee. (I warrant he never told his master he earned it.) And while he shaved me, I turned over that other matter which still unsettled me.

I had not been drunk last night, neither had I felt ill.

Moreover, the strange events only took place in Caroline Square and only near *that* house. I wondered what Esther Jerdoun had seen – merely a man stumbling and falling? Surely if she had seen anything else, she would have commented upon it. Had the spirit in the square seen anything? (And would he make sense if I asked him?)

There was one solution to the problem – avoid that square. Avoid Lady Anne and her schemings too. But Lady Anne was not the only occupant of that house and I found myself reluctant to avoid Esther Jerdoun. No, this would not do. A man may admire but he should not entertain preposterous notions which are beyond his reach, however pleasing they may be.

I dressed neatly, though not ostentatiously, and supervised George's preparations. He had spent the time while I was being shaved in leafing through the volume I had brought home from Lady Anne's.

"These are much better, master," he said with enthusiasm when I called him over. "When did you write these?"

"They are not mine, you dolt."

"But it is your hand, master."

I should have been glad to own to the authorship of them if I had been able. I turned George round, brushed him down, and made him put on his tow wig. His own straggly hair showed beneath the wig; I trimmed the ends and tucked them in. By all commonsense, he should have shaved his head entirely but his scalp was so scabby that it was patently out of the question. Still, he looked presentable. I combed my hair (for like Le Sac I too wear my own) and we set out for the rehearsal.

Hoult's Long Room was engaged for a dinner on this night so the concert was to be held at the Assembly Rooms on Westgate. I had misjudged the time and we were almost late for the rehearsal. I was surprised to be met at the door by the Steward. "Ah," he said with a sigh of relief. "You're here at last."

I was about to offer apologies when we heard loud voices from the upper room; I thought I recognised one or two directors of the Concerts. And was that Claudius Heron speaking more moderately? That murmur certainly belonged to sly Mr Ord.

"You had better go up," the Steward said. "Try your hand with them. I can't calm them down."

In trepidation, I went up, followed by George in an even worse state. "It's *him*," he quavered. "He doesn't want me here."

I emerged into the Long Room. The music stands had been set up at the end of the room in their usual places, with chairs for the two cellists and a stool for myself at the harpsichord. But only Henry Wright hung awkwardly over his music, his tenor violin in his hand and an air of embarrassment about him. The other gentlemen were in huddle near the top of the stairs, each trying to speak the loudest.

For a moment, my arrival went unnoticed. Then Mr Ord darted forward and seized my arm. "Here he is! Now all shall be well."

A silence. "Good," Claudius Heron said in his usual severe manner.

"Is something amiss?" I asked.

Mr Jenison (one of the minor scions of the celebrated family of that name and the prime mover of the Concerts) said, with ill-concealed irritation, "First violin's ill."

"I understand," Mr Heron elaborated, "that he was caught in the rain on his way home last night."

What a wealth of meaning there was in that simple

sentence! First, a reminder that Le Sac had made his way to his hostess's house on foot, which clearly marked him as inferior. Second, a reminder of my own status, for I too had done the same. Third, Mr Heron had of course been warm and dry in his carriage, driven by servants – the mark of a gentleman.

"Burning up with fever!" Mr Ord did not sound distressed but quite the opposite, almost merry. "Out of the question that he should play today. So you see," his plump fingers dug into the flesh of my arm, "we have no musical director."

Another silence. A stray slant of watery sunshine chanced through the windows and lit the empty music stands. The floor, polished for dancing assemblies, smelt of beeswax. I was conscious of a great feeling of relief.

"You must stand in, Patterson," Jenison said. "Mr Wright, will you do me the kindness of fetching the music-books from their cupboard? I have unlocked it already. The programme is decided. We will be short of violins, of course." His gaze lingered on George. "Is this the boy?"

His slight emphasis on the definite article suggested he too knew all George's history.

"Indeed," I said, seizing my opportunity. "He has had a good solid foundation in music. He will do very well on the back desk." They were all looking at me for direction, I realised, and I felt a surge of exultation. "Perhaps Mr Heron," I went on, bowing, "will consent to lead the band?"

"Certainly not," he said firmly. "Quite out of the question for a gentleman. Put the boy there." But he was plainly pleased to have been asked.

So we settled ourselves to rehearse. I ordered the harpsichord to its proper place at the centre of the band

and sat down to make sure it had not gone out of tune in the moving. The gentlemen shuffled music on the stands. At least the bad weather had kept all but the players indoors so we had had no spectators to witness our wranglings, and the petty humiliations that I suffered even in this moment of pleasure. Jenison, for instance, would never have ordered Le Sac to play this piece or that; he would have made *suggestions* in quite a different tone of voice. It was perhaps fortunate, therefore, that I had no quarrel with Jenison's choice of music; he was an excellent judge and knew what audiences liked to hear.

George settled himself in the leader's place, a small figure compared to the gentlemen looming behind him. He cast me a sly look of satisfaction; I would have been better pleased to see some nervousness there. But off we went into an overture by Mr Handel and to my surprise it went rather better than I had hoped. George played well and the gentlemen were agreeable to watching for my nod. Even more fortunately, Mr Ord was not particularly familiar with the piece and, in his concentration, quite forgot to trill except upon the last possible occasion. The gentlemen seemed subdued without their idol; I, on the contrary, was elated. I had not been fully aware of how lowering an effect Le Sac's presence had upon me.

In the middle of the rehearsal, we broke for wine that was carried in from the tavern opposite. When two or three gentlemen accosted Jenison to plead for their own favourite pieces to be included in the programme, I took the opportunity to stroll across to Wright – who stood a little apart, regarding his tenor violin with some dissatisfaction.

"Patterson," he greeted me. "I cannot get any notes out of this thing. I've half a mind to give it up altogether – I'm sick of it."

Young Mr Wright is one of those gentlemen who never picks up his instrument to practise but nonetheless fancies himself a great expert. The instrument itself, needless to say, is to blame for every fault; it is badly made, the bow-stick is too light or too heavy, the strings will not speak properly, &c., &c. But the prospect of losing our only tenor, no matter how erratic his playing, filled me with alarm.

"How odd," I said swiftly. "I was only just reflecting how greatly improved you are upon the instrument."

He turned on me a startled expression and a hopeful one. "You think so? I thought, from the way Monsieur le Sac sighs over me, I was as bad as ever."

For once, I sympathised with the Swiss. But I merely said, "If I may be so bold as to offer a suggestion?"

"Yes?"

"A small alteration in the position of your hand upon the bow-stick." I demonstrated what I meant; he copied my instructions, then tried it upon the strings.

"Good heavens! Why, that is much easier!" And he ran off a passage with a great deal more pleasure.

We resumed and went through the remaining pieces with such ease that we finished long before our usual time. The rehearsal broke up in as high spirits as it had started, though in considerably better humour. I was even more pleased to be accosted by Jenison just as I was about to leave, and asked to put in a solo of my own.

"The audience expects some fire, Patterson," he said. "Play something to take their fancy."

Something like Le Sac's vapid, showy pieces, he meant. Over ale in Nellie's coffee-house, I contemplated what I might play. I could not compete with Le Sac for virtuosity, and in any case I would prefer to play something with more heart. Yet a slow piece, no matter how moving, would not please an audience. Finally, I decided upon a piece I had written some years before – a lightweight piece intended to amuse rather than edify, based upon some popular Scotch tunes. Perhaps, in the audience's enjoyment of recognising favourite melodies, my lack of virtuosity would go unnoticed.

I drank my ale and contemplated the prospect with pleasure. At least Lady Anne's petty games had produced an unexpected result in my favour. I must make the most of the opportunity and show the gentlemen there was more than one musician in the town. As for that other matter – well, no doubt there was some perfectly rational explanation. All things are susceptible to explanation, or so the Steward of the Assembly Rooms insists.

I had told George to get himself some small beer and a pastry, and to keep out of my way (for I had no wish for company while I considered my music) but I heard a commotion at the door and he came pushing through the crowd to reach me.

"Have you heard the news, master? About the dancing fellow?"

I was seized with a sudden fear. "Which one? Nichols?"

"The other one, master." I recognised George's look, the way he leant upon the table, the way he rushed at his words. The eager gossip. Telling tales that he knows will be unwelcome, and greedy for the effect he hopes to produce. He really was an obnoxious boy. "You know him, don't you, master?"

Even as Le Sac's apprentice, he must have seen me about the town with Demsey a dozen times. "Slightly," I said. "Go on."

"Caught them red-handed, they did!"

"A full tale, George," I said. "And *now*, before I send you back to your father with a letter like Le Sac's!"

He drew back at my vehemence and hurried on. "There's another word for it, a French one. Mr Sac used to talk about it. Her mother walked in on them."

Dear God, what was he suggesting?

"He was giving a lesson." The stench of George's breath washed over me. "A private lesson at the lady's house. And the young lady's ma walked in. Kissing and cuddling, they were."

"Rubbish!" I said sharply. "Where was the chaperone?"

"The what, master?"

"The governess! The married sister!" Two or three fellows nearby glanced round curiously at my raised voice. I said more quietly, "No one would leave a young woman alone with any man, let alone one who is personable and unmarried. Where did you hear this?"

"Everyone's talking about it, master."

"Damn it, it's mere gossip!" I did not believe it, could not believe it. If it were true, Hugh was ruined. No parent would allow their daughters to be taught by him.

"No, it's true, master. Really."

I sent him off with a flea in his ear and a threat that if he spread the rumour further, I would turn him off straightway. The story was preposterous. Demsey was no scoundrel to take advantage of a girl's innocence, nor a fool to be trapped into a compromising situation; he had nothing but contempt for the silly girls he taught. Moreover (I had reassured myself greatly by this time), even if the governess had been got rid of on some spurious excuse, even if Hugh had been trapped into some indiscretion, no family would allow the story to become known. The girl's reputation would be lost for ever.

The obvious explanation occurred to me as I got up to

leave. This was Nichols's revenge for the attack upon him. He had spread these rumours to discredit Demsey. Well, it was none of my business. Demsey had brought this trouble upon himself and he must deal with it. He had made it amply clear it was nothing to do with me.

So I went off to the concert; the gentlemen played with spirit, George acquitted himself well and my solo piece was well-received and much complimented.

"All in all, not a bad night," said Mr Jenison, handing me my wages and George's. He felt it necessary to point out that he had rewarded my services that day with an extra payment of two shillings and sixpence. He was, after all, although he did not say so, saving ten shillings on the Swiss's wages that night. I thanked him but he waved away my gratitude.

"And thank goodness," he said, "Mr Le Sac will be well for our next concert."

12
CATCHES AND GLEES

As I entered the Printing Office the following morning I encountered Nichols, counting through some coins as he walked. He sneered when he saw me. "In alt this morning, eh, Patterson? Think a good deal of yourself now, do you? Applauded by all the ladies and gentlemen? Well, enjoy it while you can."

"Le Sac is on the mend, I take it?"

He looked me up and down. "Compared to him, you're a nobody."

"Oh, I quite agree," I said cordially. "But at least I know my own limitations." I smiled with meaning. "Some people never recognise their inferiority."

I was feeling, I admit, very pleased with myself and life. I had woken, late, to hear from Mrs Foxton that a lady had called for me and left her card. The card, on the table at the foot of the stairs, read *Mrs Jerdoun* in flowing script; underneath, the lady had written in an elegant copperplate: *Mrs Jerdoun much enjoyed the Scotch airs last night.* I laughed at this reminder of our argument over the value of music.

Then Mrs Foxton had offered me the second-floor room at the end of the week when the present lodger vacated it. It would be a shilling a week extra but was a great deal bigger. So I had come out in a good mood, determined to forget that parting comment of Jenison's.

Nichols leant closer. "I got Demsey and I will get you, Patterson. Make no mistake about that."

Suddenly chilled, I caught at his sleeve. "Is that an admission that the accusations against Demsey are untrue?"

He laughed and shook himself free. "Ask the young lady."

Thomas Saint, the printer, watched him go, shaking his head. "I try to be Christian, Mr Patterson, but there's a man I can't abide."

"An acquired taste," I said lightly. "Mr Saint, I wish to put an advertisement in your paper."

He lifted the sheet I gave him to the light, reading it barely an inch from his face.

Proposals for Publishing. That favourite harpsichord piece played lately at the Subscription Concert, the Subject of the Rondeau, the favourite Song of Lewie Gordon.

He stared into the air for a moment while his lips silently performed calculations, then named me the price. "I like a good Scotch tune myself."

Outside again on the Key, I paused. I had some time before my first lesson of the day and I was tempted to go down to Westgate to see Hugh. Nichols's certainty of success made me uneasy. Surely he did not have the girl's co-operation in the matter? While I stood irresolute, I heard the rattle of carriage wheels on the cobbles of the Key and was surprised to hear my name called peremptorily. Turning, I saw Lady Anne framed in the window of a carriage door. As I made my bow, she flung open the door and jumped down. Her servants, I noticed, made no attempt to offer assistance but began to root under the box for a number of parcels.

"I called upon you at your rooms, sir," Lady Anne said gaily, "and was told you had come this way. My compliments on your performance last evening."

"You are most kind, my lady." I bowed once more. "I did not see you in the audience."

She laughed. "When you sat with your back to us, sir? I am not surprised. Of course I was there – to see the results of my plotting."

"I fail to understand –"

"Had you not guessed, sir? I sent Monsieur le Sac home in the worst of the rain without offering a carriage." The breeze drifted a strand of hair across her face. Behind her, the river glittered in the sunshine; her servants carried parcels into the Printing Office. "Did you not know he was susceptible to chills and fevers?"

"He has never confided in me, madam."

How odd to find myself suddenly indignant on Le Sac's behalf. Lady Anne had behaved abominably towards him. And for what? Merely her own mischief. She stood as if expecting me to comment further, a vision in a gown of severe cut, burgundy-red touched with white lace; jewellery of gold and diamonds hung about her neck and wrists. She seemed extraordinarily overdressed for a mere ride about town.

I would not let her go unchallenged. "I do not understand, Lady Anne, why you should disadvantage your protégé in my favour."

She smiled at me impishly. "But you know what we fashionable idlers are like! Always in search of novelties. We are wild for one thing today and tomorrow are looking for some new distraction." She turned to her servants and instructed them to drive to the coaching inn to send the remaining parcels on to London. "I have an appointment at the Guildhall," she said. "Walk me there, Mr Patterson."

No, I refused to be a distraction, or a novelty. Musicians must always be polite and fawning to the gentlemen and ladies who pay their wages, but against this I rebelled. "I have a lesson to give here, madam."

"Come, you will be only a little late."

I drew back. "I regret, my lady, but a prior engagement must always take precedence."

She regarded me coolly and I thought for a moment that my favour with her would be short-lived in the extreme. Well, so be it. But she smiled again and said, "Very well. But come to me for tea again tomorrow. This time I will promise you no surprises."

Tea? In Caroline Square? But before I could refuse, she walked away.

It was a trying afternoon. I could not get the lady out of my mind. I was irritated by her games and by her arrogant assumption that I would do as she wished and be grateful for it. And the invitation to the house in Caroline Square! I had decided that I would not go there again, but how could I refuse? If I found some excuse to stay away, the lady would merely issue another invitation.

Then, as I was about to go off to another lesson, I discovered that I had left at home some music-books I needed. To go to the lesson without them would be more than inconvenient, for I had intended to introduce a good pupil to a new composer, but to go home for them would make me late. There was nothing for it but to rush back – and I dashed up the stairs to my room, only halting as I came to the last landing and saw Hugh Demsey standing against the railing, looking down at me.

"I have been waiting for you, Patterson." His voice sounded strained but his face was calm and composed. "I would be grateful for a word; I will not keep you long."

I performed my sleight of hand with the door wedge. "I am late for a lesson."

He followed me into the room. The grey daylight was

somewhat dim (the houses opposite blocked out much of the brightness) but the room was still clearly untidy. I snatched George's abandoned blanket from the floor and tossed it upon the bed, then started looking through the volumes on the table for the books I wanted. Demsey did not speak but I was damned if I would prompt him. But as he continued silent I turned, books in hand. He was staring down at the floor and I saw only the top of his black head and the bow in his hair at the nape of his neck.

"So," I said, irritated by his silence, "you've come for my help, have you? You want me to speak for your character, against this accusation dreamt up by Nichols?" I waited but he stood still. "It's nonsense, man, and everyone will know it. The girl will protest her innocence!"

He lifted his head but still said nothing. Stung further by annoyance, I said, "You have only yourself to blame –"

He said in a low voice, "I came to apologise," turned upon his heel and walked out.

I sank down upon the bed. I cannot express how poor an opinion I had of myself at that moment. To take out my own frustrations upon him… I leapt up and hurried after him.

As I started down the stairs, I heard the street door slam.

A succession of pupils on Pilgrim Street kept me busy until the evening. In this, the smartest end of town, the rich shopkeepers and tradesmen believe that their sons and daughters will be taught better if their teachers are given a proper sense of their place – that is, if they are kept waiting in a draughty hall for an hour or more. The young ladies and gentlemen have rarely put fingers to harpsichord or violin since their last lesson and can be heard running furiously through the piece (skipping the most difficult passages). A man has plenty of time to sit and contemplate how abominably he has behaved. To abandon a friend in need is unforgivable; I could not imagine that Hugh would abandon me. How could I have allowed my own preoccupations to affect me so?

So I found myself, not long before midnight, climbing down the hill from Northumberland Street towards Westgate and Harris's old dancing school. I had no expectation of finding Demsey at home – even if I did find him, it was unlikely he would talk to me – but I had a note of apology in my pocket to slip under his door.

The house was quiet as I climbed the stairs to the dancing school. It was that rare thing – an unspirited house. As indeed, now I came to think of it, was Lady Anne's house. The silence was almost palpable, and made me uneasy. Such loneliness, such emptiness, seemed almost unbearable. How could Demsey tolerate living here, constantly alone? Even the floor above was silent; the widow and her children were clearly not at home.

The door to the school room stood ajar. The lock had been turned but had failed to catch, as if it had been done in a hurry. A stray streak of moonlight laid its finger across the floor and showed dim shadows of chairs lined against the walls. I bent to pick up a curl of orange peel. Something about the room disturbed me; I stood for several minutes before realising what it was. The floor was unpolished. Surely it should have been readied for tomorrow's lessons?

I climbed to the top floor, almost expecting what I saw. The door to Demsey's attic room was closed and locked but I knew where the key was kept, prised up a length of broken floorboard and found it. It turned smoothly; I ducked inside the room, nearly banging my head on the low ceiling. A table, an unsteady chair, a bare bed beneath the oddly shaped window in the eaves – nothing else.

Demsey had gone.

13
CONCERTO FOR SOLO VIOLIN
Movement 1

By the time I reached home, I was too low in spirits to be annoyed at seeing Bedwalters the constable and Le Sac outside the door, arguing with Mrs Foxton. Of the neighbours, only Phillips the brewer hung out of his window with a guttering lamp, to advise Bedwalters not to allow dead women to interfere with the law.

"Mr Patterson," said Bedwalters formally, "I must again ask your indulgence but I am investigating a most serious matter."

"What is it this time?" I asked wearily. "More music disappeared?"

"*Mon violon!*" Le Sac cried hoarsely.

My heart turned over. I think there are few people in this world who can understand the attachment a musician has towards his instrument. That black violin of Le Sac's would have been worn to his hold, fitted snugly upon his shoulder. His fingers would instinctively have known their places upon the strings; his ear would recognise its every tone. It would have travelled with him from town to town and country to country, lying on the seat by his side like a companion; its surface would have been polished lovingly by his hand. To lose it would have been like losing a child. I know the fondness I have for my own fiddle, though I am principally by nature a keyboard player. How much more violent then must have been Le Sac's emotions?

He was shaking and red-faced; by the light of Phillips's wavering lamp, I could see sweat dripping down his round cheek. Even from this distance, I could feel the heat burning from him. "You have it stolen," he croaked. "You want I should leave this town. I *will* leave – only give me back my *violon*."

I knew it was not a bargain he would keep, even if I had been in a position to agree to it. Once he had the violin in his hands again, he would refuse to go. And, oh God, why had I not thought of it before – the violin was gone and *Demsey* was gone. Had he stolen it, in some obscure plan to punish Nichols by attacking his friend? Or did he intend to trap Nichols as Nichols had trapped him with the young lady? Would the thing be found hidden in Nichols's lodgings? No, surely not. It made no sense. But my tired, befuddled mind was beyond making sense of anything.

Bedwalters was regarding me mildly. "I regret to have to ask you this again, sir, but it would be most amiable of you to agree that your rooms be searched."

"*I* cannot agree!" snapped Mrs Foxton.

"See – he has it!" Le Sac cried and fell at once into a fit of coughing so loud we had to wait until the fit died away before we could hear each other speak.

I was too weary to argue. "Come up, then," I said. "Have your search and be gone. I need to be up early tomorrow."

We climbed the stairs, Le Sac panting and wheezing like an old man. By the time we reached my room, he was a flight behind us and Bedwalters stood at the banister with a candle to light his way. I rapped upon the door and a sleepy voice said, "Master, is that you?"

"Yes. Let us in."

I heard the soft pad of footsteps and the click of the

wedge being removed from the inside of the door. The room was in darkness and little of Bedwalters's light from the landing seeped in. I felt my way across to the table. It took me three attempts to make a spark from the tinder-box but when the candles were alight, they showed me George, seated upon the edge of my bed, yawning widely, his feet kicking at the rumpled blanket on the floor. Then his eyes widened and he scrambled back upon the bed towards the corner of the wall.

"He's come for me!"

"You!" Le Sac declaimed from the doorway. He stood with one hand upon the jamb, a picture of scorn. "What use are you to me? You have no musical Genius! Give me my *violon* and I will not care if I ever see either of you again."

"I haven't got it!" George quavered. Tears squeezed down his face, glittering in the candlelight.

The search did not take them long. A glance in the few cupboards, a turning over of the mattress, a shifting of the books on the table. George huddled in a corner, shivering in his nightshirt, while I leant against the table and tended the candles to prevent them from being blown out by the draught of their movements.

"I don't have your violin," I said at last as Le Sac prowled restlessly about the room. "I am sorry for its loss – "

"Hypocrite," he spat and turned on his heel.

By mid-morning, the theft was posted all over the town; Le Sac must have persuaded Thomas Saint to open up early to print the bills. I first came across a copy on the wall of Barber's bookshop in Amen Corner behind St Nicholas's Church, and stood reading it in the spit of a cold rain that was already staining the paper.

Whereas an old Violin, black, without a Maker's Name, and the Bow of spotted Wood, fluted from one End to the other, in a black Case, has been stolen from the Home of its Owner, in Low Friar Street, this 16th Inst. Whoever will deliver it whole to any of the undermentioned Persons shall receive one Guinea Reward and no Questions asked. At M. Le Sac in Low Friar Street; at Mr Barber's, Bookseller and Stationer; at the Golden Fleece in the Sandhill. NB No greater Reward will be offer'd.

The matter of the violin and Demsey's disappearance weighed heavily on me all day, so I walked down to Caroline Square in an uneasy state of mind. I was not inclined for company, and I did not trust Lady Anne not to spring another surprise. But it was undoubtedly true that her favour could do me great service professionally; and I found myself anticipating with some pleasure the opportunity to talk again with Mrs Jerdoun.

Still there was that other matter, which endlessly troubled and mystified me. At the entrance to the square I hesitated, looking across to the house with elegantly proportioned windows, sweeps of expensive curtains just visible through the glass. I did not wish for the repetition of the strange events that had happened to me there, yet I found myself thinking that perhaps only by such repetition would I find out their true significance. If such an event did occur again, I resolved I would face it in a rational manner, calmly looking for an explanation. So I hesitated, but went up to the house with resolution.

Nothing happened.

The footman showed me to the library to await the tea tray. I occupied the few minutes I was kept waiting by browsing through some of the volumes absentmindedly, still distracted by the one puzzle when I came upon another

– an inscription in a commonplace book, in manuscript. The book looked very much the sort of thing an organist might keep to record short pieces or to note down the works of other composers. In the front was inscribed: *Thomas Powell, organist, St Nicholas, 1725.*

I had never heard of such a man. Unless, of course, the name of the church misled me. There was also a St Nicholas church in Durham, but surely it had no organ. The book was much the same size as the book Lady Anne had lent me and I stood for a moment, fingering the cover, wondering. And then, inexplicably, shivering with sudden cold.

I looked up and saw in front of me a door standing open into a small room, very elegant in pale golds and blues, the sort of room in which a lady might sit. A book was laid closed on a small table, needlework beside it as if the lady had only just laid her work down and got up. I stared blankly at the room, knowing it had not been there before. Taking a deep breath, I moved forward. The carpet was thick beneath my feet; the delicate scent of dried herbs drifted from a bowl on a mantelshelf over an unlit fire. I reached down and opened the book on the table. It was a prayer book, of the kind often used for private devotion, and inside the cover had been listed the names of children with the dates of their births. Lady Anne was there, but not Mrs Jerdoun. The old paper was darkened where fingers had stained the pages.

A glimpse of movement in the corner of my eye. I glanced up and saw, through the window, a carriage pass down the street.

For a moment, I stared out into the street where there should have been a square. Then I thought I heard a voice; I turned and went back into the library. And as I passed through the door between the two rooms I shuddered again, as if with cold – and turned to see no door, no blue and gold room, only a wall behind me.

The ladies came out of dinner together, amiable and talkative, although I sensed some constraint on Mrs Jerdoun's part. Lady Anne was anxious to ask after my health, having heard from Mrs Jerdoun that I had felt unwell on my last visit to the house. "I do trust," she said wickedly, "that you have not caught Monsieur le Sac's chill."

"Not at all, my lady," I returned, choosing not to rise to her bait. "I have been admiring your library. I had no chance to look closely on my previous visit but I had thought there was another room, there." I indicated the wall behind us. "In that corner of the library."

She stared at me, astonished. "No, never. Only the servants' stair. Are you certain you are quite recovered?"

Somewhat irritated, I reassured her. She then asked after my apprentice, whose playing at the concert she commended. "Though I fancy, if he intends to make a living out of his skill, he will need to grow up a great deal more handsome than he promises to."

The lady herself, of course, was exquisite as usual, the splendour of her gown and jewels and the subtlety of her rouge almost making me forget that she was remarkably plain. Something in the animation of her face and the glow of her skin in the brilliant light of many candles was infinitely becoming.

Esther Jerdoun said consolingly, "Children often grow out of spots. Once he does, he may not be so bad." She too was elegant in a silvery white gown and her fair hair glinted in the lights. Her manner was cooler than her cousin's; I both preferred it and trusted it more. There was a frown between her eyes as she regarded me, before flicking her gaze towards the corner of the room I had indicated.

I was tempted to raise the matter again, but Lady Anne was already speaking.

"If Mr Patterson can but persuade the boy to wash more often, I shall be pleased. Tell me, sir, what do you make of this business of the stolen violin?"

Suspecting Demsey as I did, I did not wish to discuss the matter. I made some bland remark about how grievously musicians feel such losses.

"That must be it, then," she said thoughtfully. "I offered to buy him another but he rejected the idea so vehemently I feared for his health!" There was an edge to her voice which suggested she had not liked Le Sac's manner. "Well, Mr Patterson, this may work in your favour. You may yet direct more concerts."

"I would dearly love the chance to direct the Concerts, madam, but I would like to earn the place through merit, not at the cost of another man's misfortunes."

"Regrettably," Mrs Jerdoun said, "we often prosper at other people's expense."

Lady Anne laughed and tapped my arm. "That is a jibe at me, sir. I was very ill when I was a girl, and if I had died Esther would have inherited my father's wealth."

Flustered by her frankness, I glanced at Mrs Jerdoun. "My cousin likes to tease, Mr Patterson," she said imperturbably. "She is fond of games." And I fancied she cast me a warning glance.

What the devil was I to do about Demsey, what indeed *could* I do? The more I considered the matter, the less likely it seemed that he would have taken the violin. His quarrel was with Nichols, not Le Sac; if his intention had been to place the blame on Nichols (by secreting the violin in his rooms, for instance), surely something would have been heard of it by now? But if it had been an attack on Le Sac, the only enemy I could attribute to the Swiss was myself; and I had not taken the violin nor asked anyone else to do it for me. So was it merely a simple matter of a thief making off with the instrument? And why did I feel that there was something deeper – something as yet unknown – about the affair?

As to the matter of the house in Caroline Square…

Early on Sunday evening I went out with determination, as if I was merely taking the air, walking with my prayer book in hand to give myself an air of respectability. The ladies were out at church; I saw them walking sedately down to St Nicholas together. Few of the servants remained, by the look of it, and the square was altogether quiet.

I walked round the square twice. Nothing happened. I walked past the house, turned and went back again, to no purpose. The square remained silent, the chill was merely the chill of the first hint of frost and the flickering lanterns remained in place. Even the spirit was silent.

On Monday, I received a kind note from a Mr Parry, player of the treble harp, who was evidently visiting the town.

Sir,

Your Name has been mentioned to me as one of the musical Gentlemen of this Town, who may do me the Honour of accompanying me on the Harpsichord at the benefit Concerts I intend holding in Hoult's Rooms at the Turk's Head on the 22nd and 25th Inst. I would of course offer the customary Rates, &c. I would be much obliged if you could send me at the Turk's Head, whether you are able or no.

Yr. Obt. Servt.

Thomas Parry.

I scribbled a note, dragged George from the copying upon which he was engaged and told him to take the note to the inn. He looked at me with big anxious eyes.

"I haven't finished the concerto, master." He was copying one of the pieces from Lady Anne's book.

"There is no hurry. You can finish it later."

"I don't feel well, master. I think Mr Sac passed on his illness to me."

He was clearly making excuses. "You have nothing to fear from Le Sac, George," I said wearily. "He cannot make you go back to him."

He took the note unwillingly and went out, dragging his feet. But he came running back before long, out of breath and more eager than before. "The gentleman asked if I played too, master, and when I said yes, he said to bring my violin and he'd hear me and say if he wanted me to play! Oh, and he sent this note –"

Parry's brief note appointed a time on Wednesday the 21st, two days hence, for a rehearsal. I folded the paper into a book where I generally keep such things and George went back to his copying.

We neither of us slept well that night. As I lay in the darkness, I could hear George wriggling upon the floor, constantly turning over. It seemed strange to me that he should still fear Le Sac. To be honest, I thought the less of him for it; he must know that Le Sac had no legal hold over him any longer. As for myself, I was preoccupied by puzzles that nagged at me night-long: Demsey, the violin, the strange room I had seen, the games Lady Anne insisted upon playing. And a growing conviction that all these things were somehow connected.

And – the last thing I recall before an uneasy sleep claimed me, just as the sky was lightening into dawn –

that peculiar inscription in Lady Anne's music book. The elegant flourish of an unknown signature: *Thomas Powell, organist, St Nicholas, 1725…*

14
CONCERTO FOR SOLO VIOLIN
Movement II

I woke the following morning in a determined mood. I might not be able to do anything about the strange events I had experienced in Caroline Square, or Lady Anne's games, but on some matters I could take action. Fortunately, one of my pupils sent word that she was taken ill, so I had time and leisure to act. George was sullen and sour-faced; I could not bear his fidgeting and sent him off to Akenhead's, the stationers, to fetch more paper and ravens' quills.

In the affair of the violin at least, I could see my way clearly. How could any thief have imagined he might dispose of it? It was a Cremona fiddle and would fetch a pretty penny, but only if sold to some person with musical knowledge. And such a person would at once be suspicious, particularly if the violin was offered by someone down at heel. Of course there were unscrupulous gentlemen who would accept goods without asking questions, but then the payment offered would be much lower.

And where might the thief offer the instrument for sale? Not in Newcastle or Durham or even Sunderland, in all of which places Le Sac had played; the violin might be recognised there by its unusual colour. Somewhere further afield, then – Edinburgh or York? London would be the safest place of all, but a thief would surely want to dispose of his booty as quickly as possible and not sit in a post-chaise with it for days on end.

I inscribed my first letter to Mr Ambrose Brownless, organ-builder of the City of York, reminding the gentleman of his kindness to me a year or two before, when I had been travelling north from London, and thanking him for his hospitality on that occasion. "And if I may trouble you further, sir," I wrote. "I am in search of a violin which has gone astray, (no one is quite sure how)..."

Finishing the note, I added the address and sealed it, then wrote another letter to an old acquaintance in Edinburgh. When George returned, I gave him both notes together with a shilling, and told him to make haste to the Post Office to send them off. He laid the bundle of quills upon the table. "Out again, sir?"

"Now," I said sharply. "And then meet me on the Sandhill. It is time you had your lesson."

He hung back. "Why not here, sir?"

"Because I have no instrument, fool! We'll use the harpsichord belonging to the Concerts – the one stored at Hoult's." (I was not sufficiently aforehand with the world to afford such an expensive instrument.)

His face fell further; he hated the keyboard and played it only under protest, because I told him no musician could hope to earn a living knowing one instrument alone. I planned to start him on the German flute, too; it is an instrument many gentlemen play, and can be very profitable. I said nothing of that, however; he was surly enough already.

"Go," I said.

He went, although it was plain he was mutinous.

After putting ready the books I needed for George's lesson and the practice of my own which I intended afterwards, I walked to the foot of the Side, to the office of

Mr Jenison's agent, who keeps the key to the Concerts' instruments, feeling a good deal better for having done something about at least one of the matters that besieged me. There was a great bustle about the Golden Fleece next to the office. A coach stood ready for departure and I found George already gawping at the preparations. I left him there while I went up the stairs to the agent's for the key; perhaps letting him gaze his fill on the commotion would put him in a better temper.

I came to the foot of the stairs again just as the coachman climbed into the box of the coach and decided to stay where I was rather than struggle through the crowd. And while I was standing there, my attention was caught by an ostler leading out a glossy chestnut horse; behind him came a lady, striding out to mount the animal, flouting the proprieties outrageously by wearing breeches (although a long, full greatcoat somewhat disguised the fact) and flinging herself astride a man's saddle. Surely only one woman could scorn convention like this and face down any criticism – Lady Anne.

But as the lady turned to send her horse trotting along the Key, I saw that I was wrong. Not Lady Anne but her cousin, Esther Jerdoun. I hardly knew whether to admire her or condemn her. The women in that house were altogether out of my common experience. As was the house itself.

Fortunately, George was full of the joys of the coach. We made our way to the Sandhill in silence; I was thinking of one thing, George was talking of another, and he was in such good humour that he submitted to his lesson upon the harpsichord with at least tolerable willingness. I felt giddy; my head was full of Esther Jerdoun's figure, still most shapely for a woman of forty. But after all, a man may admire where he chooses, provided he keeps his admiration a secret to all but himself.

Our rehearsal with Mr Parry the following day went well. He was a large man, fair in his colouring though I had imagined all Welsh quite dark. He was also blind, or very nearly so, but a casual observer would not know it, for he found his way about easily by keeping very near to the wall and running his fingertips lightly along it. Those hands were huge yet very delicate, and to see such large fingers plucking the finest of harp strings and producing soft tender tunes was disconcerting. He had adapted some violin airs of Handel and Purcell to his instrument and required us to provide the accompaniment; he himself played all by heart, and was very clear in what he wanted and very complimentary when we provided it. All in all, we had a merry time of it, playing happily for several hours.

But, alas, when it came to the concert itself, Parry's better judgment deserted him. We played two pieces by Handel which went very well, and the first solo airs Parry performed were Scotch and very pleasant. But an entire concert filled with airs and jigs, and reels and strathspeys, and strange Welsh tunes the like of which I had never heard before and never wish to hear again (and which I suspected Parry of fabricating himself, though he claimed they were so old that their origins were lost in the mists of time) – well, there are limits to how much one wishes to hear of such short pieces.

The audience, which was happily large, applauded enthusiastically; many hurried forward at the end of the concert to chat to Parry who towered over them all. I saw Nichols hanging about with a request that Parry might play for his class the following day. And Mr Jenison was also there, hands in pockets, frowning.

"That boy of yours, Patterson," he said suddenly. "Very tolerable player. I warrant it was you who taught him to play an adagio like that. That French fellow just rushes at adagios – I've always said foreigners can't play them well. Haven't the sensibility for it."

He did not meet my eye. *That French fellow* – hardly the way to refer to a favoured employee. (I prevented myself just in time from murmuring 'Swiss'.) Had Le Sac offended Jenison in some way? I caught Claudius Heron's gaze instead as he walked past; "Very good," he said, and walked on.

Esther Jerdoun came up to me with a smile as Jenison turned away. The lady was dressed in grey but the light caught the shiny fabric and turned it to shimmering silver; sapphires glittered in her ears and around her throat.

"I enjoyed the Handel greatly, Mr Patterson," she said in a tone of voice I thought rather loud. "Tell me, what opera was that overture from? I had not a handbill – they were all gone before I arrived."

But she did not allow me to answer; she lowered her voice and spoke swiftly. "You need not concern yourself about the violin. It is recovered." She raised her voice to its former pitch. "I have always thought Handel's instrumental music much under-rated. Do you not agree?"

I answered mechanically, hardly knowing what I said. Her mouth smiled; her head nodded, her elegant hand drifted across the decorated lid of the harpsichord. And her eyes were sharp and warning.

"Now it's to the bottle!" Parry said suddenly and swept his arm round George. The contrast between the giant and the child was ludicrous. "Shall we introduce this lad to the pleasures of fine wine, Mr Patterson? Oh, I beg your pardon, madam."

Perhaps he had caught the soft sound of the lady's dress

sweeping the floor as she turned. Mrs Jerdoun inclined her head. "I merely lingered to express my pleasure at your playing, Mr Parry."

She was an astonishing woman, I thought, as Parry, George and I went down the back stairs of the inn into the parlour. She was capable of surprising me in a way that, oddly, her cousin did not. I supposed outrageous acts were expected of Lady Anne. But I longed to ask a host of questions. Where had the violin been found? Was it known who had taken it? Why did she clearly intend its discovery to be kept a secret? Or was it merely the *manner* of its discovery? I had a sudden recollection of her riding out the previous day; had she herself found it?

And, above all, was Demsey implicated in the matter?

I was in a fever to know what had happened. But it was not until mid-morning of the following day that I had any further news. I was not in a good temper and the first lesson of the day had been with a recalcitrant unco-operative girl who had grown up sufficiently to discover the benefits of charming men into doing as she wished but not sufficiently to be able to work the trick. The day was sunny, although a chill breeze blew a hint of winter into the brightness, and after the lesson I went down to the Key to the Printing Office to buy a copy of the last week's *Courant*, which I had missed. Thomas Saint, in handing me my change, said, "I hear that French fellow has his fiddle back."

"Swiss," I said automatically. Then, recollecting that I was not supposed to have heard of the matter, I added, "Indeed? How?"

"One of the grooms belonging to Lady Anne found it." The breeze took hold of the outer door and gently tapped it against the jamb, sending quivers of sunshine across the papers stacked on the office floor. "Lady Anne's cousin had sent the fellow on an errand to Darlington. He stopped for a bite at the Post House and saw them carrying out the parcels for the coach. The wrapping on one of them was torn and he thought he saw a violin case within. Of course, he raised the alarm and they opened the parcel and there it was. Addressed to some rogue in London, I hear."

I was astounded. "Do you mean to say the thief put it on the coach as if it was an ordinary everyday parcel?"

Saint chuckled and seized at some bills that lifted from his desk in the breeze. "Some folks have a good helping of audacity, do they not? That's the top and tail of it. Of course the groom brought it back with him, the French fellow parted with the reward without a murmur and Lady Anne rewarded the groom as well. Everyone's happy – except the thief, of course."

I listened to the tale with mounting incredulity. I had never heard such nonsense. If the thief had rid himself of the instrument as soon as possible, which would have been sensible, it would have got much further south than Darlington. Five days since it had been stolen – almost time to reach London. And to send such a delicate item by a coach was unthinkable. The instrument would have been smashed to pieces before Doncaster or Newark; ostlers and inn-keepers have clumsy hands. But if the tale was not true, what had really happened? I knew of only one person who might be able to tell me.

I begged a piece of paper from Saint and penned a letter to Esther Jerdoun.

Madam,

At our last conversation you referred to a matter about which I would be grateful to have further information. I would appreciate your being so amiable as to indicate the truth of matters which are currently the subject of much unreliable gossip in the Town.

I remain, madam,

Y^{r} most ob^{t}. Servt.

Chas. Patterson.

I sent Saint's boy with the note; when I returned home that evening, a reply was waiting for me.

Sir, it read, *I do not believe there is any advantage in discussing the matter further.* It was signed *E. Jerdoun.*

With such a curt dismissal I was, I supposed, meant to be satisfied.

I was not.

15
CONCERTO FOR SOLO VIOLIN
Movement III

Before I went to bed, I scratched out letters to two or three acquaintances whom I thought might know Demsey's whereabouts. Mr Hesletine, for one, organist of Durham and a man whom it is well nigh impossible to avoid offending. His temper was like an ague – swift to come on and slow to mend again. Seven or eight years ago, he was nearly dismissed his position for abusing one of the prebendaries of the Cathedral. But he and Demsey, for some reason, have always dealt very well together, which is more than might be expected from the disparity in their ages (Hesletine is near fifty) and the similarity in their tempers. Last time I was in company with both of them, a year back, the whole afternoon was occupied by them shouting at each other with the greatest goodwill in the world. They parted the best of friends.

So one letter went to Hesletine asking if he had seen Demsey in the last week. Another went to the Post House in Durham, in case Demsey had passed south. A third to the Assembly Rooms in Sunderland, in case he lodged in that town, and a fourth – I considered briefly – to the publisher Hamilton in Edinburgh. My request in this last letter I mixed in casually with an enquiry over publishing terms for my *Scotch Songs for the Harpsichord*, performed at the last Concert. I left the letters on the table with a note to George to dispatch them and went to bed, if not satisfied, at least content I had done all I could.

The next day was the day of Parry's second benefit and I rose early to be done with all my errands before the evening. We had rehearsed our pieces the day of the first concert so there was no midday rehearsal to distract me. I went first down to Caroline Square, with some considerable trepidation but equally with determination, to see Esther Jerdoun, tucking Lady Anne's book of concerti under my arm as an excuse for my visit.

It was a dull grey day and the spirit in the square was muttering morosely. That particular patch of ground upon which I had twice stumbled looked like every other part of the road; I stood looking at it for some time. Then one of the other gentlemen who lived in the square came out and gave me a measuring look, plainly wondering if I was a thief. Heart pounding, I walked up to Lady Anne's door. Yet again, nothing happened.

A footman answered my knock but before he could speak, I heard a shout from within the house. Lady Anne, berating some unlucky servant. An object crashed to the floor. The footman flinched.

"Is Mrs Jerdoun at home?" I asked.

"She has gone out, sir. And –" Another shout arose behind him. "Lady Anne is not receiving visitors."

"I'll return another time," I said, and made a relieved retreat.

Thwarted in my attempt to press Mrs Jerdoun for an explanation, I went about my other business of the morning, walking down to Thomas Saint's to find out whether there had been any replies to my advertisement for subscribers to my Scotch music. Without at least two hundred or so, I could not hope to raise the money to have it engraved and printed. Eight subscribers had kindly put their names down. I put a brave face on it and told Saint to run the advertisement a second week, but I was plainly going to have to call upon the ladies and gentlemen personally to obtain their patronage.

As I walked back along the Key, through the busy bustle of carts and yellow-waistcoated keelmen, the smoke drifting along the river caught in my throat and made me cough. I climbed up to Fleming's shop on the bridge – I had yesterday snapped the topmost string on my violin and used the last of my stock to replace it – and at the door, stood back to allow a lady to leave the premises. It was Mrs Jerdoun, in a sensible if drab gown of a chocolate-brown colour. She clutched a parcel of books.

"Mr Patterson," she said coolly, and made to walk on.

"Madam." I stepped forward. Her quick frown of annoyance was not encouraging. "I have heard wild tales about grooms and Darlington Post House, and I had hoped you at least would tell me a true tale."

"A true tale, Mr Patterson? Do any of us know the truth?"

I thought she was trying to avoid answering me. "I would have thought you would, madam, better than anyone." She hesitated. "You recovered the violin yourself, I believe," I added.

"Very well, Mr Patterson," she said curtly. The wind – it is always windy upon the bridge – whipped her hair about her face. "I did indeed find the *item* in question, in Darlington Post House where it had, most fortunately, been overlooked for several days without being sent on to London. The landlord of the Post House had been somewhat exercised by the handwriting upon the label. I, on the other hand, recognised it at once."

She glanced round as two gentlemen walked past and waited until they were out of earshot. Then she turned her cool grey eyes upon me once again.

"It was *your* hand, sir."

I could think of nothing to say. I had not even wit enough to protest my innocence.

"I felt it wisest to disguise the matter as best I could," she said. "I told the landlord the instrument had been sent on by mistake, bribed the fellow into silence and brought the violin back with me. The label – I daresay you will be relieved to hear – I tore into pieces and buried deep in the bogs of Gateshead Fell."

She glanced away to the shops on the other side of the bridge, her cheeks flushed. "There is, I assure you, sir, no reason to fear. My cousin's groom is a reliable man and does and says as he is instructed, and acts the fool if he is challenged. He will not say anything outside the script I gave him. You may rest easy – your name will never be associated with the matter."

I found my breath at last, though I felt my cheeks blanching. "Madam…" I began, but she turned away.

"There is nothing more to be said, Mr Patterson. I would be obliged if you do not refer to the matter again."

She walked quickly away, crossing the bridge towards Gateshead Bank. I could only stand and stare after her, my clothes tugged by the river breeze and my mind in a turmoil. She thought *I* had stolen the violin.

I shifted as another customer came from the shop, and numbly went in to complete my own errand. Fleming is taciturn; I think I left without exchanging more than a dozen words with him. I walked down from the bridge and up Butcher Bank towards Pilgrim Street, hardly noticing the passers-by. Esther Jerdoun's opinion of me distressed me but I did not find it strange that she should suspect me. Everyone associated with the Concerts must be aware of the argument between Le Sac and myself. My friend was known to quarrel with his. But the label – that was the puzzling thing. I knew, as Esther Jerdoun could not, that it was a forgery.

Kicking at the leaves that had fallen from the trees in the gardens between the houses, I contemplated Light-Heels Nichols. He would have had access to Le Sac's lodgings and might have been able to contrive a means of carrying the violin off even with Le Sac lying ill there. But why should he do such a thing? To implicate Demsey, since Hugh's disappearance at the same time as the violin must inevitably have lent credence to any such tale? But then why my handwriting on the label?

And – I halted beside a garden wall – what proof did I have that the label had ever existed? Or that the violin had ever been in Darlington? Lady Anne was plainly playing games with me for her own pleasure; why not her cousin too? Were the ladies cut from the same material?

I was not at my best during the lessons that day and my pupils came off rather easy. Nor was I in a good mood for Mr Parry's second concert. I had made a firm decision. That house in Caroline Square, and the ladies in it, was the centre of all my present woes; its owner was intent upon setting me at odds with Le Sac, Mrs Jerdoun either believed me a thief or was playing a game of her own, and even the house itself was playing tricks on me. I would certainly go there no more, whatever invitations I might receive. I would avoid the ladies, except for the demands of common politeness when we met, and that would be the end of it.

Old Hoult sensed my black temper as I climbed the back stairs to the upper room of the Turk's Head. "Cheer up, lad," he said from the banister at the head of the dark steps.

"His tunes aren't *that* bad – although some of them may be a bit outlandish."

The thought of two hours of reels and laments set my spirits plummeting.

The Long Room was brightly lit, every candle in the glittering chandeliers flickering gently in the draughts. Some of the audience were already gathered in clumps in window embrasures and around some of the most comfortable chairs. George stood near to the music stands, frowning at a handbill; I was pleased to see that the boy had dressed in his best and had managed to desist from scratching his spots. He smelt rather better, too, so he must have followed my orders to wash. He started when I came up to him and was clearly only a little relieved when he saw who I was. His irrational fears still annoyed me, but I chose to ignore them for the sake of peace.

"Is that the bill for the night?"

"No, master." He held the paper out to me. "Mr Nichols gave it me at the door."

It was an advertisement for a concert the next day. With profuse apologies for the shortness of the notice, M. Le Sac offered a benefit concert at the Turk's Head, and extended his grateful thanks to Signor Bitti, of the York Concerts, who was travelling between that city and Edinburgh, and who had kindly consented to play upon the harpsichord and to offer several solos upon that instrument.

"Sig-nor Bit-ti," George read laboriously. "Do you know him, master?"

"I know of him," I said grimly. "Hebden of York speaks highly of him. But then he has a wild fancy for anything Italian." John Hebden is not above calling himself *Signor Hebdeni* in the wilds of Scarborough where he fancies they will not be quick-witted enough to recognise his Yorkshire accent. Still, he is an excellent judge; no one can ever accuse him of hiring a bad musician. But it mattered not to me whether Sig-nor Bit-ti was excellent or not; this was one concert I would not appear in.

There was a numerous and brilliant company at Hoult's that night. Some I recognised from Parry's first concert; others had heard of the gentleman's powers and come to see for themselves. Young Hoult had to fetch in extra chairs from below and, when they had been disposed around the walls and across the place, the room looked very full indeed. The bright, warm glow of satins and silks under the candlelight was very fine, and there was only a faint miasma of sweat overlaid by perfumes of musk and lavender.

As rooms filled with a multitude of people will, Hoult's Long Room became hot and the air stale; I saw George surreptitiously slipping a finger under his cravat to ease it, and felt the sweat trickle down my own cheek. Unluckily, the members of the audience were almost all clutching Le Sac's handbills and used the papers to fan themselves, so universally that our renderings of Handel were accompanied by a regular flap, flap, flap. But once the music was begun, my mind settled, for it is impossible to play well with only half a mind on the job. Parry performed much the same pieces as before, with a few Irish tunes thrown in, and I saw one or two ladies wipe away tears at his most plangent melodies.

I occupied moments when the harpsichord was silent by looking about the audience. Mrs Jerdoun I spotted at once, seated against the far wall; she was dressed in palest lavender and did not look my way. Her cousin, I saw to my surprise, sat across the other side of the room conversing with Mr Jenison. Had the ladies quarrelled? Well, it was none of my business any longer; I was resolved to avoid them altogether.

One person I did not see until the interval between the acts was Mr Ord; indeed, I did not see him at all until he clutched at my sleeve. Parry had generously provided refreshments and Ord held a glass of Hoult's best wine between his fingers. He waved Le Sac's handbill at me.

"This – this Bitty fellow. Do you know him?" His round red cheeks were glistening with heat.

"I have heard he is an excellent player."

Ord pursed his lips. "And do *you* play in this concert, sir?"

"I am not needed," I pointed out. "Signor Bitti is to play the keyboard."

"In the band as well as the solos?"

"I have not heard precisely, but that would be my understanding."

"Ah," Ord said and nodded. "Well, Patterson – what do you say to that Irish jig in the second selection of airs? Most excellent, eh?"

"Very unusual," I said, temporising.

At the end of the concert, I sent George off to bespeak one of Hoult's pies – there is nothing like extended playing to work up an appetite – and started to pack away my music while the crowds thronged around Parry. Jenison's crisp voice sounded above all, offering congratulations. Then, as I turned to lower the harpsichord lid, I was startled by Lady Anne who swung up behind it and leant towards me. She was clearly in a better temper than she had been in the morning, her face flushed and laughing, her hair in elegant disarray. Leaning forward upon the closed lid, she afforded me a view of her slight breasts, enclosed in gold satin. Diamond drops lay on her white, flawless skin.

"I have been doing you a good turn," she whispered, with a quick dart of her eyes here and there as if to ensure she was not overheard.

I was annoyed by the way she seemed constantly to seek me out, and alarmed too that others might draw erroneous conclusions from her behaviour. We had already attracted some attention. "How so, my lady?" I asked warily.

"I have been extolling your qualities to Mr Jenison."

"I am most grateful, madam," I said dryly.

"And I have been pointing out how admired the Italian players are in London nowadays."

I realised she had not been glancing round to ensure that no one overheard but quite the opposite, for Jenison himself was walking up behind me.

"I fancy, madam," he said with some directness, "that I do not need fashionable fribbles in London to tell me what is good and what is not."

She inclined her head. "I think we both agree, Mr Jenison, that *certain persons* have a natural judgment that can recognise quality wherever it appears."

When she said *certain persons*, she clearly meant *you and I.* Her smiling glance indicated that I also was to be included.

"I have always been entirely sure, Lady Anne," Jenison said, "that England produces talent to match anything that is found abroad."

"Better, on some occasions," the lady agreed and cast another significant glance in my direction, which caused me both embarrassment and annoyance.

"English musicianship," Jenison pronounced, his gaze momentarily fixed upon the visionary distance, "is of a more solid and durable quality than that found anywhere else in the world. Lady Anne, may I escort you to your carriage?"

"Why, thank you, sir. But I seem to have mislaid my cloak. I think I left it in the window embrasure."

"Allow me, my lady." He bowed.

Lady Anne watched until he was out of earshot before leaning closer. "Wait until tomorrow, Mr Patterson, and you will reap the full benefit of what I have done."

"My lady –"

But she was gone and I was left, annoyed and irritated, to dwell on Jenison's doubtful compliment (to be *durable* is all very well but who wishes to be regarded as *solid*?), and to worry over what Lady Anne might have done this time.

16
BASS SONG

Parry was a sociable man and kept me eating and drinking in Mrs Hill's until the small hours of the morning. I was a willing participant, drinking more than I ought in order to forget my worries. George fell asleep after a huge piece of pie; I roused him after a while and sent him home, too sleepy to protest. When Parry did at last tire, I bade him a cheerful goodbye and lurched off to tell Lady Anne and Esther Jerdoun exactly what I thought of them and to insist that I would have nothing more to do with them. I saw hardly anyone in the darkness, except for the women of the streets; I don't recall what I said to those who accosted me but they went away in flounces of anger. I was fortunate that no thieves attacked me, though I heard someone yell at me as I walked into Caroline Square.

I would not be intimidated, I would not be manipulated. I walked straight across the square to the house, making sure that I lingered on that particular place in the road. And when the familiar shiver took me and I saw first darkness and then the tall looming presence of the houses in that elegant street, I was exultant. I stood in the middle of the street and I shouted at the top of my voice…

And then I shivered again and stared stupidly at the man who was shaking my arm. "For God's sake, man!" Claudius Heron snapped. "Be quiet!"

I squinted at him. "What are you doing here?"

A shade of annoyance crossed his face, no doubt at my disrespectful tone. I ignored it, laughing drunkenly. "Been out on the town? Entertaining some lady?"

His lean pale cheeks reddened. "Patterson," he said, "you will regret this tomorrow. Let me take you home."

"I hope she was worth the money," I said. Heron, I dimly remembered, was a widower. "Would it not be more convenient to find a servant in your own house?"

"Patterson!" he said, scandalised, then sighed. "Come with me. No –" I had attempted to extricate myself from his grip. "Aren't you cold? It's a cold night. You must go home."

"A cold night," I said. "Made me shiver... Didn't you feel it?"

He frowned. "There was something odd – "

"Cold and dark – and a street, not a square. And when I shouted, windows went up and someone shouted back and... and then you came. You must have seen the street! Old elegant houses."

Another sigh. "*I* shouted," he said. "I saw you reeling drunkenly down the street and came after you. For God's sake, man, think of your reputation!"

I considered this. He was right. I nodded. "You'll be dismissing me again."

He swore and slung my arm over his shoulder.

After that, I remember nothing.

I was woken at an appallingly early hour by a loud voice. When I struggled on to my elbow, wincing at the bright sunshine slanting into the room, I saw George backing away from a large presence.

"Patterson!" the presence cried. "Still abed? For God's sake, man – it's a wonderful day!"

I groaned and tried to pull the sheets over my head. My eyes were sore and my head was one huge, throbbing ache. And I was remembering the encounter with Heron, wondering if there had been more I *didn't* remember. I had invited him to dismiss me, I recalled. In heaven's name, how had I allowed myself to be so foolish?

"Get up and dressed, man," the presence said. "We're wasting drinking time!"

My stomach churned as I struggled to sit up. The last thing I needed was an encounter with Tom Mountier – good friend though he was, and in my opinion the finest bass voice in England. But he has a habit of not confining his singing to his professional duties at Durham Cathedral, or at our Concerts, but of breaking into song on the least pretext. And my tormented head wanted no recitals that morning.

"In heaven's name, Tom, do you never think of anything but drink? George, fetch me washing water."

The boy disappeared downstairs and Mountier perched himself on my chair while I hunted beneath the bedclothes for my breeches. Thomas Mountier is a fleshy man; his height enables him to call himself well-built but another few years of indulgence will make him fat. If the drink doesn't kill him first.

He contemplated me while I dressed. "Who's the lad?"

"He's my apprentice. Le Sac passed him on to me, in a way."

His black eyebrows shot together and apart again, and his wig bobbed. Mountier's face could never hide his feelings. I peered at him. "Are you here to sing at his benefit tonight?"

"Purcell," he agreed. "'To arms, Britons, to arms!'"

"You could sing that in your sleep."

"I have." He grinned.

"How was Edinburgh?"

The grin became a grimace. "Full of censorious tradesmen. *Mr Mountier, could you not sing somewhat more softly?*

Mr Mountier, that song you propose – is it not a little, er, wanting in gentility?" His imitation of a pedantic Scotch accent was excellent. "And then you go along to their so-called concert and face an audience of no more than five 'gentlemen' who can't even play instruments but talk so learnedly you'd think they'd invented the science."

"Ah, a private meeting. But they paid you well?"

"Hah!" He made a parsimonious pout. "*But you're not Italian, Mr Mountier.* I may not be Italian, I told 'em, but I was the rage of London concerts a couple of years back."

I buttoned up my waistcoat. "What then?"

"Damn it, Patterson, you know *what then.* They asked me why I hadn't stayed in London and I said, there are times when a man has to put devotion before fame, and they pursed up their presbyterian mouths and said that in that case I ought to be satisfied with the piddling salary the Dean and Chapter of Durham pay me for singing in their heathen cathedral." He made another face. "I beat them up to what they pay their precious Italians."

George came back with the water and I rinsed my face and hands. "Piddling salary, the man says! I'd accept fifty pounds a year if offered it."

"You should have seen what I was getting in London," he bemoaned. But we both knew he could not go back to that; the drink was catching up with him much too quickly.

"When did you get back?"

"Yesterday."

"And came straight here? Aren't you supposed to chant the psalms at evensong at least now and again?"

"I get one of the others to do it for me. He's glad of the extra money. But I must be back tomorrow or I'll miss matins at St Nicholas. Can't neglect my other pious duties as parish clerk, you know."

"Do you *ever* sing in the cathedral?"

"Not if I can help it, my boy. Those prebendaries – they believe in it all, you know. Po-faced, the lot of them. And talking of someone else who can't abide all the posturing and posing, Hesletine gave me a note for you."

I unfolded the paper, edging away from the too-bright shafts of sunlight that dazzled from the page. The note from Hesletine, the Durham organist, was brief. He had unfortunately not had the pleasure of Mr Demsey's company for several months.

"Are you ready, man?" Mountier said impatiently. "No, not you, youngster, we're going to drink far too deep for you!"

We walked out, leaving George pouting. As always I felt dwarfed by Mountier. He cleared his throat as we came into the sunny street and stood on the doorstep humming and watching a carter trying to negotiate a pack of dogs outside the tavern.

"Now I come to think of it," I said, "I had forgot you were parish clerk at St Nicholas. So you'll know it well. St Nicholas in Durham, I mean, not St Nicholas here."

"Charles," Mountier said severely. "You're babbling."

"Damn it, I'm making perfect sense. I've heard of a fellow called Thomas Powell who was organist at St Nicholas's church. But he was never organist at St Nicholas's church in this town, so I wondered if he was organist at St Nicholas in Durham. See, it is all perfectly clear." Oh God, my head ached.

"If you say so," Mountier said with good humour.

"Well, was he?"

"Was who what?"

"Was Thomas Powell," I said very carefully, "organist at St Nicholas's church in Durham?"

"You're still half asleep, Charles," Mountier said with

delight. "He can't have been. Church hasn't got an organ. I suggested a violin once." Mountier shook with laughter. "Should have heard the churchwardens – shocked to their core. *A violin in church, Mr Mountier? How can you suggest such a thing?*" He slapped me on the back. "Come on, man, we have some serious drinking to do. And don't worry – we'll not lose track of time. We'll be there for the rehearsal."

"You may be," I said. "But I am not invited to play. Signor Bitti from York plays the harpsichord."

"Bitti? Very tolerable player. Pleasant fellow, too – speaks damn good English. But surely he doesn't play with the band?"

"Mountier," I said wearily, "if I were to explain all the intricacies of the affair, we would still be standing on this doorstep next month."

"But we have time!" he cried. "We have all morning to drink in!" And with the carter at that moment passing us, we strode off along the street.

We spent the morning in Mrs Hill's in the Fleshmarket. In daylight, when the butcher's stalls are set up, the street stinks of offal and buzzes with flies that have constantly to be waved away. Mountier, with his unquenchable interest in food, insisted upon examining the choicest cuts of meat until thirst drove him at last into Mrs Hill's. Yet neither food nor drink had caused him to forget what I had said. He made me tell him everything (although I remained silent upon my suspicions of Demsey and mentioned Mrs Jerdoun as little as possible) while he downed a great quantity of ale and grew steadily more cheerful, if such a thing was possible. He called for his tankard to be filled again and again, yet it was remarkable that when he arose finally and went for a piss in the necessary-house behind the inn, we had precisely the time required to get to the Turk's Head for the beginning of the rehearsal.

Against my better judgment, I agreed to accompany him. I was interested to see Signor Bitti; anyone of whom Mountier spoke in favour must be excellent. A large number of people had turned out for the rehearsal, the day being fine, and I was happy to be able to lose myself in the press at the side of the room, although my view of the harpsichord was not as good as I had hoped.

Contemplating the very small band of players gathered around Le Sac, it was clear that the other performers were not as prompt as Mountier (although doubtlessly they would be more sober). I was just wondering if Signor Bitti had after all cried off, when Mountier came into the room by the rear stairs. He was all smiles, his arm around the shoulder of a slender fashionable gentleman of tender years, eighteen at most. The young gentleman wore an embarrassed smile but when he laughed at some joke of Mountier's his entire demeanour changed. He was really astonishingly handsome.

They weaved across the room – in part to avoid the congregated ladies and gentlemen, in part (I was certain) because Mountier could not walk a straight line. I realised to my horror that I was not as well hidden as I had hoped and that they were coming straight towards me. I glanced in Le Sac's direction and saw him staring at us, his face twisted with anger.

Mountier introduced us, voice as loud as a bugle horn, and the gentleman – who was indeed Signor Bitti – and I made our bows. He was, I saw, nervous and Mountier's next words made him more so.

"Patterson is our *usual* harpsichord player," Mountier roared.

"Oh? But I would not wish..." Bitti stammered. "I – If you –"

"I am greatly looking forward to hearing you play," I said warmly, to put him at his ease. "It is not often that we have the chance to hear someone so up to date with the latest London novelties."

This was something of a lie, as we flatter ourselves on our knowledge of the metropolis, being in regular contact with all the best publishers in London and corresponding regularly with promoters of concerts in the capital. Le Sac's presence, too, must indicate that I had understated our pretensions. But Signor Bitti clearly recognised what my words were meant to convey – a disclaimer of offence. He bowed and went with Mountier to talk to Le Sac. I heard Le Sac loudly ask after the health of his 'good friends' – a number of eminent musicians whose names clearly impressed such listeners as Henry Wright.

Time wore on and still the other band members did not arrive. Signor Bitti tried out the harpsichord and frowned over its tuning; Wright attempted a passage, unsuccessfully, on his tenor. Dr Brown rubbed a speck of dust from the impeccable polish of his violoncello. A gentleman with a German flute edged in with an apology for his lateness, and two cellists arrived breathless ten minutes later. But it soon became clear that no one else would arrive, leaving the band woefully thin and bottom-heavy; indeed, I thought the rehearsal could hardly go on. With only one violinist apart from Le Sac, and a poor player at that (for it was Nichols), how could they maintain the accompaniment while Le Sac played his solos?

And as I looked round the impatient ladies and gentlemen, my eyes set upon Lady Anne standing by the entrance door. I looked away at once but not before she had given me a mischievous look. I recalled her words the previous night: *Wait until tomorrow and you will reap the benefit of what I have done.* Was this her doing? But why should she wish to humiliate Le Sac in this way?

They were forced at last to begin, starting with a solo of Mountier's so that Le Sac could play in the band. No doubt they hoped that latecomers would arrive before the violin solos needed to be rehearsed. Le Sac was red-faced with anger. I looked about the room as they tuned, searching for those regular members of the band who had not yet arrived. Mr Ord and Mr Heron, for instance – where were they? Not that I looked forward to meeting Heron after the events of last night. I had written him a note of apology from Mrs Hill's, but I was certain there would be undesirable consequences from that incident. How in heaven's name had I allowed myself to become so drunk!

Despite the gross deficiencies of the band, Signor Bitti played quite brilliantly. In Mountier's songs he was reticent, allowing the soloist to dominate, never intruding. In his own solos he combined both dexterity and expressiveness, not indulging in virtuosity for its own sake but always subordinating technique to the demands of the music. I was so taken with his playing that I hardly noticed Le Sac sawing away on his precious black violin or Mountier, with perfect diction and pathetic delicacy, first rousing tears in the eyes of the ladies, then, with bellicose bombast, inciting us all to warlike and patriotic sentiments. No one could have imagined him drunk. But Signor Bitti took my chief attention and, at an interval in the rehearsal, I went to him to express my appreciation and, greatly daring, to ask for a lesson.

"But I leave first thing tomorrow," he said, the radiance dying from his face. "And I cannot put it off, for I am contracted to the Musical Society in Edinburgh."

I apologised for inconveniencing him and attempted to withdraw. "But I return in a month," he said. "And we may meet then. I will write to you from Edinburgh and tell you the date of my return."

I had no expectation that he would remember but I thanked him and withdrew, unfortunately not looking where I went. I walked straight into Le Sac.

His face was livid with fury. "I will break you, Patterson," he hissed. "I will break you for what you have done here today."

17
QUARTETTO

I had not intended to go to the evening concert itself but the prospect of hearing Signor Bitti again was irresistible. I walked into Hoult's Long Room close to the starting time. The room was crowded and noisy, and more than a little stuffy; on such occasions no one will open windows for fear of draughts. It was strange to find myself on this side of the music stands, and I looked about for a seat close to people who could be trusted not to commiserate with me upon my exclusion from the band. A movement caught my attention: Lady Anne was beckoning to me from the far side of the room. I was annoyed to have fallen so quickly into her clutches but I could not ignore such a direct invitation.

I went across to make my bow and she patted the chair next to her.

"Pray sit down, Mr Patterson. You may keep me right and tell me where I should applaud and where keep silent."

She was in no need of such elementary tuition. "You must show your appreciation, Lady Anne, where you feel it to be deserved."

She considered me for a moment, then, with a bow of her head in my direction, softly tapped her hands together.

"Madam –" I protested.

She held up a hand to silence me. "No, no, you are quite right. I must show approbation for all things Le Sacian, must I not? I am after all his patron."

I hesitated but could not keep silent. "When we spoke

last night, my lady, you implied I would reap the benefit of your actions."

She fanned her hot cheeks gently with the handbill. "A word or two in the right ears," she agreed, smiling. "A hint to the gentlemen that they might not like to be connected with foreign interlopers."

"Do I take it then, my lady," I persisted, "that it is as a result of your hints that the band was so thin at the rehearsal?"

"I flatter myself that certain gentlemen –" she was nodding in Jenison's direction – "seem to find my reasoning sound."

I stared at the empty end of the room where the stands, loaded now with music, stood deserted. I found myself resenting such interference when it disadvantaged a player as good as the Italian.

Lady Anne was smiling at me, but watchfully, I thought.

"Will you inform me, my lady, why you take such an interest in me?"

She tapped my hand playfully with the handbill. "Every good musician needs a patron."

"I thought, madam, that you were Le Sac's."

"I grow weary of foreign airs, Mr Patterson. I find myself more and more appreciating good honest English virtues."

I would have liked a generous patron, but not Lady Anne. A woman who deserts one man in favour of another – without first making the situation clear to the deserted party – may do so again.

At that moment, Mrs Jerdoun walked past. I saw her glance our way, then walk on without a word. Lady Anne chuckled. "My cousin is out of charity with me. We have quarrelled over a trifle; she will have forgotten by tomorrow."

A lady and gentleman of her acquaintance came up and she turned to converse with them. She did not introduce me; I was a tradesman, to be patronised but not indulged. Across the room, Mrs Jerdoun had settled herself in a window embrasure and I was briefly distracted by a fugitive memory. Yes, of course, the two ladies had also sat apart at Parry's concert; the quarrel must already have lasted rather longer than Lady Anne cared to have known. Perhaps Mrs Jerdoun was avoiding us both.

The seats were filling up and the first musicians came in. Le Sac had evidently persuaded a number of gentlemen to change their minds and the band was almost its usual size. In fact – I looked at all the heated faces, earnest and nervous, behind the stands – yes, almost all the usual players were there, Wright and Ord among them. The only one who had not yielded to persuasion was Claudius Heron. I did not know whether to be glad or sorry that he was not there; I had not received a response to my apology.

Mountier came panting up the back stairs, hesitating by the harpsichord with an air of panic. He hurried across, leaning over me with a waft of stale ale. "Patterson, Patterson, what am I singing?"

I gave him my handbill and he tottered off with it, only to come back several minutes later to ask the same question again. I reminded him as best I could, given I had not read the handbill, being too preoccupied. When he was gone, Lady Anne tapped my arm.

"That young thing over there, with pink ribbons. That is the Lindsay girl, the one your friend was accused of making fast and loose with."

I looked round and saw the 'young thing' Lady Anne described, all white and virginal, a halo of yellow curls, a round, smiling face and a sideways, knowing look. Who was she smiling at? Yes, to be sure – Light-Heels Nichols, just walking up with his fiddle in his hands.

The concert was a great success. From the opening notes of the full piece which began the first act, the numerous company was plainly prepared to be pleased. With great good humour, Mountier treated them to a simple, rollicking Scotch song, then Signor Bitti played a solo of his own composing. Le Sac, smiling serenely, sat through it all, keeping himself low and quiet, leading the band with such ease that he had time to glance around and nod at acquaintances at the front of the company.

Some confusion arose over Mountier's next song; he stumbled forward and started on a hunting song, which he was supposed to sing in the second act. The rank and file in the band were startled and there was much hasty (and noisy) sorting of music, some worried looks and hurried whispering. Signor Bitti, however, played on with unruffled composure, although I knew he must have had quite another song in front of him – playing from memory (and faultlessly) an accompaniment which he had seen only once before, at rehearsal. Le Sac too was unperturbed; he sat back at his ease, violin under his arm, as if he had never intended to play in this song.

And then Le Sac rose magnificently, silencing the last ripples of applause for Mountier, and launched into what I must – if I am to tell the truth – describe as some of the most brilliant playing I have ever heard. It was as if Signor Tartini himself had come among us. I warrant no one in the room paid one moment's attention to the band's soft accompaniments; Le Sac dominated the entire company with that black violin and the bow of spotted wood. A rolling, dancing, sparkling scatter of notes spilled from his hands and from that instrument of mere, once mute, wood.

And when the display was over, I sat back both elated and cross. Elated by the virtuosity of it, and cross because I was excited by empty passage-work. Admiring of his technique, and low-spirited because I recognised that I would never have such skill. Uplifted by the mob crying for more, and saddened that *I* would never know such applause for my playing.

I slipped from my place. Lady Anne did not look round. Outside, in the Bigg Market, a cool breath of night air only dampened my spirits more. I could hear the applause echoing from the room behind me. The music began again as Le Sac encored the piece.

I wandered down the length of the Bigg Market and came to where the church of St Nicholas stood darkened and silent. A torch burned outside Barber's bookshop beyond. Nichols's brother, the organist, still lived, still deep in debt and drink, and had hired a young man from Gateshead, the son of the organist there, as deputy. I had not the skill of Le Sac or Bitti, nor the patrons, nor the position.

I do not recall ever being so downcast.

The next day I occupied by moving my few possessions to my new room – an undertaking that would have been frowned on by many people (had they known it) as it was a Sunday. The room was larger than my old lodging, and rather more regular in shape; I was able to set one corner aside for George, which delighted him. Mrs Foxton had provided the room with two chairs so that George and I were able to work at the same time and, as the window opened, which my old one had not, I was better able to bear George's smell. He had given up his fear of Le Sac at last, I noted, and ran out on an errand without complaint.

When he did not return immediately, however, I glanced out into the street and saw him in conversation with Lady Anne in her Sunday finery. Lady Anne again! No doubt she had been to church at St Nicholas, but what could be her business with George? I expected her to come up but George came back alone.

"What did the lady want?"

"Lady, master?"

"Lady Anne."

"She wanted to know if you were well, master. She said you left the concert early last night."

I only half-believed him; he would not meet my gaze. I suspected something more; perhaps Lady Anne had given him a penny for some information. She was a fickle woman whose interest must always be engaged by something or someone new; she had tired of Le Sac and I was her latest toy.

A note from Mountier came as I was about to step out to take the air after my labours. The note was addressed from Hoult's.

My dear fellow. Come and haul me out of my bed and drink an hour or so with me. I cannot bear to go back to that sanctified nest of colliers and prebends without good ale to fortify me.

Yours,

Thos Mountier.

Despite my depression, I was forced to laugh over the note and its writer's fecklessness. I had no doubt that the prebendaries had told Mountier to be back for matins and that he would be expected at his St Nicholas to line out the psalms for evensong. Or possibly the other way round. Indeed, he should have gone back last night immediately after the concert; the prebendaries would be horrified to believe he contemplated travelling or, indeed, drinking on a Sunday. But one cannot tell a good and generous friend that he is behaving stupidly and will one day pay for it. I scribbled on the note: *Alas, some of us do not have such strong heads!* and sent the messenger back with it. After my experiences in Caroline Square with Claudius Heron, I was wary of drinking too much.

I set aside the unsettling thoughts that reflection brought on and spent most of the rest of the day composing. The work went well and I had scrawled several sheets before the evening, leaving them for George to copy neatly the following day. Then in the evening I went out to take the air, and encountered Claudius Heron on the doorstep, about to knock and leave his card.

We looked at each other in some confusion; I started on another apology but he waved me to silence. "There is a difference between foolishness and malice," he said. "We all do *foolish* things." And he walked away, leaving his card in my hand. When I looked at the back of it, he had scrawled *Mr Heron expects Mr Patterson for his lesson at the usual time.*

Monday was chill and blustery, as unpleasant as its predecessors had been inviting. On the Key, the wind blew in the smell of the sea, and the seagulls wheeled and screeched overhead. The smoke from the salt-works at Shields rolled in clouds upon the horizon, great billows and waves such as the sea exhibits on stormy days. Sulphur caught in my throat. But I was in a better mood today after my efforts of the previous day.

If my compositions were not as good as Le Sac's and my performance poorer – well, the Swiss was twenty years or so my elder and had more experience in these matters. I must have faith in my own abilities and not allow unjust criticism and opposition to deter me. And when I came to the Printing Office, Thomas Saint's smiling face as he presented me with a sheaf of letters seemed to reward me for my new spirit of determination. Fifty-four new subscribers for my music! I had despaired too early. I would ask Mountier to mention the matter to his fellow members of the cathedral choir. Hesletine might subscribe too. And Hebden of York was fond of Scotch tunes.

I went to Lizzie Saint's lesson much restored.

18
DEAD MARCH

But when I came out of doors again, the stink of sulphur almost overwhelmed me; the alley that led down the side of the Printing Office was dark as midnight. I stood at the entrance to the alley, covering my mouth with my handkerchief, and stared appalled upon the scene before me.

The Key was a river of smoke, eddying and drifting in a wind that dragged at my clothes and hair. As the smoke swirled, it covered everything in a pall of dark grey, then tugged itself apart again, offering glimpses of cobbles, heaps of coal, bundles of charcoal, ballast stones abandoned in huge hillocks. The screams of seagulls echoed as if from a great distance; faintly I heard shouting – confused and alarmed, frightened even – as if some calamity had occurred. A man stumbled out of the smoke, coughing and retching - a collier by his clothes and the ingrained black lines on his hands and face. He pushed past me, swearing through his coughing, and stumbled on.

At last I understood. No seagulls made those unearthly noises but the spirits of drowned sailors, calling from the water for assistance, pleading to be lifted from the river, crying out for rescue. Sailors who had fallen from the keels, or cast down by wreck, or thrown over by drink or malice or the impenetrable workings of fate. Each of them tormented, each crying for help.

I thought of following the collier. Behind the Printing Office, an alley twists round to the back of All Hallows Church; from there it climbs the hill to the more salubrious areas of Pilgrim Street, where the smoke and stench would be far below. But I had told George to wait for me outside the office of Jenison's agent, so we could collect the harpsichord key for another practice. So, feeling my way with one hand on the wall of the house to my right, I edged forward into the smoke – and fell over a coil of rope into a pile of grimy empty baskets.

I lost my handkerchief when I fell, scrabbled among the baskets for it in vain, finally picked myself up and started off again without it. A mountain of ballast was piled up ahead of me; I was forced to leave the wall to go round it and was immediately unsure of my direction. The shouting persisted all around me now, disorientating and unnerving. A blurred darkness loomed; cautiously I went on and the smoke eddied and parted, and showed me a knot of seamen sprawled upon the cobbles, as if taking their ease in a meadow, smoking begrimed pipes phlegmatically.

"Watch your step," one called to me. "Spirits are up."

I went on, feeling for every step. In the darkness of the smoke ahead, I saw a still darker shape – the scarecrow-thin figure of the rector of St Nicholas, the Rev Moses Bell, standing at the side of a huge upturned basket. He was lifting a hand in blessing and consolation, muttering prayers in tones that varied between compassion and fear. Beyond him, in billows of smoke, nuggets of black soot seemed to drift, sometimes plainly visible, sometimes almost illusory.

The Rev Mr Bell saw me, raised his hands helplessly, murmured his endless prayers. I stumbled on into the mist. I knew that my way must be in a straight line along the Key, and so I kept a straight line. Or so I thought until a voice spoke at my feet.

"Come you to join me, sir?"

I looked down and glimpsed a ripple of dark water barely

inches in front of me. Another step, and I would have fallen into the river.

"If you'd just oblige me, sir –" Did the spirit have a Scotch accent? "If you would help me up. This place stinks like a shithouse."

"I cannot," I said. "There is nothing I can do."

"Come, sir. Ain't it our Christian duty to help them in need?"

"Yes, but –"

"It's little enough I'm asking. Just a helping hand."

"You cannot leave this place," I blurted helplessly, wanting to help, wanting to flee. "You're dead. A spirit."

Silence. I heard the slap-slap of water against the Key and I thought *One day someone will say the same to me,* and *Dear God, let me never come to this.* I have never given much thought as to where I would prefer my spirit to linger its hundred years or so beyond death; but, God, let it not be in the river, among the smoke and the lost souls, the sailors who babble in foreign tongues and cry out for lost familiar scenes, the lunatics who fling themselves into the dark poisonous water and regret it at once as they sink deeper and deeper into death.

I heard a voice raised behind me and, edging round, saw Mr Bell gesticulating a yard or so away. I stumbled back to him and together we fumbled our way along the cobbles.

"Two or three times a year I am called to this unpleasant duty," Bell said. "My predecessor, Mr Greggs – when I was a chaplain – told me not to worry over it. Tell them you can do nothing, say a blessing or two and go home. But it goes against all I believe in, Patterson, to be so uncaring."

"Yet there *is* nothing to be done," I said. The wailing of the spirits, drifting all around us, was still unsettling me. The black specks in the smoke came so close I instinctively tried to knock them away; looking down, I saw my sleeve speckled with black and did not know whether the marks were made by spirits or mere flecks of soot.

"There was one there..." Bell jerked his head. "He was murdered, pushed over the side of his ship. He knows who did it but the villain was never brought to justice; he ran off to Bristol and sailed to Barbados, it seems. The spirit asked me when the villain was coming back. Do you know the worst of it, Patterson? The murderer sailed with the Quaker fellow, Fox!"

Full seventy years must have passed since George Fox left England for Barbados. Seventy years in which to bemoan unfinished justice. It would, I reflected, be all the same in another seventy years when the cheated spirit had faded beyond even a whisper in the wind and no one would know his story; but nevertheless the tale struck me cold. There must always be a lingering fear that one day such a fate will befall oneself.

I hesitated but the need to ask was not to be denied. "You must get into every part of the town?" I said.

"Of course," he said, surprised.

"I wondered –" There was no help for it; I plunged on. "If you had ever had a glimpse, however strange and unexpected, of – of another world..."

His face lit up with radiance and delight. "Indeed, Patterson, indeed I have. It is all that sustains me at times like this. The glimpses we are all vouchsafed of God's heaven, of the saints sitting at his right hand..."

With sinking heart, I realised that he was talking of something altogether different. Well, it had always been the faintest of hopes.

The Rev Mr Bell turned towards the Side to climb the hill and the smoke soon swallowed his dark figure. I felt my way along the walls of the Sandhill and found the Golden Fleece by the sound of horse's hooves and the chinking of harness. As I came to the arch into the inn, the stench of horse dung briefly choked me. A few yards further and I saw a hunched figure low to my right. A quavering voice said, "Master?"

George was sat upon the lowest step of the stairs to the agent's office, hugging himself in his fright. "I heard voices!"

"Just the spirits."

"In the river? I hope I don't die in the river."

I stood, listening to the cries and shrieks still echoing from the pall of smoke around us. "Amen to that," I said.

We climbed the steps to the agent's. A lamp hanging above loomed out of the thinning smoke, shedding a miasma of oil and lavender from its guttering wick. Lavender bunches had been hung outside the door at the top of the stairs and rustled as I brushed against them. I was about to open the door and go in when I heard voices.

"Why don't we go in, master?" George said, his voice muffled through his hand cupped over his mouth against the smoke.

"Shhh."

We bent our heads to listen. I felt guilty at setting a bad example to the boy but was unable to resist the temptation. For the voices – a trifle hoarse from the stench and the smoke – were Jenison and Le Sac.

"I will not be refused," Le Sac said.

"It is most unreasonable." Jenison's annoyance was evident in his voice. "The usual rate is ten shillings. That is more than adequate."

"Fifteen," Le Sac said peremptorily. "I will accept nothing

less. It is the fee paid in London."

"This is not London," Jenison said. "Thank goodness. I flatter myself we have a better idea here of how much money is really worth. And fifteen shillings for one rehearsal and a concert is asking a great deal, sir. You are already paid ten and I for one am of the opinion that *that* is generous."

I struggled to stifle a cough – the damn oil and lavender were clogging my throat as much as the smoke. Le Sac was continuing.

"Ten shillings is nothing."

"It is ten days' wages for one of my labourers, sir."

"Any man can shift stones or till the land. Is there another who can lead your band for you, and choose your music, and entertain you?"

A pause, before Jenison said, "I daresay Mr Patterson could have a good stab at it."

George prodded me with glee but I was cursing. This could only increase Le Sac's antagonism towards me.

"In any case," Jenison went on, "we have to remember, sir, that music is not one of the necessities of life. Can you eat it, drink it, shelter under it? Oh, I grant you, it has its uses, else I would not be one of the directors of the Concerts. It encourages trade in its way and provides an employment for the ladies who might otherwise be idle, and it gives a place a good character when visitors find we are so respectable as to have a set of concerts. But it is not *necessary*, sir – it is a luxury. And to be spending fifteen shillings on a luxury when I have the other performers to pay, and the room to hire, and the candles to buy, and all the rest of it – no, sir, you ask too much."

"Then I will not play," Le Sac said with an air of triumph. "See then how many people support your *luxury*."

"They may do what they choose," Jenison said. Le Sac

had plainly forgotten that the music lovers had already paid their subscriptions and the money was safely in Jenison's pockets.

"You cannot do without me, sir!" Le Sac cried. "You saw last night how they adore me!"

"Well, if I cannot," said Jenison, "I will happily do nothing at all. I would rather abandon the Concerts altogether than pander to a – a French –"

The door of the office was thrown open and Le Sac stalked out, head held high. We drew back quickly. He smiled coldly when he saw me and said something in French. As I have said before, my knowledge of that language is abysmal but I gathered the general meaning of his remarks from his tone and the expression upon his face.

"Mr Patterson," said Jenison from the office. "How opportunely come."

So I came into the direction of the Concerts, for a while at least, since I was certain that either Le Sac or Jenison would give way within a few days. And I had no doubt that Jenison saw me as someone he could control more easily than the Swiss. When I suggested I had works that might grace the Concerts (thinking of Lady Anne's volume of pieces), he frowned as if I was guilty of great presumption and was only mollified when I offered to send George's copies of the volume to him, implying that his judgment was better than my own. (I vowed to slip one of my own pieces in with the volume.) Demsey may be right in saying I know how to handle such men as Jenison, but it can be hard and dispiriting work.

Nevertheless, I was pleased when Jenison promised me seven shillings and sixpence for each concert day. With George's three shillings and sixpence for playing as leader, each concert would earn me as much as Le Sac's despised fee. I hoped merely that they would not come to an agreement until the passing of at least one concert, so I could show what I could do and flatter the gentlemen into thinking me the better bargain. At last one thing was turning in my favour.

I had reckoned without sly Mr Ord.

19
CANZONET

I would have been still better pleased had the concert been on its customary day. But it had been put off a day for the convenience of several of the gentlemen players who had another engagement. I calmed my impatience, though not without difficulty.

In the morning, a reply to one of my letters came from Mr Hamilton, the publisher in Edinburgh. The letter was welcome in two respects. First, he sent me a list of twenty-six subscribers for my music, which I carefully added to my ever-growing store. Second, most astonishingly, he told me he had seen Demsey.

> *I had the honour* [he wrote] *of Mr Demsey's Company at Dinner a se'nnight ago.* [I checked the date of the letter – last Saturday.] *He was, I thought, sombre but in good Heart and gave me much lively Intelligence of Affairs in your Town, the which I was glad to have for it is many Years since I was there, and, owing to the present uncertain State of my own Health, unlikely I shall ever be there again. Mr Demsey was, he informed me, on his way to Aberdeen, although what the Purpose of his Visit was, and how long he intended to remain there, I cannot tell. I have recently receiv'd by Ship from France, several of the latest Concerti…*

I scanned the rest of the letter; it consisted of business matters only. What the devil was Demsey doing in Aberdeen? And at this time of year? Thomas Saint's wife comes from Dundee, I recalled, and she has often spoken of the winter gales and snows in that part of North Britain.

Perhaps Demsey intended to set up there as a dancing master; but what call could there be for the elegancies of life in such a god-forsaken spot?

I was pondering whether to go and quiz the good lady when George came in, clutching the latest edition of the *Courant.* Thomas Saint has evidently taken to publishing on Tuesdays as well as on Saturday. George was looking puzzled.

"I saw Mr Ord, sir, and he asked if I'd read the paper yet. When I said I hadn't, he bought me a copy." He sounded both awed by such largesse and uneasy over the possible cause of it.

I took the paper from him and scanned the front page; it was crowded as usual with advertisements. Did Le Sac plan another benefit, perhaps for the week of Signor Bitti's return? It would be too hard upon the heels of the first concert, but perhaps he wanted to convince Jenison of his popularity.

The faintest gleam of light slid between the hinges of the door. Mrs Foxton said, "The third page, sir, at the bottom of a column."

I passed over the national news upon the second page and glanced at the local correspondence. An account of a high wind at Morpeth, tragic death at Sunderland, three drowned at Shields, the Bishop's return to Durham, births, marriages...

"Which column did you say, Mrs Foxton?"

"I know not. I saw Mr Phillips reading as he passed the window and noted how he had the paper folded. He seemed to find the matter amusing."

My heart sank as I found the piece at last. It was a letter, printed in the smallest type Thomas Saint had, for it was a long letter and he had been hard put to to get it all in.

Sir,

Pray allow me the advantage of your columns to put forward the case of a modest young man who has been most harshly treated.

Oh God, I thought, the writer cannot refer to *me*? Other phrases leapt to my attention. *Where Genius can command, it has the power to be generous to those less fortunate.* A reference to Le Sac clearly, and a less than happy compliment to myself. Yes, and here was the demand for fifteen shillings – *only, we are told, what is commonly offered in London.*

I was reading snatches aloud. Mrs Foxton snorted at references to Genius. George was staring open-mouthed; no doubt he didn't understand half of the rolling, pompous phrases. The writer must have spent his entire day on this rubbish, and poor Thomas Saint must have been up half the night setting it in type. Unless, of course… I scanned the column again; there was nothing in it that might not have been written last week, except for the matter of the fifteen shillings; which might have been inserted at the last minute. But *that* would imply a well-planned campaign against Le Sac.

To make such Demands is unworthy of one whose Heart ought to be softened by the divine Art of Musick… No, no, never mind all that.

The affair of the missing Music Books [oh God, not that again] *transpired to be a mistake – the books, we are told, were merely mislaid. As for the Violin, we shall doubtless never know the thief who sent it on its journey south, but the Swiss Gentleman should think twice before he makes Accusations. He should recall that the Instrument was stolen from his own Rooms, under his very Nose, while he lay ill in Bed; and that the modest young Man he hints about never had access to those Rooms.*

I stopped reading. How *had* the thief taken the violin?

"Go on, master," George urged.

"Read it all." Mrs Foxton had moved to the table next the door and gleamed upon the unlit tallow candle. "It is best to know everything, however bad."

I read the rest of the column, preposterous as it was. "There is much written of Le Sac's manner," I said. "It talks of *an insult to the young man* – that is supposed to be me, clearly – *in not asking him to play at his benefit Concert.*" I stopped, amazed. I had been disappointed, yes, principally for the sake of the money, but how could anyone say it was an insult when the substitute was Signor Bitti?

As for righting the supposed insult – this letter was more likely to send Le Sac running in alarm to make his peace with Jenison and I would lose my chance to direct the Concerts. I was seized by a sudden rage and tossed the paper into a corner of the room. "How can anyone write such drivel? It can only make matters ten times worse!"

The letter was signed *AMATOR JUSTICIAE.* Lover of Justice. "Amator Discordiae, more like," I said in disgust.

I was not left in doubt of Le Sac's reaction for long. He sent me a note scribbled in an execrable hand and in French so colloquial I understood less than one word in ten. I pondered long over whether to seek a translation. I could not ask one of the gentlemen of the Concerts in case the note contained wild accusations against me; moreover, I doubted such men as Jenison and Ord would know any language but their own. Claudius Heron might, I supposed, but after our last encounter I judged it best not to test his good will too much. A pity Demsey was not here; his French was fluent (and colloquial) to a degree – all those visits to Paris to learn the latest dances.

I was tempted to throw the note into the fire but Le Sac

was devious enough to send me a letter I could not understand and then claim he had told me this or that important fact. I had but one alternative; only one person could oblige me with a translation without exclaiming over the contents of the note. Lady Anne, despite her plottings, or perhaps because of them, would understand any accusations Le Sac might have made.

I was conscious of the irony in asking Le Sac's patroness to decipher the threats of her protégé but I felt reckless. I was surrounded by people who wished to take my life into their control and to use me for their own purposes, and I was not inclined to allow them to do so. I had had enough of mysterious plottings. If I had a quarrel with Le Sac, I would prosecute it myself.

My first lesson of the day was in the upper reaches of Northumberland Street, almost upon the Barras Bridge. After the lesson, I was walking down towards the town through a stiff breeze blowing leaves about me from the gardens, when a horse clip-clopped to a halt beside me. I looked up into the face of Claudius Heron.

"Do you go to the Key, Patterson?"

"To Caroline Square."

"I will walk with you."

He swung himself down and fell into step beside me, leading his horse and glancing about. Not, I fancied, out of interest in the few passers-by, but as an excuse not to look directly at me. The embarrassment of that last encounter still hung between us.

"I am very pleased with my son's progress," he said. "His harpsichord playing is much improved."

"He works hard."

"Of course." Heron's profile, which he kept turned to me, was in the classic style, most elegantly proportioned;

his figure was trim despite his age (he was forty-one or two) and his demeanour as cool as ever. "He has expressed a wish to learn the German flute."

That I doubted but I did not say so. "A very gentlemanly instrument."

The wind lifted the skirts of Heron's riding coat and slapped them about his thighs. The horse tossed its head and tugged at the reins. "You will start him on the instrument the next time you come."

I was about to speak when he added, "And I will have my lesson first."

"*Your* lesson, sir?"

"Upon the violin."

"I had thought –"

"Yes?"

"That you studied with Monsieur le Sac."

"I am of the opinion," he said, turning his head to me for the first time, "that music is an art for gentlemen. Monsieur le Sac is not a gentleman."

"Indeed," I murmured.

We soon parted, and I turned west to walk down towards St John's Church and Caroline Square. The prospect of instructing Mr Heron was daunting, and would require every ounce of tact I had; it was a challenge, however, that I found myself anticipating with some pleasure. What I did not look forward to was Le Sac's reaction to losing a pupil, especially a wealthy one.

Caroline Square was quiet, touched only by the rustling of the leaves on the trees in the central gardens. I walked boldly across the square towards the house. If the strange events were to happen again, so be it. Every time they happened, I gathered more information. (Would not the Steward of the Assembly Rooms congratulate me on my 'scientific' attitude?) I had learnt that within those events I could see other people but apparently was not seen by them; I could walk about and touch and hear, and feel the ground beneath my feet. The events could occur as well within the house as without and no one else experienced such events (remembering Lady Anne's astonishment at my hints). But wait, had not Claudius Heron felt the chill too? Had he not heard me shouting?

Still, at least these strange events had never yet threatened me with any danger, merely discomfort and confusion. And today, as on the last occasion, they did not occur at all. I cursed. I had steeled myself to confront the mystery, to no purpose.

A servant answered the door; Lady Anne, he informed me, was absent on business and not expected back for some hours. I stood irresolute.

"Very well," I said at last. "Ask Mrs Jerdoun if she will spare me a few moments of her time."

I was left to wait in the withdrawing room while the servant went in search of Esther Jerdoun. I was conscious of my temerity in approaching a lady with whom I was on bad terms – worse, one who thought so ill of me – but there was nothing else to do.

She came into the room quickly, dressed in a gown of pale green, with tiny embroidery of white. "Mr Patterson," she said brusquely, "I must apologise to you."

Disconcerted, I stuttered. "Apologise, madam?"

"I have been most unforgivably rude with you, and with no excuse other than my own ill humour."

I was silent, remembering what she believed me capable of. Her cool direct gaze creased into a frown.

"Are you well, sir?"

"A trifle – distracted. No matter."

"You were unwell the other day."

That was my opportunity. "There is something about this house –"

She nodded. "My cousin likes it greatly but I confess I feel it has a cold air. I am never quite warm here. Are you sure you are not ill?"

"You have not seen anything *unusual* here?"

She frowned. "Of what kind?"

No, she had seen nothing unusual; I knew that by her puzzled manner. And she had her own preoccupations. When I merely shrugged, she went on. "Do you come about that letter in the *Courant*? I assure you I had nothing to do with it. Indeed, I thought it most ill-judged and told Mr Ord as much."

Ord! I sighed and explained about Le Sac's note. She took it from me, exclaiming at the handwriting and frowning over one or two words that are evidently only to be found in the Swiss form of the French language.

"I suppose we are lucky he did not write in Romance," she said. "Though I daresay it would still have shown the same poverty of mind, the same ungentlemanly character, the same conceit."

"If you could just give me the general meaning, madam?"

She did so, glossing over the worst of it, by her own admission. It was of no moment. Le Sac claimed that I was the author of that 'scurrilous nonsense' in the *Courant* and accused me of being intent, out of jealousy, upon destroying him. In short, he accused me of all the evil designs he himself had conceived against me.

I folded the paper away and rose to take my leave. Mrs Jerdoun asked if I would take tea with her, but I could not regain the easy manner I had had upon my previous visits. Despite her apology, I could not forget her suspicions of me. I declined. She looked as if she would say something more, then merely nodded. Yet, on the threshold of the room, she paused, hand upon the door.

"Mr Patterson," she said. "What I am about to say may seem ungenerous, bearing in mind whose house this is, and whose guest I am. But I *must* warn you, sir – beware of my cousin."

Our gazes met – my own astonished – and she added, simply, "She is a dangerous woman."

20
CHORUS

Le Sac's supporters did not wait for the next week's paper but instead had a broadsheet printed indignantly refuting Mr Ord's claims. I read it on the coffee-house wall at mid-day; by the time I reached the spot, the paper was already tattered at the corners by the wind. All the insinuations of AMATOR JUSTICIAE were rejected; the paper claimed that fifteen shillings was not an unreasonable wage for so distinguished a performer and asserted that Le Sac was not in the least motivated by greed or vanity. All these slurs, I read, were put about by a so-called modest young man who was jealous of Le Sac's eminence.

There was some truth in this accusation, I had to confess, but none of it was my doing. I could not be blamed if certain gentlemen chose to exert themselves on my behalf, or rather – for I had no illusion about the matter – if they chose to exert themselves against Le Sac. For the one thing no gentleman will tolerate is hubris on the part of those that are his inferiors.

I went into Nellie's coffee-house and found a quiet place by the window to drink and muse on my present situation. Esther Jerdoun's words the previous evening still astonished me. She had gone on to warn me that Lady Anne loved to make others dance to her own tune, reminded me of the trick she had played on Le Sac the night he came to play and hinted that Lady Anne had her own aims with regard to the gentleman, and that I was part of her schemes. Nothing of this was new to me.

But the harshness in Mrs Jerdoun's voice had taken me

by surprise. Why should she speak so vehemently against her cousin? Was this merely another game that the ladies were playing against each other? Many an apparently loving pair of sisters or cousins have hated each other with cold passion.

I drank coffee and idly observed the streets. The mysteries seemed insoluble; if only I could be clear of them... But I knew I did not wish to be clear of Esther Jerdoun at all. In an effort to distract myself, I pulled from my pocket the list of subscribers for my music. The list numbered more than ninety now and the prospects of publication were increasing. Perhaps this would be a good day to canvass more support. After all, patronage of my music would imply rejection of Le Sac.

When George and I came to Hoult's for the concert rehearsal at noon, only half the gentlemen were gathered. I found Mr Ord tuning his violin ineffectually and wondered whether to mention AMATOR JUSTICIAE. But a fear that Mrs Jerdoun might be mistaken held me back. Instead, I pulled out a copy of the proposal for my harpsichord pieces.

"My dear fellow," Ord said as soon as he saw the paper. "Of course I shall subscribe. Put me down for six copies – my nieces are wild about all things Scotch and the music will make delightful presents for them. Heron, my dear fellow, you will put your name down for Patterson's music?"

The gentleman inclined his head.

"And Jenison – you too."

So I found myself patronised by Mr Ord and gathered ten names for a total of eighteen copies. All the time, however, I was watching the faces and counting those who did not arrive. It was inevitable that some of the gentlemen should support Le Sac; Henry Wright, for instance, was absent, which left us with no tenor violin. I had been prepared for that, but the woeful state of the cellists (only one arrived out of four) left us with almost no bass. We had the instruments themselves, of course, and Mr Ord volunteered to play the tenor, but the defect in the lower parts was very audible.

Apart from that, the rehearsal went tolerably. George had gathered confidence as first violin but his youth and inexperience left the way clear for me to direct from the harpsichord unchallenged. Jenison had perhaps anticipated the problem with the performers and had chosen music we knew well.

We worried over Mountier, who did not arrive until the end of the rehearsal, apologising that "the damn horse had gone lame"' (by which we guessed that he stopped too long in Chester le Street for refreshment). He was almost drunk as usual and, as the gentlemen wished to leave, we agreed that I alone should accompany his songs. We rehearsed only a short time, since we both knew the songs well, then parted; I went to a lesson; Mountier (as it transpired later) went to get even more drunk.

So to the evening. Jenison arrived with the son of his agent who played very loudly upon the cello with a poor tone, but in excellent time, and Mountier stumbled in noisily in the middle of the overture but sang his songs perfectly. All in all, it went a great deal better than I had feared. It was inevitable, however, that the next morning should bring crowings of delight from Le Sac and his supporters. I saw the man himself as I was about to step into Fleming's for harpsichord wire; he lifted his head, smiled triumphantly and strolled on. By the time I reached Nellie's, a second broadsheet had been pasted over the first.

To read it, you would have thought the concert a disaster.

Mountier's drunkenness I could not deny, nor the raucous quality of the cellos, but Mr Ord upon the tenor was most unjustly vilified. (Did they suspect, perhaps, that he had written the letter in the *Courant*?) He had in fact been much better than upon his usual violin and had rather enjoyed the responsibility his sole possession of a part had given him. As for George – poor George. His age was enough to condemn him. *What can be the quality of a Concert led by a twelve-year-old boy?*

At Jenison's agent, where I went for the harpsichord key, I found Ord seated at a desk under a window smeared with drizzle, a pile of paper stacked in front of him and a quill laid beside it. He chortled at me as the agent sent his boy for the key.

"Have you seen their latest efforts, Patterson?" His round face was shiny with excitement; the lamp which the agent was lighting against the gloom outside glinted in his eyes. "They are struggling, are they not? They say anything to keep their man in the public eye. After all, his absence was not much remarked upon last night, was it?"

I had, in fact, been asked three times if Le Sac was ill and the audience had been noticeably thinner after the interval when it had become obvious Le Sac did not perform.

"Well," Ord said, puffing himself out, "I flatter myself I have a better way with words than these foreigners and a better case too. We shall see what they think of my next offering."

I looked with foreboding at the pile of paper, gleaming in the lamplight. Rain splattered against the window.

"Would it not be better, sir, to treat their accusations with the contempt they deserve and remain silent?"

"My dear Patterson!" he cried in horror. "And let the whole town think I have run away defeated?"

Not much of the 'whole town' was interested in the matter, judging by the slight interest shown in the broadsheets. But Ord was plainly set upon the matter; there was nothing I could do but murmur, "I defer to your judgment."

He twinkled at me as the agent's boy brought the key. "Oh, I have plans, Patterson, grand plans." He tapped his nose. "But more of that later."

I left the office with foreboding and a sure knowledge that I would not like Ord's plans. In heaven's name, was the whole town mad over plotting and planning?

I was glad to see one or two people at Hoult's who complimented me upon the concert, particularly the harpsichord solo I had played (a piece from Lady Anne's volume). Several remarked that George had played very well and if they added "for a boy of his years" I could not take offence, for I thought the same myself. The praise was enough to encourage George to concentrate upon his lesson on the harpsichord and then to send him willingly home afterward to practise on his violin. I spent the afternoon practising on the harpsichord at Hoult's, much to my benefit, and turned out to go home in the early evening. The drizzle had not long cleared and a warm dampness was fragrant in the air. A spirit spoke to me from the arch of an inn.

"Mr Patterson, sir? I carry ye a message from Dick Kell."

"The fiddler? At Mrs Hill's?"

"The same, sir. He wonders if you would come and see Mr Mountier on to his horse."

I sighed and turned back. What in heaven's name was Mountier still doing in Newcastle?

The last butchers' stalls were being packed away as I came into the Fleshmarket and Mrs Hill's was full of company in bloodstained aprons. Half the butchers, it seemed, congregated here after a long day's business. I stood upon the doorstep, almost gagging at the stink of old meat.

Dick Kell spoke from a barrel to one side of the door. "Charlie lad, well met. How's that father of yours?" Kell was as bluff-voiced and beery as he had been in life.

"I don't know. I haven't spoken to him for years." My father, luckily, died in Durham, at the Red Lion there – a place which I take good care to avoid on my rare visits to that city. We were not on the best of terms in life and he has not changed his opinion of me since.

"Pity," Kell said. "Many's the good chin-wag I've had with him over a pint of ale."

"I was told you wanted to talk to me about Mountier. I can't see him."

He snorted with laughter. "Over by yon wall."

Pushing through the crowds, I found Mountier lying face down upon a bench, a hand trailing to the ground. He was snoring. A bloody handprint marked his coat in the small of his back; when I eased him over, I saw his watch was gone.

Dick Kell was a grease stain on Mountier's shoulder. "His horse is in the stable. I've had one of the lads saddle it up if you can but get him sober enough to mount it."

"Why on earth call me? One of the ostlers could have done it."

"Too busy, Charlie lad. Now how d'you want to go about it? Water? There's some in the rain butt out back."

The stink of bad meat was making me irritable. Worse, I saw, as I looked down, a thin trail of sinew and gristle trailing from the skirt of my coat in a smear of blood. "Let him sleep it off."

"Nay, Charlie. He'll just wake up and ask for more."

"Then let him get drunk again."

"Weeelll..." Dick Kell was keeping something from me. He had always been a protective man, lying easily, with a chuckle, to keep his friends in good odour with those who might otherwise hurt them. "As a matter of fact," he went on confidingly, "he said the high-ups there at the Cathedral –"

"The Dean and Chapter?"

"If you say so," he said doubtfully. "You know I never did get the hang of anything to do with the church." Kell had always been one for whom religion was a harmless mumbling. "Anyway, they've said he has to be back. Don't trust him, I reckon."

No one could blame them, I thought. The Dean and Chapter are always jealous of their reputation and Mountier's increasing drunkenness would have exasperated a far more lenient body. I sighed. "Very well, show me the water butt."

I threw water over Mountier – three bucket-loads before he stirred and then he only mumbled and shook himself to be rid of the moisture. By the time I had got him upright and forced him, with Kell's encouragement, to stagger out to the horse in the yard, it was dark. I saw him trot off down the Fleshmarket with some trepidation. The horse, however, seemed to know its way and was a great deal more sober than Mountier.

So I was late and yawning when I let myself into the house. Mrs Foxton's voice drifted from the back of the house, from the room behind the stairs where the seamstress lodged. The silence upstairs seemed to suggest that George had long since fallen asleep over his practice and I was eager to follow his example. I came to the door of my room – and heard a creaking of floorboards. Looking up, I saw two men on the landing above.

I knew at once they were trouble. They looked very like the ruffians Demsey had hired. I grabbed for the wedge in the door of my room. No, of course, I now had a key. I fumbled in my pocket, felt the metal slip out of my fingers and settle deeper. Then they were upon me. Their silence was terrifying. I opened my mouth to call out, tasted rancid cloth and stinking flesh. An arm forced my teeth against my lip. I struck out wildly, heard a grunt. Then something rough caught around my neck and tightened, so that I could not breathe…

21
SOLO

I came to myself slowly, aware only that I lay upon a hard surface and that my throat burned. I opened my eyes to darkness that hurt, and squeezed them shut again.

"Mr Patterson," a voice said insistently. "Mr Patterson!"

Wood. I lay upon a wood floor. And the voice, yes, that was Mrs Foxton. I rolled over with a groan. My head pulsed and throbbed.

"Can you rise, sir?" Mrs Foxton said. "Mr Patterson!"

I crawled into a sitting position against the wall.

"Find your key, sir," Mrs Foxton said patiently. She was somewhere above me – on the door perhaps, or one of the paintings on the stairs. "Your key, sir. In your pocket. That's it. No, don't go to sleep. Put the key in the lock."

Struggling to my feet would have been impossible. I dragged myself on to hands and knees, and poked tremulously in the direction of the lock. The movement set me retching; the coughing set my damaged throat on fire. I found the lock at last and turned the key. The door swung open. I toppled into the room.

By stages, I got myself to the chair by the table. The chair scraped away from me and I almost fell to the floor, but finally got myself on to the seat. I dropped my aching head into my hands.

"Well done, sir," Mrs Foxton said approvingly, as if I was a child. "And well done too for fighting off those brutes."

My memory was hazy but I knew I had done no such thing. "I thought –" But all that came out of my bruised throat was a hoarse croak. The villains must have been disturbed; perhaps they had heard Mrs Foxton and run off. I crept to the bed, crawled on to it and curled up, struggling to ease my pounding head.

I remember little after that. At some point, George came in; I heard him say something. Perhaps I mumbled something in return. But nothing was clear until I woke to find sunshine lying aslant my bed, stinging my eyes. A man was leaning over me, and after a moment I recognised Claudius Heron. The sunshine gleamed on his lean face and on his fair hair that, unusually, was a trifle disordered, as if he had been hurrying. But he was outwardly as impassive as ever.

"Does your head ache?"

"Like the devil," I croaked, trying to sit up. He made no attempt to help me but watched until I was still. He was, I noted, as impeccably dressed as always, still wearing his greatcoat.

"I have had the apothecary examine you," he said, sitting upon the edge of the bed. "He says there is nothing seriously amiss. Your landlady told me what happened. Did you see the ruffians?"

"Too dark," I managed.

"It was Mr Sac!" I had not seen George until he blurted out the words. He had been standing behind Heron and my first thought as he moved into my line of vision was how unkempt and vulgar he was, compared to Heron's cool elegance. But he was also wide-eyed and fearful. I sighed; I had hoped he had conquered his fear of Le Sac.

"It is unwise to jump to conclusions," Heron said. "Even an honest man may have rash supporters who think they know how to please him." (Did that mean he too suspected Le Sac?) "From what I've heard, this was no chance attempt at robbery. They were waiting for you."

I tried to speak, choked. Heron signalled to George and

he poured me ale. It was weak stuff but it soothed and cooled my throat. "They were outside my former room. Not knowing I had moved."

Heron hesitated. "Do you have any other enemies, Patterson?" He said *other* as if he took Le Sac for granted. "Anyone who might wish to harm you?"

"I trust not."

"You are not in debt?"

"Most definitely not," I said forcibly.

"Good." He rose. "I shall have the matter investigated. Who is the parish constable?"

"Mr Bedwalters, sir," George said.

"The writing master? I shall speak to him. In the meantime –" That impassive expression did not change; did he ever smile or scowl? "I suggest you keep yourself at home."

"I have a living to earn, sir."

That provoked some expression of emotion in him, a displeasure that twisted his thin mouth, as if the very idea was distasteful.

"Very well. Then make sure the boy is with you at all times. Boys have strong lungs and loud voices and, in my experience, need little provocation to use them."

Looking at George's fearful glance, I could not imagine he would be much use to me.

I was not wrong. When Heron had gone, I gave George money to fetch food, but he refused to leave the house.

"You went out to find Mr Heron," I pointed out.

"I didn't, sir!" George protested, on the verge of tears. "I didn't fetch him. He was walking past the end of the street."

"And the ale?"

"The seamstress went for it. I *can't* go out, sir. He'll be waiting for me."

"Nonsense!"

"It was me he wanted," he cried hotly. "He sent those ruffians for *me*!"

"George, I won't have this!" But shouting made my throat burn. I fell to coughing so hard my eyes began to water. The whole thing was preposterous; how could he think that the oafs would have mistaken a grown man for a twelve-year-old boy? I dried my eyes upon the blanket.

"Where were you last night? Why weren't you here?"

He hung his head. "I did start to practise, sir."

"And then?"

"Tommy the cheesemonger's boy came by and shouted up there was a juggler in the Bigg Market. And a fiddler, sir." That, I supposed, was intended to try and convince me he had had his musical education in mind when playing truant.

"George," I said, forcing myself to speak quietly. "When I took you on as apprentice, I vowed to myself that I would not beat you. I flattered you by thinking you were not the sort of boy that needs chastisement. After your experiences with Monsieur le Sac, I would have thought you would be eager to please me."

He took a deep shuddering breath and looked up at me from under his lashes. Then he took up the money I had laid upon the table. "Yes, master."

"Then fetch me food and do not disobey me again."

He fled from the room and I heard his footsteps clattering on the stairs.

"About time," Mrs Foxton said from the door. "Boys need beatings."

"I lack the strength," I said, falling back upon the bed.

I must have slept, for when I woke a new jug of ale and a potato pudding lay upon the table beside me, together with a note from George. The note, in the boy's neat hand, said he had gone to take a message to my pupils to tell them I could not attend them that day. I was loath to lose the money but pleased to see that George was at least trying to behave responsibly. I was even more irritated at the loss of income when, an hour or so later, the apothecary sent up a boy with his bill for attending me. Apparently Heron had not considered the expense of the consultation.

In late afternoon I woke again and took some exercise about the room. George, I saw, had been in again while I slept and spent some time copying out the concerti from Lady Anne's volume. Mrs Foxton, who came when she heard me moving about, said he had gone out to eat about five minutes earlier. After a moment's consideration, I followed him, wrapping a muffler around my throat, partly to keep warm, partly to hide the livid bruises my mirror had shown me.

The fresh air revived me, although I couldn't help looking around in case my attackers were loitering in the area; I resolved to be home before dark. I set myself the task of buying a new piece of music from Barber's bookshop behind St Nicholas's Church and sauntered that way through a crowd of Scotch carters haggling over prices. Joseph Barber himself was in the shop and I had to wait until he had finished selling a walking cane to an elderly gentleman. He is a man of much good humour and made great play with my croak of a voice.

"But in truth robbery is not to be laughed at," he said, after doing just that for ten minutes or more. "These days a man can get hit over the head for a penny or two. Though I have heard –" He looked at me thoughtfully, his ruddy face with its flaring eyebrows suddenly sober. "I have heard robbery was not their aim, in your case."

"I know not," I said, thinking hard for a way to change the subject.

"And now this duel they're proposing..."

"Duel?" My voice cracked on the word. "Who is to fight?"

"Why, the Swiss and that boy of yours."

I had a vision of Le Sac and George facing each other across a brace of pistols. Preposterous! I rubbed my aching brow.

"Mr Barber," I said, "I would be much obliged if you would explain it all from the beginning, slowly and, if you please, very quietly."

22
PHANTASIA

Lady Anne was sitting in her withdrawing room over a dish of tea with Mrs Jerdoun. In my agitation I had blundered into the house with not a thought for the dangers – which had not appeared – and now stood at the door of the room staring wildly at the ladies. Lady Anne turned in astonishment.

"Mr Patterson! My dear sir! You look exceedingly troubled. Pray sit down and tell us what has happened." She signalled to a servant to bring another dish.

I sat but could hardly restrain my anxiety. Lady Anne was as light-hearted as ever; even in my distressed state I perceived that the orange gown she wore was unflattering to her colouring and clashed with the red-and-white-striped satin of her chair. There was an air of reserve about Mrs Jerdoun.

"I hardly know where to begin."

They were startled by my croak of a voice. I outlined quickly the attack upon my person. During my tale, the servant returned with a dish and Lady Anne, listening intently, poured the tea. Afraid that its heat might scald my sore throat, I left the brew until I came to the end of my story.

"Do you know, sir," Lady Anne said at last, when I had finished, "whether this was merely an attempt at robbery, or something more sinister?"

"Nothing was stolen, madam."

Lady Anne glanced at Mrs Jerdoun – who sat upon the edge of her chair looking at me as gravely and coolly as had

Claudius Heron – then returned her gaze to me. "One name comes inexorably to mind in connection with this matter."

I forestalled her. "I cannot think, Lady Anne, that anyone would have cause to set ruffians on me."

"No? Perhaps you do not understand the continental temperament."

Mrs Jerdoun rose and walked across to the fireplace, poking with an elegantly shod foot at the desultory embers among the ash. I started to rise politely but she waved me seated again. Her face was turned away from me.

I sipped my tea warily. "Too much has been made of – of certain *disagreements* between myself and the gentleman in question. I acknowledge his superiority to me as a musician, though I confess I envy his place as musical director of the Concerts." Here Esther Jerdoun turned and gave me a steady look. "So when the gentlemen asked me to take that place, I thought it foolish to refuse, believing in any case that it would only be for a short time, until the argument between the gentlemen and Monsieur le Sac was resolved. But since that time some of the gentlemen – annoyed with what they believe to be Monsieur le Sac's presumption – have chosen to conduct their quarrel in public."

"That letter in the *Courant*," Lady Anne said, laughing. "I recognised old Ord's style at once. And there have been broadsheets posted about the town. Have you seen them, Esther?"

"I thought them too ranting and vulgar to take notice of," her cousin said. Yes, there was certainly some coolness still between the ladies.

"It is the matter of the duel that concerns me," I said.

As Mrs Jerdoun looked up sharply, Lady Anne sighed. "I have the greatest admiration for you gentlemen, Mr

Patterson, but to meet with swords at dawn seems to me to be an extreme way of settling a violinist's wages."

"Not at dawn," I said gloomily. "Next Wednesday afternoon, between two and three o'clock at Mrs Hill's in the Fleshmarket."

"You will have the watch down on you!" Mrs Jerdoun said in horror.

"They would not enjoy the experience." I had no more stomach for the tea and put the dish down on the polished wood of the table. "It is to be a musical duel. It has been proposed that Monsieur le Sac and my apprentice George compete, in the presence of the best judges of the science of music in this part of the country, to see which is the better violinist."

"The boy?" Lady Anne echoed, looking nonplussed for once. "Why the boy?"

"Monsieur le Sac is evidently aggrieved that his place as leader of the band has been taken by a twelve-year-old. He considers it an insult."

"But it is not the boy who insults him," Lady Anne pursued, leaning forwards. "The boy merely does as he is told. It is the man who puts the boy in that place who insults Le Sac and that, surely, is you, sir. Why does he not duel with you?"

She seemed disturbingly eager to see myself and Le Sac at odds but I acknowledged she had a good argument. "I have only heard of the matter at second hand, my lady. But evidently comments were made that George played as well as Le Sac and that the Swiss was no loss to the Concerts. That seems to have spurred him into action."

"He is a fool," Esther Jerdoun said contemptuously. "No one with any judgment could fail to see the truth of the matter. The boy is good for his age but he cannot match

Le Sac. The man demeans himself by agreeing to such a preposterous contest."

I nodded. "I'm afraid there is some plot behind the plot, so to speak – a plan to humiliate Le Sac."

"You fear, in short," said Lady Anne, "that the contest will not be a fair one. Tell me the exact terms."

The fire was burning more strongly and Esther Jerdoun moved her full skirts away with care. She turned to pace across the room. From the long windows at the far side of the room the gardens of the square could be seen, bedraggled by the early chills of winter.

"Each player is to bring with him an accompanist and a piece of music in which he is well practised. Each piece will be played, then exchanged and played again by the other party."

"To test their sight reading," Esther Jerdoun said, pacing restlessly. "Le Sac will give the boy one of his impossible compositions."

Lady Anne shook her head. "No, no. The boy was his apprentice, remember. He will know Le Sac's hand and perhaps even remember the pieces. But in general terms you are correct. Le Sac will produce a piece of virtuoso playing which is impossible except after years of practice. Who are to be the judges, Mr Patterson?"

I laughed shortly. "That depends upon which side you support, madam. Le Sac's partisans insist upon Mr Nichols, organist of St Nicholas."

"Brother to Le Sac's crony! And the boy's supporters?" She smiled impishly. "That is to say, Mr Ord and Mr Jenison?"

"They want Thomas Mountier of Durham."

"Known to be your friend." She glanced at Esther Jerdoun, who was shaking her head. "I agree – quite unacceptable. In any case, he is surely a better judge of vocal music than instrumental."

"When he is sober," Mrs Jerdoun said sourly.

Lady Anne tapped her fingers upon the rim of her tea-dish and bit her lip thoughtfully. "Mr Patterson, you have not finished your tea. Drink up, sir, you need strength."

The brew was chill but I sipped obediently while Lady Anne considered. Esther Jerdoun toyed with straightening the china ornaments upon a small table.

"Hesletine of Durham would be a better choice," Lady Anne said at last. "He knows both you and Le Sac, I think? And he is such a cranky, obstinate man, so confirmed in a sense of his own good taste, that it would be next to impossible to influence him. Mr Patterson, would you be distressed to see your boy lose this contest?"

"I would think it only just. But is it fair to allow the boy to compete, knowing that he must be defeated? He will lose confidence in his own ability. And he will be disadvantaged if he becomes known merely as the boy who lost the duel."

Lady Anne sighed and set down her tea-dish. "You are quite right. An effort must at least be made to stop the affair. I take it, Mr Patterson, that you wish me to undertake that task?"

"I have not come here without making the effort myself, Lady Anne. I called upon Mr Jenison. He said it was not an affair that concerned me and I should stand well clear of it. Mr Ord said that I must trust them to know what they were doing and that I could not help but benefit from the matter."

Mrs Jerdoun laughed harshly. "Such men always believe that they know best."

Lady Anne shot her a swift look. "Indeed," she said dryly, and I fancied some feeling in her voice. "But I agree that you should not be seen to be involved, Mr Patterson. If Le

Sac has taken so strongly against you, your interference can only make matters worse. Whereas I – as Le Sac's patroness – must carry some weight."

"You may as well save your time and strength," Mrs Jerdoun said. "Nothing will prevent the contest. Too much pride is involved."

Lady Anne smiled and I saw a mischievous delight in her eyes. "We shall see." She rose in a rustle of silk and I hurriedly got to my feet. "Come, Mr Patterson, I will see you to the door. You are not to worry. We shall win this particular game."

"Life is not all games," Esther Jerdoun said sharply. "We are talking of men's livelihoods."

Lady Anne cast her a mocking look. "My cousin thinks I am much too frivolous, but I assure you I take this matter quite as seriously as anyone could wish!"

Glancing back as Lady Anne laid her hand on my arm, I met Mrs Jerdoun's gaze. Her last remarks, I knew, had been intended for me, as a warning. But surely Lady Anne could not toy with us all at such a serious juncture?

Lady Anne flung open the door and we proceeded into the hallway. A servant hovered at the foot of the stairs but Lady Anne dismissed him and he walked away through the door to the servants' hall. Lady Anne turned to me.

"I fancy you think the worse of me, Mr Patterson, for not having restrained Monsieur le Sac's vanity before this time. But –"

And then the whole house seemed to shudder.

The walls wavered around me; I saw Lady Anne shiver and shimmer. I tried to reach out to her. Then the walls settled, as steady as they had been before, unchanged – no, had not a landscape hung on that wall below the stairs? It was now a portrait of an elderly man with a big old-fashioned wig. I turned on my heels, trembling, my head and throat throbbing, saw furniture that I did not recognise, a mirror that had not been there before…

And a stout, ruddy gentleman came noisily down the stairs, calling my name. I turned. It was the gentleman at the dinner party I had glimpsed – the one who had sat at the head of the table on that earlier occasion when I had looked through the window.

I could not speak a word. The pain in my head was squeezing at my eyes and making the gentleman's face blur and fade. I glanced round, looking for the only certain thing in this place, for Lady Anne – but she was gone. Had she ever been here? Had she come into this insane place with me or had I left her in the hall of her house? The man was speaking to me again and that frightened me more than anything. Before, I had been a spectator, looking on a scene as if in a theatre; but now, now I was required to speak and act…

The man took hold of my arm. I felt his warmth, the hardness of his grip, the stink of his breath on my cheek. "You have come in perfect time, Patterson. You received my note?"

I would not panic; I would not be overcome. I licked my dry lips. "Indeed…"

"You'll play for my niece's wedding, then? Good, good." He barked with laughter. "Never known a busier fellow – all those damn pupils and the Concert series. Which reminds me –"

He was walking towards the door. I went with him in a kind of fearful daze. What else could I do but walk through this strangeness, letting it unfold around me? Who was this gentleman? How did he come to know me? Why was this house both so familiar and so strange? Where was Lady Anne and the familiar reaches of Caroline Square?

The door stood open (in my daze, I had not noticed the fact before) and the day outside was chill and sunny. I looked out on the street that I had only seen in darkness before. By daylight it looked of no great significance, neither busy nor quiet, not shabby yet not especially grand. A few carts trundled up its length, followed by a carriage with the blinds drawn down. A woman who passed inclined her head to my companion; she was of a respectable middling sort – the wife of a tolerably well-off tradesman, perhaps.

Two men lounged against a sedan chair at the pavement's edge. They straightened as they saw us and hurried to the chair's poles.

"You're a good man, Patterson," the gentleman said, regarding the scene with some satisfaction. "I said as much when we appointed you to St Nicholas. And that music of yours – good decent stuff."

He seemed to wait for a reply; I said mechanically: "Thank you, sir."

"Well, I must be off." He nodded goodbye to me. I expected him to climb into the chair but no, he strode away along the street. The chair, expensive as it was, was mine.

I stood on the doorstep, looking at the bearers. What if I was to get into the chair, allow the men to carry me away? Would I find the rest of the town subtly changed, with people I did not know but who knew me, with different streets and buildings, with perhaps even stranger, as yet unknown phenomena? If I walked away from this house would I ever get back to the people and the places I knew?

I put my hand to the smooth paint of the door. It was chill under my fingers. And the chill spread up my arm, into my heart and my head, and I was falling, falling…

23
SINFONIA CONCERTANTE
Movement I

Lady Anne swept into my room, laughing aside the protests of Mrs Foxton who hung upon the door jamb. Startled, I raised myself on one elbow against my pillows. I had been lying fully dressed upon my bed, trying to ease the throbbing in my head and the turmoil in my mind, staring into the shadows of the room and the dark of that madness last night. I could still feel the light touch of Lady Anne's fingers on my arm as the walls had begun to waver, still smell the man's sour breath, still see the gaudy livery of the sedan chair bearers…

Mrs Foxton's shimmer reflected the late afternoon light and worsened the pain behind my temples. Lady Anne was dressed in a pale gown with a velvet cloak thrown about her shoulders; her face was flushed and her hair awry.

"Oh, stop your fussing, spirit!" she cried. "Go and talk to that sallow-faced seamstress. Leave us alone."

I protested. "Your reputation, Lady Anne –"

"Never mind *her* reputation," Mrs Foxton said shrilly. "Think of your own. Think of the rumours about Mr Demsey."

Ignoring her, Lady Anne produced a basket from the folds of her skirt and, from the basket, took a bottle of brandy and two glasses. Mrs Foxton made a noise between a sniff and a snort, and the gleam of her slid soundlessly between the hinges of the door and out of the room.

Lady Anne perched upon the edge of one of my chairs

and insisted I drank the brandy. It was a very fine brandy. "You gave us all a fright, Mr Patterson," she said, and there was an odd edge to her voice, a hint of – I could not be certain what. Concern? Could that be true?

"I had not intended to, my lady."

"You virtually fell into my arms." Yes – a forced edge to her good humour. "I thought for one dreadful moment that you had expired. But the apothecary said it was merely an after-effect of your dreadful experiences the other night, so we had you carried home and physicked. But I vowed to be certain you were well, so here I am!" She leaned forward. "A strange thing… You sounded as if you were speaking with a gentleman. Do you recall anything?"

Now was the time to tell Lady Anne what I had seen and heard in her house, but I looked into her face and knew I could not. There was concern in her gaze, yes, but there was mischief too, a gleam of bright pleasure. She was a woman with little to do who had therefore turned to setting one part of the town against another. She would greet my story with sympathetic understanding, no doubt, then tease me with it in front of others, embarrass me with hints. Exaggerated fears, perhaps, but I did not trust Lady Anne's understanding of how careful a man must be when he relies on the favour of others to earn a living.

So I lied. "I did seem to have a dream. But I don't remember it."

She was watching me closely. "Nothing at all?"

"An impression of sunshine," I said, sensing that she would not be satisfied with a denial. "And voices." I shook my head. "I cannot recall what they said."

She straightened in her chair, smiling at me over the top of her brandy glass. "Well, sir, I have more news for you, though I fancy you will not be pleased to have it. I have spoken to Mr Jenison and Mr Ord and they are adamant that the contest will go ahead."

I set my head back against the pillows and cursed their obstinacy. "And the other gentlemen?"

"Mr Nichols and Mr Wright are acting for our Swiss friend. They in their turn insist upon the right of their principal to defend his reputation."

"And Le Sac himself, madam? Have you spoken to him?"

"Impossible. He has gone to Sunderland for a concert and will not return until the day of the contest. Jenison and Ord are of the opinion that he has fled but I know him better than that. He is, in his own way, a man of his word. Having consented to the duel, he will not withdraw."

"Then I will forbid George to take part."

"You have that right, certainly. But I think Jenison and Ord will not forgive you interfering and you will then find yourself in a more difficult position than before. No, I have considered all aspects of the matter and I cannot find any way of preventing the contest that will not make the situation worse."

Suddenly she bent forward and laid her hand upon my arm. "Mr Patterson, I beg you to take my advice on this matter. Let the contest go ahead. Le Sac will win. The boy will be disappointed, certainly, but you are a man of tact and understanding – you can console him. I assure you I will use my influence to raise general sympathy on the boy's side."

She drank down the rest of her brandy with a mannish gesture and got up to leave. "You had better rest, Mr Patterson. I have instructed the boy to send your apologies to your pupils and I will ensure that no one takes offence at your absence." She took the empty glass from my hand.

"My cousin, by the way, has sent a potion for you." She indicated a small bottle upon the table, stoppered with cork and a twist of cloth. "It is a remedy for the headache; she brews it herself. I can personally recommend its efficacy."

At the door, she almost walked into George, racing up the stairs. But she was in a good mood; she merely chided him laughingly and submitted to being taken downstairs by Mrs Foxton.

I had not seen George for some hours and I saw a change in him. He stood in the middle of the room, panting for breath and trying at the same time to list all the people he had visited on my behalf. He was in great good humour; yes, that was the difference – I had never seen him so animated.

"You seem to have been having a good time of it," I said.

He looked guilty and his hand, all unbeknown to him, I think, crept to the pocket on his left side. What had he in there? Surely he hadn't been indulging in boyish pranks – stealing fruit or cheeses, perhaps, from some stall. Yes, I thought, resigned, that would be it.

"And I saw Mr Jenison and Mr Heron upon the Key by the Printing Office. They told me to go home and not to catch cold before the contest. At least," he amended, "Mr Jenison said so. Mr Heron just frowned."

Heron. I caught at a faint hope. He was a man of sense. Might he prevent the duel?

I struggled off my bed. The brandy had made me warm but also dizzy. "Well, if we are committed to this stupidity, we had better take it seriously. We must decide what you are to play."

"The Vivaldi!" he said eagerly.

I stared. "Which Vivaldi? I never taught you Vivaldi. I wouldn't touch the stuff."

"Mr Sac taught me it." He started rummaging among the papers on the table. (I allowed him a corner at the back of it to keep his own music.)

"Corelli," I said forcibly. Quite apart from the fact that I could not allow any apprentice of mine to exhibit inferior taste, I considered it more sensible to play a piece he had recently practised. And Le Sac himself would be familiar with the Vivaldi if he had taught it to his apprentice, and would no doubt play it excellently. No doubt he would be familiar with the Corelli too; we had played one or two of the concerti in the Concerts. But he had shown small enthusiasm for them, dismissing them contemptuously as 'simple' pieces. Such attitudes have a way of being heard in performance. And Hesletine, the proposed judge, was fond of Corelli, and would probably be offended by Le Sac's indifference.

We produced the music at the same time. I stood with my hand on a printed edition; George waved a paper filled with that lamentable scrawl of Le Sac's.

"Corelli," I repeated, opening the book. "Get out your violin."

"I don't need to practise that one," he said, looking beneath my arm. "We played it at the last Concert."

"I was there," I said. "You need to practise."

He lifted his head defiantly. "Mr Jenison says I'm an excellent violinist."

"You have the prospect of becoming so, certainly." I was feeling light-headed; the brandy, I realised, had been stronger than I had made allowance for.

"Mr Jenison says I'm going to win this contest."

A harsh retort hovered on my lips but I looked down at the boy and held my tongue. If the effects of his inevitable defeat were to be lessened, I must tread carefully. But I cursed Jenison as I looked down at the upturned face and saw the swaggering confidence there and the childish glee at anticipated victory.

"And what did Mr Heron say?" I asked gently.

"Nothing. I don't think he likes boys."

I had come to the conclusion that Claudius Heron liked nobody very well. "Mr Jenison's opinion," I said carefully, "is valuable, but he is, after all, only a gentleman amateur. If you are to win this contest, you must satisfy Mr Hesletine. And he, as I'm sure Mr Mountier's anecdotes have made clear to you, is very difficult indeed to please. Now, get out your violin."

He made a face of mutiny but fetched the instrument and I lingered at the window as he tuned the strings. The shrill sound of it made my head throb again and it seemed to me that George deliberately produced an inferior tone to spite me. I remembered Mrs Jerdoun's potion and read the instructions she had neatly inscribed upon the label. Pulling out the stopper, I sniffed at the summer scents of lime flowers and rosemary, mixed with wine.

I drank a small glass of the potion and felt the warmth of it seep down my throat. Leaning my hot cheek against the chill window glass, I gazed out into the dusk and tried to concentrate on George's begrudging lifeless attempts at the first bars of the faultless Corelli. Figures scuttled beneath me: a child with a barking dog, a woman with a baby heaved up on a hip. And at the far corner, just turning out of sight…

Demsey.

24
SINFONIA CONCERTANTE
Movement II

I heard Mrs Foxton call as I flung open the front door. The cold air made me reel; for a moment the world seemed to spin. The road was full of people – housewives coming home from markets, children shrieking, carters edging horses through the melee – and the gloom of night was gathering fast. I pushed my way down the street. A barrel rolled across my path; I leapt it, turned the corner…

Nothing. The street was empty.

It was a momentary condition; almost at once, a group of miners trudged around the far corner. Might Demsey have gone into a shop? Or a tavern? I stumbled along, glancing in at every window, staring after every dark passer-by. I even accosted two gentlemen, complete strangers.

The air was making me giddy, or perhaps it was Lady Anne's brandy. Had I merely imagined a likeness in a passing stranger? Demsey had gone to Aberdeen to make a new start, to teach young Miss Scotts their native dances or to introduce them to the civilising influence of the English. Hamilton had said so.

I wandered on as night gathered, unwilling to go back home. I'd left George without a word of explanation; he must think me mad, or ill again. But to the devil with George. An obstinate part of me whispered that I had not been mistaken; Demsey had returned. Perhaps Hamilton had misunderstood him, or he had changed his mind after speaking to Hamilton and not travelled north after all. I am not a man who likes to be at odds with his friends and since Demsey's departure I had felt acutely the need of a friend.

Moreover, I was conscious I had behaved abominably to him; I would have welcomed a chance to apologise. And a reassurance that he was well and did not suffer from the false accusations against him. Good God, what was happening? First the plot against Hugh, then the duel (besides all the mysteries happening in Caroline Square). Would there never be an end to it all!

"I am besieged on all sides," I cried aloud. "Insulted, manipulated by men for their own purposes…"

"You are drunk, sir," a cold voice said.

I looked up the steps of St Nicholas's church, to the deep shadows of the half-open door. Light-Heels Nichols stood upon the step, looking down at me superciliously.

"Brandy, sir," I said. "Fine brandy. It is beneath me to get drunk on anything less."

"And where do you get the money, sir?" he returned contemptuously. "I trust the rate of interest upon the loan was not too extortionate."

He was hardly fit to comment, considering his brother was so well acquainted with the money-lenders. But I could not quite express the thought; there seemed a gulf between my brain and my tongue.

"I intend to make my fortune," I said, waving my hands expansively. I was feeling reckless, wild enough for anything. And nauseous.

"Indeed?"

"Indeed," I cried. "I am off to Aberdeen, to write Scotch tunes and pass them off as centuries old –"

I stopped. He had drawn back. He turned his head away from me, came rapidly down the steps and pushed past. I yelled after him and was rewarded by an irate shout from the upstairs window of a nearby house. Then he was gone.

Some time later, I managed to find Mrs Hill's in the

Fleshmarket. I stumbled into the place reeking of offal, for in the darkness I had slipped in a pool of butchers' blood and sat down in discarded guts. The tavern was packed and noisy; I collapsed upon a bench and called for Dick Kell.

"You're drunk," he said accusingly from the carved handle of a tankard. The candlelight flickering from the metal and from the glitter that was Dick Kell made my head spin. I put my face in my hands.

"I'm trying not to be," I said thickly. "Wait, wait." Had I learnt nothing from that episode with Claudius Heron? When I was drunk, I did the most foolish things. And to wander around the town out of my wits when there were ruffians out to get me was more than foolish. I gathered my thoughts together at last. "Dick, you were here when Light-Heels Nichols first came to this town, were you not?"

"Lord, yes. Year before I died. Let me see. I died – um – four years back. That year we had the terrible snowstorms. Year before you came back from London."

"You don't by any chance," I said carefully, squinting at the ale-damp table to one side of the tankard, "know where he came from?"

"Lancaster."

My hopes plummeted.

"Born and bred there. Father was the organist. His brother had the post too but put himself up for the St Nicholas's job. More money. Always liked money, those two. And women. Well, Light-Heels does anyway. If you ask me, that's why he left Aberdeen."

"Dick," I said to the pool of ale on the table, "I'm tired and I can't think properly. Talk to me slowly. Nichols came to this town from Lancaster?"

"No, no," he said good-humouredly. "You are in a sorry state, aren't you? Light-Heels was *born* in Lancaster, but he spent some while as a music teacher in Aberdeen before he came here. Taught singing."

"Singing?" I echoed incredulously.

"And the violin. Can't have made much a of a go of it. Left. Oh, sorry." He mimicked Light-Heels' careful voice. "*I resigned in order to return to my native country. The Scotch were most complimentary about my playing.* Well, let me tell you, I've stood in front of Light-Heels Nichols in more than one concert and if the Scotch think a violin should sound like a nail being drawn across a metal box, they've even less sense than I've always thought – and that's not saying much! And what's up with you?"

"Aberdeen!" I said and started to laugh.

I made one last effort to prevent the contest on the Monday next, two days after I thought I had seen Demsey. Before I gave his son a lesson upon the harpsichord, Mr Heron came in to take his first lesson. I spoke directly about the matter of the duel, for I knew he would scorn subterfuge or roundaboutation. I asked him to speak to Jenison and Ord and request them to call off the affair.

He was taking his violin from its case and paused to look sideways at me. In the clear chill sunlight entering through the window, his pale eyes seemed to glitter.

"I do not think there is any point in wasting time in an endeavour that cannot possibly succeed. Why do you object to the contest?" He straightened, bow-stick in one hand and his resin-box in the other. "Do you fear your boy will lose?"

"I know he will," I said, rather more forcibly than I had intended. "As you are aware, sir, I was in London scarcely three years ago and I heard few violinists even there who could stand comparison with Monsieur le Sac."

"What, then?" He rubbed the horsehair over the resin.

I hesitated, but still judged it best to speak plainly. "Mr Jenison and Mr Ord have been filling the boy's head with expectations that cannot be fulfilled, which will only lead to disappointment. It is not fair on the boy."

Heron did not speak for a moment. He laid the bow-stick upon the table and lifted the violin to the light, angling it as if to catch the patina of dust upon its surface. One lean finger plucked a string.

"Slightly flat," he said and glanced again at me. "I approve your good sense, Mr Patterson, but there is no avoiding this matter. I advise you to do as I do and stand well clear of it."

I considered but was not able to agree. "I cannot, sir."

"Then there is no more to be said on the matter. Shall we proceed?"

And so I gave him that first lesson, surprised by the seriousness with which he undertook the task. Teaching gentlemen is never easy, for they are rarely amenable to accepting advice, or anything but praise, no matter how undeserved. Heron, however, made it plain he expected honesty from me, and did not snap at me for giving it. It is rare to find a gentleman who takes the science of music so seriously as even to practise.

Only later did I realise that Claudius Heron had done me the honour of adding to my name the title of Mr.

I had, perforce, to accept the inevitability of the duel. Lady Anne, Heron, gleeful Mr Ord – all thought it impossible to avoid. But I was determined to enjoy the Concert upon the Tuesday night, as it might be the last I directed and I wanted to leave a good impression. It went very well, I thought, despite Mountier's absence (he had another engagement in Durham); at the end of the music, I went down into the yard of the Turk's Head, to feel the coolness of the evening air after the heat of the crowded Long Room. Despite my tiredness, and my aches and pains, there was a warm pleasurable feeling in my gut, a certainty that, given a larger opportunity, I could do very well as musical director, that this was something I could excel at.

A shadow moved beneath the arch of the inn. Then Esther Jerdoun came cautiously across the cobbles, holding up her blue satin dress from the mud and horse manure, stepping in and out of shafts of moonlight, her shining shoes bright. She stopped in front of me but said nothing. She dropped her skirts and smoothed them down, then looked into my face with a directness that disconcerted me.

"Did you never consider staying in London, Mr Patterson?"

I was astonished; her hint was unmistakable. "Are you advising me to consider it now, madam?"

Her ash-blonde hair gleamed in the moonlight; her bare arms, white and slim, lay smooth against the satin. She was without a cloak but did not seem to feel the cold.

"I wish I could say there is no danger to you, sir, but I would not be honest."

"Do you mean to warn me against your cousin again?" I said boldly.

Her face hardened.

"Forgive me," I said. "But I am well aware that Lady Anne enjoys playing games with lesser mortals. She –" I searched for polite words, then recklessly plunged on. "She finds everyday life tedious and seeks to enliven it. I do not like that, I confess. Nor do I like being embroiled in your quarrel with her."

She was contemplating me, expressionlessly.

"For you do have a quarrel with her, do you not, madam?

You seem to disapprove of almost everything she does. Well, madam, if you wish to play your games, and try to diminish your cousin's standing with the world, I cannot prevent you. But I will not be caught up in it."

I stopped, appalled to hear my own words, the force and the anger behind them. Esther Jerdoun regarded me for a moment, then reached to lift her skirts again.

"You are a fool, Mr Patterson," she said, and turned away.

25
SINFONIA CONCERTANTE
Movement III

And so to the duel.

I rose early on the Wednesday morning, looking out of the window on to a gloomy drizzle; a thin layer of mud gleamed on the street below. George still snored, entangled in his blanket on the floor, and I kicked him awake before splashing my face with cold water from the previous night. He was full of glee and talked incessantly of how he was going to defeat his old master. I curbed my impulse to speak to him sharply – now was not the time to weaken the boy's confidence – but I inwardly cursed Jenison and Ord. Vanity should not be encouraged, particularly where it has no basis in fact.

"I must give my lessons as usual," I told him. "I've lost enough money recently as it is. You will stay here and practise the Corelli."

"Master –"

"Put on your best clothes just before you go. When you get to Mrs Hill's, speak to Dick Kell. He knows what's what." I buttoned up my waistcoat and glanced down at his eager face, wondering how it would look when I saw him next, after the defeat Le Sac would inevitably inflict on him.

"Play as well as you can, George. I cannot ask more than that. I'll meet you here tonight and you can tell me all about it."

"Yes, master."

As I left, I wished he had been more sombre and thoughtful.

He had that look of mischief that always bodes ill.

I spent the morning teaching on the Westgate and, on my way back into town, looked in again at Demsey's school. The room itself was as it had been, except for a thick layer of dust on the chairs. But, as I turned to go back down to the street, I saw something catch the light on the stairs to Demsey's rooms above; I turned back. The fragment of a bright button, twisted and broken. Perhaps that glimpse in the street had not been born of the brandy, after all. I looked closely and saw, in the dust on the stairs, the faintest trace of footsteps. Demsey was always extraordinarily light upon his feet. I went up to the attic and rapped on his door. Not the smallest sound. I prised up the floorboard but the key was gone. He had certainly come back.

I went down to the coffee-house to write him a note saying I had seen him, that I regretted my last outburst and wished to speak with him. But the words were impossible to find. I sat long in Nellie's, with a dish of coffee cooling before me and the ink drying upon the quill. *My dear Demsey.* Easy enough to begin, but how to continue? How many men find it easy to say *I'm sorry*?

I was biting the end of the quill when there was a great noise at the door and I saw the massive figure of Tom Mountier, rolling and reeling against the jamb. Flattening at least three men on his way, he hailed me with a roar.

"Charles, I'm parched! Buy me a drink!"

I signalled to the serving wench. "I'll buy you coffee, Tom. You're drunk."

"Nonsense!" He gave me a wink. "I can sing as well as ever. Listen."

He rollicked off the first notes of a hunting song and of course all heads turned. Some shouted encouragement and some joined in so that soon nearly the entire coffee-house was singing. I sat back and listened, with a half-smile on my lips and the cold fear of dread in my heart. For I heard today, as I had never heard before, the edges of roughness creeping into that fine polished bass voice – the suggestion of hoarseness and, worse, the lack of care he took over the shaping of phrases and the small graces that show true taste. Before, even when drunk, those things had come effortlessly to Tom Mountier, once the darling of London concert-goers.

He finished, tossed off the coffee and called for ale. Someone shouted for another song but he roared that he was too sleepy, and melodramatically flung hmself down on the table, his head on top of his arms, snoring loudly.

"Why are you in Newcastle?" I asked.

Bright-eyed and wide awake, he lifted his head and grinned. "On my way to Edin – Edinburgh. To the good gentlemen and their private concert."

"Leave of absence again? I wonder Hesletine allows it."

"Doesn't know about it, my boy! Blissful ignorance and all that. I left him a note reminding him I told him of it weeks ago; he'll not remember whether I did or no. When our esteemed organist sits down in front of manuscript paper, the outside world exists no longer. Even now, he is penning some sublime Ode."

I laughed. "'Not at this moment, he isn't. He's in the Fleshmarket, being entertained – or otherwise – by my apprentice."

Mountier stared at me. "My dear Charles, you run mad. I left Hesletine deep in the throes of composition. I had to creep past his window to avoid his notice."

"He probably set out minutes after you did."

"Nonsense. He'll not stir till he goes to conduct the rehearsal for the concert."

"Tom," I said patiently. "Thursday is concert night in Durham. Today is Wednesday."

"Not the public concert," he said. "The private one in the Deanery. Handel, Handel and more Handel, the saintly one. Charles, my dear fellow..."

I was already halfway to the door, mowing down newcomers in my turn and running for Mrs Hill's.

The butchers' stalls in the Fleshmarket were crowded so there was scarce space for a dog to run down the street. I pushed through the mob, apologising hurriedly, stepping on feet, oversetting baskets, apologising again. Someone spilt beer over me, someone else jabbed an elbow in my side. Gasping for breath, I stumbled against the wall of Mrs Hill's – and felt a hand seize my arm.

I tried to pull free, twisted and looked into the sombre face of Claudius Heron.

"It's a trick," I said, breathing heavily. "Hesletine is not coming. He probably doesn't even know what's going on."

Heron nodded. "I'm afraid so."

My recriminations died on my lips. Something in Heron's expression stopped them – a twist to his mouth, that familiar hint of distaste and... And what? I put my hand against the cold wall and drew a deep shuddering breath. "What is happening in there, sir?"

He drew me aside, to the mouth of an alley. He was perhaps an inch or two shorter than I, and his hand on my arm was chill even through the cloth. His speech was always slow but on this occasion more than usual. "I regret to say that Ord and Jenison are trying to manoeuvre Le Sac into a position where he feels so humiliated that he leaves the town. They intend to impose new conditions for the contest which he will not be able to accept."

"He will never leave," I said, recalling that night on the Side when Le Sac had threatened to force me out. "He'll not give in. He's too obstinate."

Heron nodded again. "I have told them so. But they are set upon the idea and they are the last men in the world to yield to a counsel of caution."

I gave him a direct look. "And your part in this, sir?"

"Nothing." Again that grimace of distaste.

"Then may I ask why you are here? You advised me nothing could be done."

I could not keep the anger from my voice and my tone was far from respectful. Heron lifted his head.

"Because," he said, "I have a higher opinion of your perspicacity than they do. I guessed you would fathom their plans and come here to stop them."

"You are right, sir," I said and made to push past him. He took hold of my arm again. When I tried to pull free, he bore me back against the wall, gripping my flesh with those lean fingers.

"You must not be associated with this, Patterson. No, hear me out." I had made to free myself. "If you take sides in this matter, *whichever* side you take, half the gentlemen of the town will shun you. How then will you make a living?"

"You take great care of my reputation, sir," I said sarcastically. I had had enough of being told what to do: Lady Anne, Esther Jerdoun, now Heron…

His grip upon my arm was fierce. "I am trying to ensure that as little damage as possible is done to all concerned."

I hardly heard him. "I am already associated with the matter. The boy is my apprentice."

"The boy is not here."

"Not here?" I echoed. "Then where –"

"I sent him home." He seemed to realise he still held my

arm, let me go and stepped back, flexing his fingers. "I intercepted him at the top of the Fleshmarket and told him the contest was postponed. He seemed... disappointed."

A little, a very little, of my anger was dissipating. If George was out of the way (at least for the time being), the matter might yet be mended. I murmured thanks but Heron was not listening to me. He stood under the unlit lamps of the tavern rubbing his fingers together and staring into some private thought. A strand of his fair hair had escaped from the bow at the nape of his neck and curled on the shoulder of his dark coat.

"I abominate these petty intrigues," he said. "They are set afoot by men with nothing better to occupy them than small jealousies and their own pride." That sharp gaze settled on my face. "Do not, I pray, Patterson, force me to lodge you in their company."

"I never wanted this," I said vehemently. "Everything in this matter has been forced upon me from the beginning. Even the boy."

"Then go home, Patterson. I certainly intend to."

"You do not go in?"

He laughed mirthlessly. "Sometimes my fellow men disgust me, Patterson. While I deal politely with them, drink wine with them, discuss trade and politics with them, ride with them, play music with them, go to church with them, their breath is stinking on my neck. My stomach turns with it all." His mouth twisted. "Sometimes even my son disgusts me. I was never so glad as the day my wife died, for that event absolved me of the need to act the kind hypocrite every day. No, I shall not go in."

And, brushing past me, he pushed into the mob in the street and was lost from sight.

I admitted the wisdom of all he said; I knew I could not afford to alienate any of the men on whom my living depended. But I knew too that I must see what went on inside the inn. I waited a moment or two, to be sure Heron had gone, then pushed my way into the inn-yard.

The door leading to the stairs to the Long Room was open. I leant my weight upon the bottom step cautiously, knowing the stairs creaked. A murmur of voices was audible from the upper room. I heard Ord's shrill tones and the measured low rumble of Jenison. And was that Nichols?

On the top stair, I eased myself to one side to look into the room without being seen. Mrs Hill's Long Room was not as spacious as that of the Turk's Head and there were no glittering chandeliers here, merely a branch or two of unlit candles upon the windowsills. The room was laid out for a supper; the long tables down the centre of the room were covered with white cloths and servants at the far end were clattering cutlery and uneasily tiptoeing in and out.

At the near end of the room, under windows that looked down into the street, a cluster of men were gesticulating and shouting. In their centre stood Le Sac, stocky yet elegant in his suit of midnight blue, a cravat of purest white at his throat, disordered by the imprint of his violin. That black fiddle was gripped in his left hand, the bow stick held like a cudgel in the other. He was red-faced, and I have never seen such a look of malice on any man.

Yet he was stock-still and silent. It was Nichols who made the noise, arguing his principal's case with near-incoherent rage. One of the gentlemen of the concert band stood nearby, awkwardly clasping his cello – Le Sac's accompanist, I presumed. And, standing in the full glare of the daylight from the windows was Jenison, hands behind his back, head raised, feet planted apart in a stance of stern implacability. Behind him, sly Mr Ord bobbed and grinned.

I went back down the stairs, careless of the creaking, knowing that none would hear me. Le Sac had brought the confrontation upon himself, yet of all the men gathered in that window it was he who sparked my compassion. For his dignity in fury, if nothing else.

And Ord and Jenison were the men whom Claudius Heron would have me placate, men who had decided to be rid of someone they found difficult to control and instead to put in his place another man of more pliability. And I knew I had no choice but to accept the situation. Jenison and Ord held the key not only to my successful future as a musician but to my very survival. A man must eat and thus must earn money in his chosen profession.

But it sickened me. Walking up the Fleshmarket, ignoring the children that bumped me and the carriers that barged the corners of their boxes into my legs, I felt disgusted at myself. And when a tavern presented itself with open doors, I turned into it, regardless of the urine-damp straw upon the floor and the stink of sour ale. And there, for some hours, I proceeded to drink as much as Tom Mountier ever did, and to become progressively more and more sober and morose. Who was Claudius Heron to lecture me on my behaviour? He was a gentleman with an inheritance and coal mines aplenty, stocks and shares by the hundreds, money to drop into a working man's outstretched hands. What did he know of earning a living?

Eventually I went home, walking straight, with a mind sharpened still further by the cold night air. As I let myself into the house, I could hear voices, miners arguing in the back rooms; on the first floor, Mrs Foxton called to one of the lodgers. I was in no mood to speak to anyone; I climbed the stairs wearily, searching my pockets for my key.

My gaze was arrested by the door to my room. Wood showed pale and raw where the lock had been broken. I touched the door; it swung silently open. I listened for the quick rush of footsteps, tensed myself for an attack.

None came. The door swung on, opening wide.

And showed me the boy, sprawled upon the floor amid the smashed fragments of his violin. In his right hand was clutched, not the Corelli that I had insisted upon, but the Vivaldi. And the pages were soaked with blood.

26
ELEGY

I leaned over the banister and called down to Mrs Foxton. The muffled voices from the first floor ceased; Mrs Foxton's voice came from the landing below.

"Can I help you, Mr Patterson?"

"I would be obliged if you would send for Bedwalters," I said, amazed at the calmness of my voice. "There has been an accident."

But as I stood over George's crumpled body again, I knew it had been no accident. There was nothing to explain the blood upon the music – no broken glass or fallen knife. Nor would George have been so careless as to fool around with his violin in his hand; his livelihood depended upon that instrument. And the violin itself lay oddly beneath the boy – face up, the bridge sprung free as the tension of the strings was released. The curved back had been smashed and the neck broken. I could not imagine how it might have fallen thus: because of the grip with which the player holds the neck, the violin should surely have fallen face down when George fell.

Bedwalters came up, the street girl who seemed to be so often with him treading behind. The girl carried a candle, its light flickering across her curious composed features. The intake of breath I heard did not come from her but from Bedwalters. From the door jamb, Mrs Foxton muttered.

"I have not touched him," I said.

Bedwalters nodded. He shifted forward, cautiously trod to the other side of the body and lifted an unlit branch of candles from the table. As the girl tilted the flame of her candle to them the room grew brighter and the hunched shape upon the floor more awful.

"Not much blood," Bedwalters said, looking down. "Perhaps he broke his neck in falling. But then why should there be any blood at all?"

I explained my reservations about the violin; Bedwalters nodded again. "You'll know that better than me, Mr Patterson. Since you were good enough not to touch the body, perhaps you were good enough not to touch anything else in the room? A knife, perhaps?" He must have seen my puzzlement. "Some people prefer not to be associated with suicide."

"Suicide!" I echoed incredulously. "George would not do that!"

"I only meant that it must always be considered, sir. You would be surprised how many people in this town live in quiet despair."

I glanced at him in surprise, for he had spoken with a kind of passion. And I saw too a shift in the girl's stance; she had for a moment lost her composure. But she was still again in a moment. I looked down upon the body with Bedwalters silent beside me.

"It cannot have been suicide," I pointed out. "He has the violin in one hand and music in the other. How could he also have handled a knife?"

Bedwalters nodded. "If you don't object, sir, I'd like to turn him on his back."

With considerable reluctance, I bent to help him. The movement set the candle flames leaping and the shadows moving, and for one dreadful moment I thought I saw the boy move too. But his flesh was already cold and passive under my hands; he seemed extraordinarily heavy. As we turned him, the violin slipped from his grasp and clattered to the floor. Then his head fell back against my shoulder and Mrs Foxton said faintly, "God have mercy."

His throat had been cut.

I turned my head away from the gaping maw of flesh, sinew and bone, and helped Bedwalters lay George down again. I brushed at the shoulder of my coat. There was no blood there but I fancied I could see the imprint of that bloody gaping hole, that it would be there for ever.

"Not suicide," Bedwalters said. "No boy could do that to himself."

"Murder?" Mrs Foxton said in shocked tones.

I forced my mind to work. "He would have made an easy victim – small, not very strong. Both his hands were occupied. He would have been fearful of dropping the violin too..."

I stopped. Bedwalters and I both stared at the ruined instrument that had slipped from George's limp fingers. Bedwalter's large hands hovered over the fragments of wood.

"He wasn't holding the violin," he said. "The dead don't let go of what they were holding when they died. Not at once, at any rate. Look how he grips that paper. He held that when he died. But the violin – no." He reached down to George's left hand and, to my extreme discomfort, shifted the fingers. I heard the rasp of broken bones.

"His hand was broken to force the violin into it." Bedwalters stood up, tapping his teeth thoughtfully. "And another thing. A cut throat should have covered the floor with blood."

"Yet there is hardly any at all," I agreed, still rubbing at my shoulder. "And all of it on the music."

Bedwalters bent and set his palm flat against the floor as

if feeling for moisture. He brought it up dry. "A spot or two, nothing more. So..." He gave a heavy sigh. "He wasn't killed here."

We looked unhappily at one another, but it was Mrs Foxton who spoke the words aloud. "If you don't know where he was killed, you'll not find his spirit. And if you can't find his spirit, you won't be able to ask who killed him. The murderer will get away with it!"

Bedwalters departed to inform the Justice of the death; he managed to lock the damaged door again and took the key with him. I did not wish to go back into the room, but as I stood at the door, looking out at the chill starry night, I wondered where I was to spend the night.

"Mrs Foxton, I will stay with – with friends. If I am asked after, by Bedwalters or the Justice, tell them I will return tomorrow before ten." I turned to go, then paused. "Did you not hear anyone come in?"

"Of course I heard someone come in," she said sharply. "Twenty-five people live in this house. People are always coming in."

"Thank you," I said, and stepped into the street to prevent myself snapping at her.

The cold air made me reel, or perhaps it was the lingering effects of the ale I had consumed that afternoon. I was tempted to head back to the inn but I needed rest and quiet thought, not ale. For one thing, I must be clear-headed on the morrow for the inquest. I would have to explain not only how I had found George but also when I had last seen him, and that would entail awkward questions about the duel.

A cold realisation gripped me. If Claudius Heron had sent George home, he could have been the last to see him alive. I stopped in the middle of the street, appalled by the thought that had crept into my mind. I had only Heron's word that he had sent George home. And the man had been unusually bitter, unusually discomposed when I spoke to him.

Heron?

I needed to think, in quiet, on my own. I might find a room for the night at Mrs Hill's, but there I would have Dick Kell to deal with. I turned my footsteps towards Westgate Road.

There was a frost in the air; it sparkled in the stone of the walls and gleamed off the windows. Overhead, stars glittered in a faultless sky, although to the east a heavy cloud hung upon the horizon – the smoke from the salt-works at Shields. Plenty of people were still about; whores laughed in the arms of sailors, an embarrassed chaplain hurried quickly by, children played jumping games on a grid scratched into the earth of the street. At the entrance to Caroline Square, I paused, glancing across at the dark outline of Lady Anne's house. Lady Anne, Esther Jerdoun, even the house itself, seemed to conspire against me but I would not complain. *I* was still alive.

Westgate itself was quiet, as more genteel districts generally are. The tall houses, thin-faced, marched up the hill towards the dark hulk of the West Gate itself. I passed the dark wall of the Vicarage Gardens, crossed to the guttering dying lanterns of the Assembly Rooms and came to Demsey's dancing-school. The side door was unlocked as ever; I was preoccupied as I climbed the flight of stairs. Could I conceive of Claudius Heron as a murderer? He had the coolness for it. But what possible reason could he have for harming George?

I passed the schoolroom. I had no wish to spend the

night on the floor, or on one of the damned uncomfortable chairs round the walls. ("Of course they're uncomfortable, Charles. They are designed to encourage people to stand up and dance!") I climbed to the attic, lifted my hand and tapped on the door of Demsey's rooms.

"Hugh? Hugh, if you're there I need to speak to you."

Silence.

"Hugh, for God's sake! It's not about that... that quarrel we had. It's about George." I could hardly bring myself to say the words. "The boy's dead, Hugh. Murdered."

A moment's silence, then a key clicked in the lock. The door swung open on to a shadowy room lit by only a single candle. Demsey stared at me, wild-eyed.

"Murdered?" He clutched at my sleeve. "I didn't do it, Charles. I swear! The boy was alive when I left him!"

27
SONATA

I pushed him back into the room and shut the door lest our voices echo down the stairs to any chance passer-by. In the shadowy candlelight the room looked very much as it always had; the bed was made, clothes were piled in an open chest, papers laid across the table as if Demsey had been working at them.

"When were you with him, Hugh?" I asked carefully.

He looked at me with a glimmer of amusement. "Don't use that damn tone with me, Charles. I know I'm in your bad books."

"Can you blame me? After that affair with Nichols?"

"It was none of your business!" he flared, then swore and took a turn about the room to calm himself.

"Perhaps. And I … I behaved abominably," I said, finding, I admit, some difficulty in saying the words.

He spun and flashed me a grin. "So you did. But I knew if I left you to stew a week or two, you'd come round."

"Hugh!" I exclaimed in exasperation. "Of all the –" But I could not remain angry. Our old friendship mitigated against it. I seized and embraced him, then fell to further abusing him, until we were both convinced that all grudges were satisfied. And I felt a huge relief too, that I was not left alone to cope with this mess.

"Hugh – have you ever been in Caroline Square?"

He was pouring ale from a jug on the table. "Of course. I've a couple of pupils there."

"Did you ever notice anything odd about it?"

"There's that damn spirit, in the gardens."

"No, I meant at Lady Anne's house."

He looked bewildered. "How odd? New cobbles? New railings?"

"No, no. Take no notice." I downed ale while he watched me critically. "I cannot think straight with this business of George."

"Charles –"

"Wait." I perceived he was about to ask me about the boy. "Let me take this in order. Tell me what you have been doing since I last saw you." There was fear in my mind, if truth be told – fear of finding out what had happened to George, of discovering Hugh had played some part in it.

He ran his hand through his black hair. "I went to Aberdeen," he said, "to chase after friend Nichols's past." He seized my arm. "Charles! You know what they suggested of me with the Lindsay girl!"

"I have seen her," I said. "She was pointed out to me at a concert. As sly a slut as I have ever seen."

He snorted with laughter. "She is one of those that twists this way and that when dancing, always seems to be looking past her partner's shoulder, or under his arm, and when you glance round to see what's caught her attention, you see it's her own reflection in the glass!"

I sipped my ale; Demsey always bought the best, and hang the expense. The sloping roof prevented me from standing upright and I perched upon the edge of the bed.

"What happened?"

"Nothing." He shook his head at my stare of disbelief. "Honestly, Charles. I knew nothing of the matter until the day after. Her governess sat with us the entire lesson."

"Then how could anything ever be proved against you?"

"Charles, Charles. There is no need of proof. Rumour does the trick amply. The girl denied the whole thing throughout. The father – as sour-faced a bigot as I ever saw – summoned me to his inner sanctum and called upon the slut to accuse me. "Oh, father,' she cried." (Demsey's imitation was scurrilous.) "'Oh, father, how can you think such a thing. Mr Demsey is the soul of honour!' And all the time she's making sheep's eyes at me and damn near winking!"

"And you say Nichols put her up to it? What persuasion did he use? She came perilously close to sacrificing her reputation."

"Marriage." He grinned at my incredulity. "Close your mouth, Charles – it does not become you. He swore he would marry her and bear her off to the delights of London."

"Good God." I could not conceive that even the most naïve of females could tolerate the thought of marriage to Nichols. "But the fellow's a mere dancing master – she would hope to do better than that!"

I stopped. Demsey's expression had twisted and he looked upon me with some dislike. "A *mere* dancing master?"

"I was referring to Nichols," I said quickly. "You are of such a superior stamp that I had for a moment quite forgotten your profession."

He regarded me consideringly. "A tolerable retreat, Charles, tolerable. No more than that. But what can one expect of a mere musician?"

I grinned. "Touché. And what did you find at Aberdeen?"

He swung round to the table and seized up some papers.

"See here, Charles. Letters from – well, I had better not say the name. A gentleman in Aberdeen, the younger son of a trading family there, with connections in Norway and the Baltic, very respectable, well-moneyed. He has a daughter whom friend Nichols taught. Nichols tried to seduce her, promised her marriage and might even have gone through with it had not the girl confided her joy to her elder sister."

"He wanted the money, I suppose."

"No," Demsey said grimly. "What he wanted was the title of *gentleman.* He tried to bargain with them. He said they could tie up the largest part of the girl's dowry so he could not gain access to it, provided they gave him an allowance, accepted him at dinner parties and introduced him to polite society. It was *politely* suggested to him that he should return to his native land."

"Where he thought to try the same trick again for a different purpose – to be rid of a rival."

Demsey stood, papers in hand, the animation dying from his face. "I brought the whole matter on myself, did I not? Rising to his bait, arguing with him, setting those ruffians on him…"

"Indeed," I said.

He laughed shakily. "Damn it, Charles. A friend's supposed to say something consoling in a situation like this."

"I cannot feel consoling. My apprentice has just been murdered."

"Damn, I forgot." He tossed the papers down upon the table. "I saw him this afternoon and he was alive and well. Obstreperous, but well."

I drained the ale. "Do me the favour of an explanation."

He shrugged. "No sooner had I returned than I heard about this so-called musical duel. Why in heaven's name did you agree to it, Charles?"

"I never did. It had gone too far before I knew of it. Ord and Jenison are the guiding hands of the affair. Le Sac made the mistake of injuring them where it hurts them most. He asked for fifteen shillings a night."

Demsey whistled.

"Of course he is the darling of the audiences."

"What do *they* know about music?" Demsey retorted.

"Enough to recognise my worth, I hope," I said dryly. He made a mocking bow to me. "Go on, go on," I said irritably. "You had returned and heard of the duel."

He perched upon the edge of the table, gathering the skirts of his coat away from the flames of the candle. "I thought you might appreciate some support, so I went along to see the affair, thinking I would find you there. Only I arrived at the very moment Le Sac and Nichols stepped across the threshold, and I hung back. I didn't want to see Light-Heels. Those papers go to lawyer Armstrong tomorrow and I fancied I might be inclined to gloat and arouse Nichols's suspicions."

I nodded. "And then?"

"I walked up and down the street to waste a minute or two. I planned to slip in under the arch and go in the back way. But then I saw your boy running along the Fleshmarket, violin case in one hand and music in t'other – till he ran slap-bang up against Claudius Heron. God knows what *he* was doing there."

"He was, I believe, trying to prevent the affair." Or rather, I thought, trying to prevent my becoming embroiled in it. But why, I asked myself, should Heron take such care over me?

"That would accord with what I saw," Demsey said thoughtfully. "He exchanged a few words with the boy and sent him away. I was too far away to hear what was said but I could see the boy didn't want to go."

I sighed. "Jenison and Ord had worked on him. He thought he could defeat Le Sac."

"That boy? Then he is a bigger fool than I thought."

"He *was*," I agreed.

Demsey winced. "I thought he looked rebellious still, even as he turned back, and then he went charging off at such a pace I was at once suspicious. Do you remember that narrow lane down beside Humble's stationers?"

"In heaven's name! The boy ran round the corner, dashed down the alley into the back street, then cut into Mrs Hill's yard from the rear!"

"Out of Heron's sight," Demsey agreed. "I knew I hadn't time to follow him – I could never have got through the crowds round the butchers' stalls. So I slipped into the yard when Heron's back was turned and caught the boy as he came down the alley. I got him by the collar and marched him back out into the street again." He shifted the candle and glanced at his coat for signs of singeing. "I knew the affair would do you no good, Charles, and I thought that if the boy went missing for an hour or so, the contest could be called off with no blame on you."

His tone was mild but so like my late unlamented father's way of reproving me for some foolishness that I at once bristled.

"They would have said I instructed the boy to stay away! And how did you ensure he kept away when Claudius Heron could not?"

He looked shame-faced. "I took him into the nearest tavern."

I looked upon him with foreboding. "Hugh!"

"I told the landlord the boy was trying to get up courage for an important performance and treated him to strong spirits."

"Good God, it's a wonder he wasn't sick. How much did you ply him with?"

"More than I thought I'd have to. That boy was no stranger to strong drink!"

I started to speak, then shook my head. "I cannot berate him for it now. So how long were you there?"

He shrugged. "I didn't watch the clock. I fed him enough to get him well away, then steered him in the direction of your lodgings. He was singing," he added with some asperity. "He was a damn annoying child!"

"Where did you leave him?"

"At the end of your street. I didn't go to the house in case that landlady of yours saw me. But I watched the boy to the door."

"Did you see him go in?"

"No," he said reluctantly.

I was too restless to sit still any longer and started to pace the room. "Could he have decided to go back yet again? He was drunk, after all."

Demsey straightened the papers on the edge of the table, which I had knocked against in passing. "Charles, why do you not ask the boy's spirit when it returns?"

"We found the body in my room but he was not killed there."

"Where, then?"

"We do not know. But there would have been a great deal of blood – his throat was cut."

"Poor bastard." Demsey restlessly straightened papers again, trimmed the guttering candle. "Charles, I can't see Le Sac killing the boy. He had nothing to fear, surely – he would have won the contest."

"It is not as straightforward as that." I explained what Heron had told me. "Ord and Jenison never intended the duel to go ahead. They were merely manoeuvring to get Le Sac into a position from which he could not withdraw with honour."

"He will not accept defeat," Hugh said decisively. "Perhaps

he killed George to revenge himself on you, thinking that the gentlemen are acting out of partiality for you."

I laughed harshly. "They are partial to men they think they can control. No, no, I cannot believe it. Le Sac is too proud a man. He thinks George beneath his notice – that's what galled him about the duel. He did not kill George, I'm certain of that."

"Then who?"

"God knows."

A silence. A rumble of wheels from the street outside.

"Charles," Demsey said at last. "Are you certain George was the target?"

"Who else should it be?" I asked bewildered.

"Damn it, you were attacked only days ago! Yes, yes, I've heard about that too… Charles, what if the killer was after you?"

I stared at him. "What was that you said about friends consoling each other?"

"Damn consolation. I'm talking about your life."

"I cannot believe it! How could anyone mistake the boy for me, even in the dark? And remember, he wasn't killed in the room – he was placed there afterwards."

"To incriminate you."

That suddenly struck me as uncomfortably likely. But my head was aching again, and I was abominably confused.

"That would give Le Sac a good motive," Hugh pressed.

"Only a moment ago, you said you couldn't see him as a murderer."

"Well, he – no, I – damn it, I can't think straight, Charles." He swept a hand in a melodramatic gesture at the shadowy room. "It is all hidden in darkness."

"It will not be," I said. And in that moment I determined to discover the truth of the affair. George had been an innocent child – offensive and unattractive, yes, but he had not deserved to die.

I accepted, without reluctance, Demsey's insistence that I stay the night with him, though I anticipated lying awake tormented by dark thoughts. But I fell asleep quickly, waking only once to wonder why the ceiling was so low. Then I heard Demsey's breathing steady beside me, and the soft patter of hailstones outside, and I remembered where I was. I turned over and slept again.

In the morning, we heard that Le Sac had disappeared.

28
SONGS AND AIRS

As I lay in bed, staring at the ceiling, I heard a murmur of noise from the street, like a multitude of soft voices.

"What in heaven's name's that?"

"Rain, you fool," Demsey said, his voice muffled by the bedding.

"Rain!" I crawled over him to peer from the narrow window; Demsey muttered and tried to push me away, dragging the blankets about his ears. The glass was speckled with water and, outside, rain drove in visible sheets across the houses; a small stream trickled along the centre of the earthen street.

"Damn!"

"Go back to sleep," Demsey said indistinctly.

I collapsed back upon the bed in despair. I had dreamt in a curiously logical fashion. In my dream, I had followed George as he crept to the end of the street to check that Demsey had gone; from there, I had seen him hurrying back to Mrs Hill's, determined to take part in the duel. And from some dark alley, Le Sac had stepped out, pulled George into the darkness and slit his throat. Blood had sprayed out, soaking the walls, the earth, the rubbish lying in the alley.

Waking, I had imagined I dreamed the truth. City streets are an eminently sensible place to commit a murder. Slit a man's throat in a house or even a public building and his blood and his spirit will remain to condemn you. Use some anonymous alley in a lawless part of town where respectable men refuse to go, and it will be much harder to discover the scene of the murder.

So I had decided to make a start in looking for George's spirit by walking back from my own lodgings towards the Fleshmarket, investigating every alley for blood. But the rain would stir the streets into mud, wash the walls of the buildings and drench the rubbish in the gutters. All I could hope to do now was to repeatedly call out George's name. And the spirits of children are notoriously slow to appear; two or three days perhaps might pass before George's spirit came to itself. In the meantime, if Demsey was right and the murderer hoped to kill me as well…

In a soft, drenching drizzle we set out, an hour later. Demsey was bound for lawyer Armstrong's office with the papers that might help clear his name, I for the Fleshmarket. I called first at my own house and spoke to Mrs Foxton, who informed me that the jury had viewed the body in my room and it had now been carried to a neighbouring inn where I was expected to attend the inquest that afternoon. She said also that Claudius Heron had called and had insisted on walking up to my room and looking about as if for some clue. I went up and looked about the room myself, but nothing was out of place or changed.

I promised my attendance at the inquest and set off again, following what I thought to be George's most likely route, walking into every dank, muddy alley, calling for the boy's spirit. To no avail. Then I went to Hoult's tavern to request old Hoult to ask the other spirits if they knew where George's spirit was. But the spirit demurred.

"Much too early, Mr Patterson, sir," he said soothingly. "You know children never disembody quickly. Ask again in a day or three."

It was what I had expected but the outcome depressed me nonetheless. I went on to Mrs Hill's, tired and discouraged, ready to snap even at good-humoured Dick Kell.

"What a to-do," he said cheerfully, accosting me the moment I emerged by the back lane into the courtyard of Mrs Hill's. "Never heard anything like it."

I leaned against the wall of the yard morosely. Rain dripped upon my head from the eaves; the yard was covered with a slick, greasy patina of silver upon the cobbles. Above me, Dick Kell hung on a torch bracket, chuckling rustily.

"Read the broadsides," he advised, almost giggling. "There's one on the front wall. One of Jenison's men put it up an hour ago."

"I am not interested."

"You know what they say: if you win, rub it in."

"I can imagine."

"Read it!"

"Damn it! A boy died last night because of that duel!"

"That brat," Dick said, still good-humoured. "Couldn't play the fiddle for love nor money."

I pushed myself from the wall. If he had been alive, I would have punched his face to a pulp. "He was twelve years old," I said. "And he could have outplayed you any day!"

"Rubbish music," Dick Kell snapped. "He couldn't have played a decent tune to save his life."

I flung pebbles at the wall-bracket. Dick Kell slid higher up the wall, taunting me with childish noises.

"Jigs and reels, a good strathspey, a proper country dance," he said. "That's your decent music. Not that la-de-da, ever so po-lite music you play, all die-away airs and scraping to see how high you can play, and setting people's teeth on edge with the screech of it. Kill a pig and you'll get the same noise."

"You can't even read music," I said contemptuously.

"Who needs to? Music's in your hands, and in your head, and in your heart!" He was yelling at the top of his voice now, for I had walked away from him, out across the slippery yard, dodging a carter who clattered in under the arch as I reached it. The horse was blowing and sweating, steam rising from its flanks in hot gusts; the clop of its hooves drowned Dick Kell's last shouted taunts.

The broadsheet was short and extremely nasty. It purported to be an account of Le Sac's 'defeat' at the duel and had been written in a gloating frame of mind by one of Le Sac's detractors (Mr Ord?). It was in the form of a mock obituary – surely penned before George's death was known, for no one could have been callous enough to have written it afterwards. *We write to tell of the death of a cholerick little fiddler, a nimble-finger'd Swiss...*

No, I would not read it. I walked away, heading down the Fleshmarket, through the air that smelled of rain, somehow accentuating the smells of the blood and offal. Le Sac, I thought, was as much a victim as George – manipulated by Ord and Jenison, idolised and humoured so long as inclination lasted and occasion demanded, then humiliated as soon as he became inconveniently demanding, even though the gentlemen's flattery had encouraged those demands.

Yet, I reflected as I walked through the last of the rain on to the Sandhill, the gentlemen might have been too clever for their own good. Once they succeeded in being rid of Le Sac, I became their only recourse if they wanted the Concerts to continue. In disposing of Le Sac, they had strengthened not *their* hand but mine. And I would not give in to them. Brave words, I know, but I had no doubt of adhering to them. I had such contempt at that moment for Ord and Jenison that I could not have lived with myself had I yielded to them.

I had engaged to meet Demsey again at Nellie's but I was early for our appointment and paused in thought, staring absently across the Sandhill to the ugly mass of the Guildhall and its double staircase. Claudius Heron was standing at the foot of one of the stairs; he seemed to be staring across at me. When he saw I had recognised him, he crossed the Sandhill towards me. He seemed ill at ease.

"I called to see you earlier, Patterson."

"So my landlady informed me. You wanted to see where the boy died?"

"I feel some responsibility," he said. "That I did not talk some sense into him that day at Mrs Hill's."

"You think the matters are connected? The duel and the boy's death?"

His lean face hardened. "Do you not suspect Le Sac of this?"

"I cannot imagine him a murderer. What danger was George to him?"

His fingers tapped the edge of his thigh. "Could he not rather have seen a danger in you?"

He and Demsey were thinking alike. "No one could mistake George for myself!" I said, exasperated.

"Give the man some credit for subtlety, Patterson," he said with a trace of sarcasm. "Perhaps he intended a warning – a suggestion of what might happen if you did not mind your own business. Perhaps he did not intend to kill the boy, only to frighten both him and you. You were yourself attacked only a few days ago – was that not for that very same purpose?"

He leant closer. "Someone is after you, Patterson. I think it is Le Sac; if you choose to believe otherwise, so be it. But I would advise you to be careful, very careful."

And he walked away.

Devil take it, was that a warning from a genuinely concerned well-wisher? It had sounded almost a threat. What in heaven's name was Heron doing – first searching my room, then this? For God's sake, where was the truth in all this?

I pushed through the crush of merchants and clergymen in Nellie's in search of Hugh. As I reached the window, a figure rose up and seized at my arm; I turned to find Demsey mouthing words in my ear. I could not hear him in the noise and shook my head. We struggled through the crowds into the passageway at the back of the house and thence into the street at the rear.

"Le Sac has gone!"

"I am not surprised. Have you seen the latest broadsheets?"

"Not *left*. Disappeared!" Demsey ran his hand through his hair. "His clothes are still in his lodgings – most of them, at any rate – and his music books. And they found a bag of money under his mattress. But he himself is gone."

"How do you know this?"

A carter turned into the end of the street; we pressed ourselves against the wall until he had passed. A trail of smoke from the Key seemed to drift after him, along with the smell of horse dung.

"They came to Lawyer Armstrong's while I was there."

"They?"

"Light-Heels Nichols and Le Sac's landlady. It was damned awkward, I can tell you, in view of my conversation with Armstrong. Anyway, I hid in Armstrong's office until they were gone – or, as the lawyer put it, I retired to allow him to consult with his clients. The landlady had the money and didn't want it on her hands, afraid someone would rob the house and she'd be accused of stealing it. Made Armstrong's clerk count it there and then."

"How much?"

"One hundred and fifty guineas."

"Good God!" I had not made a third of that these last five years, let alone saved it.

"And, of course, while they were counting, the whole story came out. Nichols was extravagantly wild. 'Find my friend!' he cries. 'Find my friend!' Armstrong told him to call out the watch."

"Did Le Sac take his violin?" I said.

"It wasn't in his rooms." Demsey grimaced and kicked at a stray dog that came sniffing round his ankles. "Armstrong more or less said outright that the fellow had run off in panic. Threw out broad hints about George's death."

"What does Armstrong know about that?"

"He's presiding over the inquest this afternoon."

"So he thinks Le Sac murdered George, then ran off in fear of being taken for it."

"Exactly. But he's not right, is he?" Demsey snorted and thrust his hands into his pockets. "What fool flees for his life leaving a hundred and fifty guineas behind him? With that kind of money, he could be halfway to London or even St Petersburg by now."

A flurry of soot settled upon my sleeve. Smoke blew across our faces. Demsey swore and waved it away ineffectually.

"So what say you?" I asked. "Is Le Sac murdered too?"

"Why? And by whom? Ord? Jenison? Can you think of anything more preposterous?"

"Nichols?"

Demsey screwed up his face. "I won't deny I'd like to think so, but half of Light-Heels' importance comes from his friendship with Le Sac. And you didn't see him this morning, Charles. I would swear he was genuinely distressed."

"And if Le Sac is dead, then it is likely his killer killed George too. Two murderers stretches credulity."

"Nichols kill George?" Demsey snorted with laughter. "By cutting his throat? That prancing fool would probably faint at the sight of blood."

"I agree it sounds unlikely." I sighed. "But who else might do it? Heron?"

"He would have the coolness and wit for it. But why, Charles?"

I kicked through the mud; Demsey took my arm. "Charles," he said, "stop blaming yourself for George's death. Come back inside and take coffee with me."

We went back into Nellie's, to see Claudius Heron sitting in a corner, taking coffee and reading the London news in the latest edition of the *Courant.* He did not seem to see us. We sat and drank a dish of coffee in some despondency, offering each other fragments of ideas. Perhaps Le Sac had hired ruffians to kill George, then been killed in turn when he refused to pay them. Perhaps the two matters were unconnected, and Le Sac had met with an accident somewhere. Or he had ridden off into the country to give a lesson and been delayed in his return.

"You know..." Demsey sat up with an arrested look. "That last idea has a ring of truth to it. The weather was dreadful last night – hail, then heavy rain – and the fellow is vain about his appearance. Suppose he begged a bed for the night from a country gentleman rather than get wet? Especially after the last time he was out in a downpour, when he caught a chill from it."

"But Nichols must surely have known if Le Sac was merely off giving a lesson."

"I don't know every lesson *you* intend to give. Where did the fellow hire his horse?"

Now I sat up too. "At the Golden Fleece, I should think."

We got up together. From Nellie's we hurried to the Fleece, scarcely a hundred yards away. When we came under the arch into the yard, an ostler was grooming a horse there and offered at once to help us. He remembered Le Sac very well.

"Yes, sir, indeed, sir. Came in here last night in a great rage. Wanted a horse straight away."

"Had a violin with him, did he?"

The ostler looked doubtful; Demsey sketched a shape in the air.

"Oh yes, sir. He had a case that shape. Yes, sir. Strapped it very careful to the saddle. Struck me, that did, him being in so great a rage yet so careful with the case."

"Did you see which way he went?"

"Off towards the bridge." He jerked his head in that direction. "To Durham, he said."

"Durham!" I exchanged a glance with Demsey. "To the city itself or somewhere in the country?"

The ostler shrugged.

"And has he come back?" Demsey demanded.

"Not yet, no sir. But the rain was so bad and he went so late, he probably stayed over. He'll be back. Reliable gent, Mr Sac."

"No one has ever before called Le Sac reliable in my hearing," I commented as Demsey and I walked out onto the Key, "but I suppose he is. He has never missed a concert, never turned up late; I have seen him play – and play excellently – when he was streaming with cold. Odd how you never notice such things, or never give credit for them, at any rate."

"Durham," Demsey mused, staring up at the bulk of the bridge with its haphazard roofline of houses and shops.

I heard a noise behind me, glanced round and saw Heron walking away from Nellie's. "What's so attractive in Durham, I wonder?"

"Hesletine, I daresay. The fellow's touchy. If he thought Ord and Jenison had been taking his name in vain, he might support Le Sac out of spite."

"A big fuss about nothing, then," Demsey said.

"Looks like it."

We were, of course, wrong.

29
CATCHES AND DUET

I came away from George's inquest greatly depressed. To stand in the presence once more of that small body, to see that head lolling at an odd angle and presenting the gaping slash in the throat to the ceiling of the inn and the fascinated horror of the eight jurymen – that was an experience I fervently hoped never to repeat.

Armstrong the lawyer was a gangling individual whose build suggested a boy growing too tall, which sat oddly with the weather-beaten face of a middle-aged man. He was the sort of man who uses silence to provoke witnesses into saying more than intended and into his silence I poured the story of George's fear of Le Sac, the things he had said, those occasions the boy had seemed afraid to go out for fear of meeting the Swiss. Armstrong complimented me on my Christian behaviour to a sad child whose life had been so villainously cut short. Neither Demsey nor Heron was called to speak but Armstrong questioned Tommy the cheesemonger's boy, who told him lurid tales of beatings and threats, and a thin woman who said she had seen Le Sac beat George. As Demsey said later, the verdict brought in by the jury – murder by Henri Le Sac – had been inevitable.

We both thought the verdict incorrect. Claudius Heron, who had sat silently through the inquest, apparently did not. He accosted me outside the tavern, stared Demsey into moving a step or two away. "The boy's death was a warning, Patterson," he said shortly. "Keep out of the affair. Leave it be."

I shook my head. "I cannot, sir."

He walked away.

In the Bigg Market, Demsey and I encountered Mr Ord hurrying down towards St Nicholas's Church. "Well, well," he cried, on seeing me. "You must be gratified, Patterson. Good news, good news indeed. I am hurrying to tell Jenison, you know. Good day, good day."

"Gratified," I repeated as we watched Ord's plump figure disappear into the crowds in Amen Corner. "Gratified that a child has lost his life?"

"I hope I never make such efficient enemies," Demsey said.

We passed Barber's bookshop and were turning from the vestry door of St Nicholas's when it opened and a man came hurrying out. Light-Heels Nichols. I bowed to him and made to pass, but he cried out shrilly, "I trust you're satisfied!"

"Leave it, man," Demsey said wearily.

"Leave it? When my friend cries out for justice? His reputation is ruined!"

It was damnably difficult to push past him; he seized my coat and for fear of tearing the cloth I was forced to turn back. His thin features were pinched, as if he had not slept nor eaten. But he had, by his breath, drunk a great deal.

"Condemned as a murderer!" he said shrilly. "For a dirty, poxed brat and a notebasher like you! Oh, you saw your way clear, didn't you? You saw how to make your fortune at the expense of his!"

"Shut up, I say," Demsey said through clenched teeth.

I tried to speak soothingly. "I had nothing to do with the matter." I put a hand on Demsey's arm, looking to deflect his rising anger, conscious of faces shifting behind windows, Barber staring from his shop door.

"Nothing to do with it?" Nichols shrieked. "Ord and Jenison are your cronies, the boy's your apprentice. You arranged the whole thing. *You* killed the boy!"

Demsey swung his fist. I lunged to prevent him but too late – bone crunched as the fist connected with Nichols's jaw. His grip on my coat loosed; he toppled into the mud of the churchyard, cracking his temple against a tombstone. Demsey was all for going for him again but I dragged him back and pinned him against the church railings.

"Leave him," I said.

Nichols lay at our feet, moaning.

"He accused you of murder!"

"He is looking for someone – anyone – to blame. After all, his prospects disappear with Le Sac."

"Damn it, Charles!" He rubbed at his bruised knuckles, and smiled sweetly at an elderly man who hovered in uncertain curiosity. The man hurried off.

"What do you say to a ride in the country?"

His brow creased. "Are you raving?"

"A trip to Durham."

We left Nichols groaning in the mud and walked down the hill towards the Key. A curl of sulphurous smoke came up to meet us, yellowy-black like a bruise; the narrow curves of the Side seemed to sink into it, as if burrowing into a fragment of hell. Demsey coughed as we came into the first tendrils of the smoke but they curled up and away from us and left a mere thickening of the air, a haze as on the outskirts of a fire.

"Charles," Demsey said, "do we go to capture Le Sac or to warn him?"

At the foot of Butcher Bank, a quack was trying to sell potions to a little cluster of women. The Row, climbing from our left up towards All Hallows Church, stank with decaying meat; a rivulet of blood came down the gutter to meet us. Demsey stepped fastidiously across it.

"Which do you suppose?"

"I suppose you're a fool," he said tartly. "I admit I don't think Le Sac a murderer, but you will never persuade Ord and Jenison of that."

"I do not look to save the man's reputation. But his life is a different matter." I stopped, astonished at myself. "Do you hear me, Hugh? Did you imagine you would ever hear me speak of helping Le Sac?"

"I wish I could decide who did kill the boy," he said. He was still rubbing at his sore knuckles. "That's more important than Le Sac's affairs. For all you know, Charles, you might be the villain's next victim."

"Or you," I pointed out. "If the villain is Nichols, for instance."

We turned into the yard of the Golden Fleece, and Demsey went to bespeak two horses. I lingered under the arch on to the Key, watching the wisps of smoke drift along the river, hearing among the clatter of loading and unloading the whispers of spirits and their pleas for help, and involuntarily shuddering again at the thought of dying in that water, drifting in the mad babble of confused spirits, even being borne out by the tides into the desolate seas. The clatter of hooves behind me raised me from my reverie; I turned – and saw Claudius Heron outside Nellie's. He nodded and moved on.

"That fellow's haunting us today," Hugh said, leading a pair of horses out to me. They were not the finest pieces of horseflesh I have ever seen but they looked sturdy enough. Hugh handed me the reins of a bay and kept a grey for himself. "This expedition has all the marks of a fool's errand," he said. "We are not dressed for riding, there's a wind from the sea and a smoke coming with it – and rain too, damn it. We are not even certain the fellow went to Durham, or if he merely said so to deceive the ostler. And it's so late in the day we will never get to Durham and back in the light!"

He hauled himself into the saddle of the grey. As in all things, he did it gracefully.

"I for one, Charles, do not intend to ride back in the small hours of the morning. The post boy was robbed of six letters beyond Chester le Street last week and I don't want to meet the fellow who did it. I shall lodge in Durham overnight, at the Star and Rummer in the Market Place."

I shuddered. "What, with that fellow Blenkinsop? Have you heard him sing, Hugh?"

"I don't care how he sings. He does very good beef."

I climbed into the saddle of my own horse, with rather less grace than Hugh. We rode up the slope on to the bridge and wound our way through the crowds of passers-by. A few raindrops splattered on my hand. "I told you!" Demsey said triumphantly.

We urged the horses up the bank in Gateshead, past St Mary's church and its tilted, uncertain gravestones. From there, the roads diverged; we took one that led away from the town and climbed on to Gateshead Fell. We were above the smoke now; looking back towards the river, I saw it hidden beneath twisting yellow clouds. The houses on the bridge seemed to rise out of the smoke as if they floated upon it; all else was hidden.

We kept silence awhile, lost in our own thoughts. Then Demsey said, "I'm glad I hit him. Nichols, I mean. I have longed to do that for months." I nodded absently, but my thoughts were elsewhere – wondering where poor George's spirit wandered.

The rainstorm came upon us more quickly than we had anticipated. A great bank of dark cloud on the eastern horizon seemed to well up and race to overtake us. A blue-black pall flung itself across the sky and tossed driving torrents of water over us, stinging our exposed hands and faces. We galloped for a stand of trees a little aside from the road; the foliage had been thinned by autumn but kept the worst of the rain away. We shivered as water dripped from the trees and slid coldly down our necks. The horses shifted restlessly.

"This is dangerous, Charles," Demsey said uneasily. "God knows what thieves might be lurking in this murk."

"They won't want to get wet any more than we do." But I too fell to scanning the shifting shadows in the rain.

We sat on in gloomy silence, every so often imagining that we saw a lighter patch of sky behind the black clouds. The horses fidgeted and tossed their heads against the rain. I was inclining to Demsey's view and contemplating a return to Newcastle when suddenly lightning streaked out of the clouds and thunder clapped hard upon its heels. My horse started and it was all I could do to prevent it rearing. I could feel it trembling between my legs.

"We can't stay here! The trees will draw the lightning!" I jerked my head into the darkness. "Let us try to get to Gateshead. I teach the Hawks family there – they will shelter us."

Demsey yelled agreement and we turned our horses into the fury of the rain. Then came another streak of brightness, simultaneous with the clatter of thunder, and Demsey's horse reared up. He cried out, hauled back on the reins, fought the frightened brute. But it bolted away into the darkness, running like a pale wraith into the black moor.

I urged my horse after them, praying there were no

hidden obstacles, no rabbit holes or abandoned mine workings. I could hardly see the ground beneath the horse's hooves, reined him back to a canter. I felt him quiver as the thunder cracked overhead.

Then to my right, I saw a patch of even greater darkness. It puzzled me, even as the horse veered away from it. It was a pond, I realised, folded into a dip in the fell. Lightning flared over our heads again. A few bushes rimmed the edge of the dark water – and I glimpsed something clinging to one of the bushes.

I dragged the unwilling horse towards the pond; reluctantly it stood shivering at the water's edge. The object blown by the wind against the bushes was only part of an old sack, after all. I was turning away when the lightning showed me another object floating near the edge of the pond.

I dismounted, groped among the bushes for a fallen branch. Pushing the branch out into the dark water, I snagged the object, pulled it ashore. So familiar an object: a little box, of the type that violinists keep their resin in. And beneath the bushes that overhung the water's edge bobbed a larger object, which came out only after a struggle.

Torn cloth, the dark edge of curved polished wood. A heavy object in which water sloshed. I tugged back the cloth and exposed the blackness within.

A black violin.

30
SYMPHONY

It was a dishevelled group that gathered at the pond the following morning. The day itself was bedraggled, overlaid by a blanket of grey cloud, damp with a drizzle that soaked our hair and clothes. The night before, we had ridden into Gateshead to David Hawks's house and he had generously offered us shelter; we went to bed to the rumbling accompaniment of the thunder. In the morning we woke to find that Hawks had called out the constable, and we all rode back to the pond with a handful of Hawks's servants.

Now one of the servants was venturing cautiously into the middle of the pond, testing his footing as he went, edging out until he was almost waist-deep. A thick rope about his waist was held by three men on the bank among the reeds; he clasped a second rope in one hand.

Suddenly he dipped, his hands splashing into the water as if he dived for a fish. But there was no silver flash of scales, no desperate flap of tail – merely a widening spread of ripples. He straightened and signalled to his friends on shore. He had left the second rope attached to something underwater. Another two fellows waded out to join him and together they dragged at the rope. It came up with a rush, water flooded away, and I saw hair hanging in rat's tails from a lolling head.

"We were too late," Demsey said laconically, touching the bruise on his temple where he had struck a branch during his horse's mad flight the previous evening. "Is it just as well, I wonder?"

"Where is his horse?"

Demsey shrugged. "Gone back to its stable?"

"Nonsense. It would have been back before we set out."

Hawks was calling to us; we went across to where the men were dragging the body on to boggy ground. The constable was bending over the body, turning the head this way and that, checking arms and legs for injuries. He, and I, saw none. Saw nothing but a parody of a man, a stocky figure hardened for ever into death, fashionable clothes torn and muddied, elegant clever fingers like claws. The constable heaved the body over; water dribbled out of the mouth.

"Drowned," said one of the men.

"Never ride on dark nights," said another, shaking his head philosophically.

Hawks nodded me to one side. He was a lean hard whip of a man, long past sixty but not looking a day beyond his prime. Every inch the gentleman.

"I have heard the rumours, Patterson." Weak sunlight glinted off the silver buttons of his coat. "I saw Heron yesterday and he told me everything that has happened – the duel, the death of the boy, the suspicions of Le Sac. Do you think he was fleeing?"

I was conscious of Demsey hovering behind me. "I cannot believe him guilty of murder, sir."

"Then what the devil was he doing out here?"

"I think he was on his way to Durham to speak with the organist there, to ask if he had anything to do with the duel."

Hawks guffawed. "Hesletine? A miracle if he could get any sense out of Old Fusspot. Still, he might have thought to try. Don't know when he left Newcastle, do you?"

"Late Wednesday afternoon, the ostler said."

He pursed his lips. "Looks like an accident, then. Lost his way. Didn't know the fell, I daresay."

"I would have thought he did, sir," I protested. "He gave lessons in several houses in the country."

But it was plain he had already made up his mind. I glanced at Hugh; I was certain an accident was much too fortuitous, and Hugh seemed to agree. But what evidence did I have to prove it?

"I'll have his body taken down into the town," Hawks said, "and we can hold the inquest this afternoon. Might as well get it over and done with."

My heart sank. The prospect of attending two inquests in two days was not enticing and would hardly do my reputation much good. But Hawks, scowling down at the body, went on. "Shan't need you, Patterson. My men will bear witness to finding him."

He strode off. Demsey came to my shoulder and together we watched the men struggle through the wet grass with their sodden burden. The body's long fingers hung almost to the ground, the head drooped grotesquely. And at the end of the short trip, only an ignominious toss on to the back of a cart, which then bumped off across the fell.

"If Le Sac was killed on Wednesday afternoon, on his way to Durham," Demsey said, "where's his spirit? A day and a half is quite long enough for it to disembody."

"He could have died on his way back – sometime yesterday. In which case, it may yet be a few hours before his spirit makes an appearance."

"Do we still go to Durham, to find out if he was there?"

"We do," I said.

We rode into the cathedral city two or three hours later, both tired and exhilarated by the ride. The horses were fresh and willing to gallop along the safer stretches of the road, and I almost – almost – rode out the frustrations in my mind and body.

Demsey insisted upon going to the Star and Rummer straightaway, for some of the famous beef, and the ride had stirred up my appetite to such a pitch that I was willing to fall in with his wishes. Durham is a tiny dirty town, full of colliers pushing through narrow streets, not troubling at all to get out of the way of the fastidious clerics who look down their noses at them. And above the thin houses crammed into their few streets looms the great church with its fortress-like towers, and the crenellations of the castle beside it.

In the Star and Rummer, Demsey was greeted like an old friend, shown to his favourite place by the window and supplied with beef before he had had time to ask for it. And before *I* could sit down, my name was shouted across the room and Mountier hurtled towards me, making the tavern seem half the size it had before. Behind him came a small man, dwarfed by Mountier but beaming. I had seen the small man once before, at a distance in the cathedral; the fellow was all nose, and I recalled that his voice came down that nose like a sheep bleating.

"Is all of Newcastle here?" Mountier cried. "We are overrun by you! Setting yourself up in competition, eh?" He ranted on while the small man smiled and raised his eyes to the ceiling.

"Friend of mine," Demsey said to me, indicating the small man as Mountier rambled on unregarded. "Met, have you? No? Charles, this is our host, Peter Blenkinsop. Blenkinsop's the best brewer of ale this side of York, you know. And the best singer in the cathedral choir."

Blenkinsop hooted with laughter. Mountier flung his arms around him. "S'right. Sing, pretty Peter, sing." And he launched into a rendering of *Te Deum, Laudamus* that was decidedly secular in spirit. Blenkinsop obligingly opened his mouth and good-humouredly joined in. I stared at Demsey, who was grinning; I had remembered correctly, for the man hooted through his nose like a penny trumpet.

"We are looking for someone," I said.

Mountier stopped in the middle of an out-of-place *Amen* and looked reproachfully at me. "You mean you seek company other than mine, Patterson? You distress me beyond all measure."

I recoiled from his breath. "Le Sac."

"Oh, the French fellow."

"Swiss," Demsey said through a mouthful of beef.

"Seen enough of *him*."

"He was here, then?"

"Yesterday," Blenkinsop said in his reedy voice. A girl slid a plate of beef in front of me. "At least, turned up late Wednesday night and was off again yesterday. And I don't care if he never comes again. Upset the Lord and Master no end. Right after Evensong when he was looking forward to a quiet evening to himself."

"Hesletine," Mountier said in confidential explanation. "Deep in the throes of that Ode still and Le Sac bursts in and accuses him of some plot."

Blenkinsop frowned. "There was talk of a duel."

"A musical duel," Demsey said, gulping ale. Mountier leapt up and pranced about the crowded room, in blundering imitation of swordplay. The serving girls fended him off irritably.

"Fiddlesticks at dawn!"

"The duel never took place," I said. "And now both parties are dead."

They were silenced, staring at me. The clatter of crockery and the raucous laughter of a party across the room seemed incongruously disrespectful.

"Who was the other fellow?" Blenkinsop asked, curiously.

"My apprentice."

"The boy?" Mountier cried. "Alas, poor Richard."

"George."

"Did they stab each other with their fiddlesticks?'"

Blenkinsop, with a quick frown, tried to sober him but he was too drunk to take notice. Demsey speared meat with his knife. "The boy was murdered. Throat cut. Le Sac was found last night in a pond on Gateshead Fell."

"Did he lose his way?" Blenkinsop asked. "There have been some devilish storms the last two nights."

"That is the commonly believed explanation," I said, exchanging a glance with Hugh.

"Poor fellow."

We did not trouble ourselves to go up to Hesletine's lodgings in the North Bailey. With the skill born of long practice, Blenkinsop banished Mountier to another party in the room and gave us a round account of what had happened on Wednesday.

Despite his voice, Blenkinsop was a sensible man. It had been his turn, evidently, to chant the psalms at evensong in the cathedral that night, and he had done so to a near-empty church, the Dean and prebendaries being at their other livings in more salubrious climes nearer London. Only the one prebendary required by statute was there, with a couple of the minor canons and Hesletine, who for all his argumentative nature was pious. On leaving the church, Hesletine had delayed Blenkinsop on some matter or other when Le Sac burst upon the scene, accusing Hesletine of all kinds of villainy.

It had taken both minor canons to separate the two but, to cut a long story short, Hesletine had said enough to convince Le Sac he had not known a duel was to take place, let alone that he was supposed to judge it. So Blenkinsop had talked the Swiss into calmness, put him up in the Star and Rummer, and with his own eyes seen him mount his horse and head northward on Thursday morning.

Soon we were riding north again ourselves. "It would have been around midday when Le Sac reached Gateshead," Demsey protested as we came close to Chester le Street. "I know the fell is a wild spot but a *daylight* attack?"

"If he *was* attacked," I agreed, "someone was audacious."

By the time we came to the bridge across the Tyne night was falling; the bridge was quiet and the town in a sleepy state. Demsey had composed a long indignant letter refuting all the accusations against him and laying out his counter-claims against Nichols, which he intended to publish in the *Courant*. He therefore went off to the Printing Office while I took the reins of both horses and walked them to the Fleece. I had hardly left the inn again when a voice spoke behind me.

"I have been waiting for you, sir." Lady Anne laughed as I started. She was impeccably dressed as always, the ribbons of her cap dancing as she moved to face me. "I have been hearing of your exploits on Gateshead Fell."

Exploits? It was an odd word to use, I thought, for the discovery of a body. I was curt. Her constant meddling annoyed me. Moreover, two people were dead and she was smiling and amused by it all. "The news has spread, then?"

"Claudius Heron came back from Gateshead with it. He is a friend of David Hawks." Another smile. "How did you discover poor Henri?"

"Demsey and I were sheltering from the storm." *Poor Henri*? I could not help but remember that she had been scheming against *poor Henri* behind his back quite as much as Ord and Jenison, and probably for much the same reason. Le Sac's greatest fault had been his failure to understand what constituted one demand too many.

"Whatever his failings," I said sharply, "he should not have died."

She opened her eyes wide in astonishment. "You call murder a *failing*?" Her look challenged me, those green eyes steady in the thin plain face. "Mr Patterson, do not tell me you doubt that Henri killed the boy?"

"I can think of no convincing reason why he should have done so."

"But surely it is clear – he murdered the poor boy, then drowned himself in remorse."

Remorse was not an attribute I had ever associated with Le Sac. "Suicide, Lady Anne? When I last saw Mr Hawks he was of the opinion it was an accident."

Lady Anne shook her head. "The verdict of the inquest was suicide."

Claudius Heron had spoken to Hawks, she said. Had he persuaded Hawks to change his mind? But why?

"And Mr Heron also believes that Le Sac murdered George?"

"From what he says, yes." She regarded me for a moment. "One should not gossip, Mr Patterson, but –"

I hated her for that *but*. She was teasing me with it, inviting me to encourage her to talk. And devil take it, I had to. I had to know what had happened to George. If there was the remotest chance that I had been in some way, no matter how small, to blame for his death, I owed him the courtesy of discovering the truth. "*But*, my lady?"

"A suggestion, no more," she said coyly, "that poor Henri knew one or two things about Heron that Heron might not wish known."

Her lack of courtesy, the way she casually referred to Claudius Heron without his title, annoyed me. And the suggestion that *Mr* Heron had guilty secrets was beyond belief. Lady Anne was playing games with me again.

No matter. The spirits on the river were whispering, calling. Tomorrow, I thought, I would speak to Le Sac's spirit and find out the truth.

31
VIOLIN CADENZA

Demsey was waiting in the street when I stepped out into the cold misty drizzle of early morning; he was so wrapped up in his coat I hardly recognised him. And he was inclined to grumble. "We'll probably find half the town waiting to talk to Le Sac's spirit."

"No one else will be waiting," I said. "Everybody thinks they know already what happened."

We hired horses again from the Golden Fleece and rode out across the Tyne Bridge. Two or three countrywomen trudged in the opposite direction, bearing on each arm baskets heavy with straw-bedded eggs or tiny black cheeses. I was tired; I had slept poorly, unable to ignore Lady Anne's hints, remembering Claudius Heron's constant coldness towards Le Sac, his refusal to play at the benefit, his warnings at the inquest, his insistence on blaming Le Sac for George's death. Had he persuaded David Hawks to regard Le Sac's death as suicide?

I had waited on Heron at his house the previous night; but he was closeted at dinner with ship-owners and merchants, an official function that had no doubt continued well into the night. After that, I had gone to old Hoult and insisted he ask the other spirits to find George's spirit. They had not been able to. I could only conclude the spirit had not yet disembodied, although so late a disembodiment was unheard of.

Where in heaven's name was George's spirit?

There were no answers anywhere. Unless Le Sac gave them.

Wind swept across the fell, shivering the reeds and cotton grass at the pond's edge; the water was misty in the early morning light. A thin drizzle dampened our shoulders; Demsey said, "God preserve us from drowning." I wondered what I was doing there, seeking to talk to a dead man, to persuade him to give up the name of his murderer. I never even liked the fellow. But I could not let the matter drop, for George's sake, for my own safety, for the safety of others. If Le Sac was not the murderer, the real culprit was free to kill again.

I raised my voice. "Le Sac! Do you hear me?"

No reply, except for the screech of a gull wheeling overhead. A rabbit burst from the cover of bushes and scampered across the fell into a burrow.

"Le Sac! I do not believe that you killed the boy. Nor that you killed yourself."

The fellow's spirit was as secretive as the man ever was. I have never known a spirit who did not want to tell the whole world how he died.

A rustling in a stand of trees a short distance off. Another pair of rabbits scuttled into the open, stood briefly twitching.

"I want to find out who killed George. If you tell me, I can bring you justice too."

A sheen upon the rippling water. A harsh voice swore in French. Demsey huddled into his coat.

"I had nothing to do with the plot against you," I said into the thick twilight. "I had no idea what Ord and Jenison were planning." I shrugged. "I know I did you no favours then; let me make amends now."

"Very friendly," Le Sac's voice, more guttural than in life, said hoarsely. "I do not trust friends. There are no such things."

"Nichols?" Demsey suggested.

The spirit cackled with laughter. "That prancing idiot?"

"Who killed you, Le Sac?"

"Why should I trust you, Patterson?"

"Because no one else believes you innocent of killing the boy."

A moment's silence. "I had not seen him a se'nnight," he said. "I rode straight from those –" he seemed hardly able to speak the word – "those *gentlemen*, to Durham. They are *gentlemen* there too," he added bitterly.

"And on the way back?"

A shot cracked in the still air.

Demsey cannoned into me, knocking me flying. I hit the muddy ground with a force that jarred my bones. Demsey grabbed at my arm, trying to drag me away. "Come on, damn it! Quickly!" Mud and reeds slithered under my hands; another shot splintered a stone inches from my face. Two shots. Surely that must be all – the attacker could not have more than a brace of pistols.

I was up on my feet at last but stumbled as pain stabbed at my right ankle. Demsey ran ahead, urging me on with a shout. Beyond him, our horses had taken fright and bolted. Hugh raced after them, and for a moment seemed to be on the verge of catching at the reins. Then another shot rang out. Demsey jerked forward, seemed to hang in mid-air...

I spun away behind a tree.

To my left, the horses galloped off like a quickening heartbeat. Demsey lay sprawled on the rough grass.

I was not rational. My mind was filled with a great rage. My heart thumped, my blood seemed to heat like a fire. If I could have seized hold of the attacker in that moment, he would not have survived. I forced myself to breathe more slowly, to concentrate on the hurried ripple on the pond, the rustle of foliage in the stand of trees to my right. Surely the attacker could not fire again; how many pistols could he have? I must do something before he had time to reload…

Le Sac called sharply, "No more killing!" His voice echoed eerily in the chill damp air, directed at the hidden attacker. "I will make a bargain with you. Go away and I will tell no one what happened to me. Until the day my spirit fades into the wind, I will be silent. No one here will endanger you. Let them go."

No hint of movement, no reply. I cursed. Le Sac's bargain might buy me my life at this moment, but if he honoured his word the murderer would go free for ever. And they say that a man who kills once will kill again.

I slipped from the tree to the shelter of a thick cluster of bushes. Crawling behind them, I crept away from the pond, closer to Demsey's sprawled body. His head was turned towards me, his eyes closed, his black hair drifting across his cheek. I found myself whispering to him – ridiculous, I don't even remember what I said – with in the back of my mind the thought that if he could hear me, he could not yet be dead.

My course of action was obvious. I must escape. I could not count on the murderer accepting Le Sac's bargain or keeping to it if he did accept. But how to escape across such open land? Only the occasional clump of bushes or trees offered cover. In any case, I could not abandon Hugh, living or dead.

Behind me, Le Sac's voice talked on into the mist, cajoling, bullying, dripping with sarcastic sincerity. I would not have accepted any bargain he offered. I began to work my way back, away from Hugh, back towards the vegetation from which the murderer had fired. If I could creep through the shrubs at the edge of the pond…

I crawled on hands and knees through reeds and gorse bushes, hardly daring to breathe. The attacker had had plenty of time to reload at least one of the pistols. Why had he not fired again? My hands fell on a thick fallen branch, half-hidden in the grass. An inch or two of it broke off, rotten in my grasp, but the rest seemed sound. Struggling along with it in my hand was even more difficult but, out of breath and bruised, I achieved the shelter of a thicket of willow.

And, in that moment, I heard the clatter of a horse's hooves.

Was that our horses? Or a passing rider? The sound alone was enough to frighten off our attacker. Bushes rustled violently; a dark figure, great-coated, broke from the shelter of a clump of trees, racing wildly across the fell, heading towards the slope down into Gateshead. There were woods there, gardens, streets in which anyone might lose themselves. Roaring with fury, I was up at once, racing after him, waving my broken branch maniacally.

The rough ground was my undoing. I put my foot in a rabbit hole, pitched forward. My foot twisted. I tried to right myself, stumbled again and went down with a force that knocked the breath out of me. By the time I had staggered to my feet, the greatcoated figure was out of sight.

I hobbled back towards the pond, to the dark huddle of Demsey beyond it. Along the track, I could see a rider on a grey horse climbing the hill from the south and leading two other horses – our horses. Even from this distance I could see the rider was a woman, sitting astride.

Esther Jerdoun.

As I stood over Demsey, she urged her horse up to me.

I was dazed, confused, in a rage, recklessly suspicious of the entire world. "What the devil are you doing here?"

Her hat was blown askew; her hair was tousled and windswept. "Mr Patterson," she said evenly, "this is not the time for argument or explanation." She jumped down from her horse and knelt over Demsey. "We must stop this bleeding."

Tugging a scarf from her neck, she reached across Demsey's back to press the material against his shoulder. The pale yellow cloth suddenly bloomed in a great burst of red. I was thinking slowly, stupidly. "I thought –"

"He was dead? Dead men do not bleed." She glanced up at me. "Who did this? Who would want to shoot Mr Demsey?"

As I stared at her, I was filled with a sudden certainty. Everything was so clear – why had I ever been confused? I knew who the villain was. I knew who had wanted to injure Hugh. I knew who had murdered George and Le Sac.

32
SONG FOR TWO VOICES (DUETTO)

The great church of St Nicholas had an eerie stillness. I stood just inside the west door, my hand lifting the curtain that hung there to prevent draughts, and looked towards the east end of the church. My view of the chancel and altar was blocked by the bulky screen on top of which the organ sat. Beyond the screen and the tall dulled pipes of the organ facade, the east window was a mere shadow.

Churches are gloomy places and on such a dreary day as this more than usually so. I listened for the shift of a footstep, the rustle of clothing. Nothing seemed to stir among the high-backed pews. Yet there was movement, sensed rather than seen, up in the organ loft. A flutter of sound, like the pages of a book being ruffled. Perhaps it was only the older brother indulging in a rare organ practice. But Light-Heels's landlord had been certain he was here.

I kept close to the church wall as I went softly up the aisle. Pew after pew of closed doors, private domains where those with delicate sensibilities need not mix with vulgar inferiors. Where the screen joined the wall, an open door showed a staircase rising through a stone shaft. I stepped carefully up the worn stairs; at the top a second door stood open on to the organ-loft. I could hear the sound of feet shifting on the floor, the thud of books. I eased myself through the narrow gap between door and jamb, taking care not to move the door in case it creaked. For a moment I looked over a low parapet to a dizzying drop to the nave below; I drew back, briefly nauseous.

Nichols stood in front of the organ stool. The manuals

were locked into their cabinet but the mirrors designed to allow the organist to see priest and congregation below were exposed, and I drew back, fearful of Nichols glimpsing my reflection. Laid out along the wooden stool were piles of music-books. Bound printed volumes stacked in one pile, manuscript commonplace books in another. Loose sheets of manuscript in a third pile, odd handwritten notes at the near end of the stool. Nichols himself held a small book that looked very like a book of psalm tunes; he clasped it in both hands and looked from one pile to another as if trying to decide where to put it. His lips moved soundlessly.

"Well met," I said, moving forward.

He started, dropped the book, stared at me.

"Thinking of taking your brother's place?" I bent to pick up the book, held it out to Nichols. He did not move.

"You do not seem out of breath."

His colour, which had receded, flushed again.

"From your ride back," I elaborated. "You did well to get back before I did. Although of course I was somewhat delayed by concern for my friend."

He seemed to pull his wits together. He managed a laugh. "You're talking nonsense, Patterson."

"I had to see Demsey to the care of a surgeon before I came to find the man who shot him."

Esther Jerdoun had seemed to wish to detain me but I would not stay, desperate to catch Nichols before he escaped. Yet here he still was, hardly seeming to hear what I said. He said mechanically, "Indeed," and turned back to his sorting of the books.

The first doubts prodded at my certainty. When Esther Jerdoun had asked who might wish to injure Hugh, I had seen at once that I had been looking at the matter from the wrong perspective. I was not the attacker's intended target;

Hugh was. And the only culprit then could be Nichols. Le Sac's contemptuous references to friendship, Nichols's antipathy to Demsey, a desire for revenge for the ruffians Hugh had set upon him – all these pointed to Nichols's guilt. True, I could not understand how George's murder fitted but otherwise I had no doubt. All this trouble had been caused by a quarrel between a man too quick to anger and another too quick to malice.

And yet, faced with the man in this dulled lethargic state, my reasoning began to seem flimsy. Did a man kill on so slight a provocation?

I was walking through a fog, trying to find my way in an unknown country; all I could do was take one step at a time. I put my hand on Nichols's arm. "Listen to me. I know what happened."

He frowned.

"In Aberdeen."

He reddened and pulled away from me, put the end of the organ stool between us. His voice raised a tone or two in pitch. "Aberdeen? Nothing happened in Aberdeen."

"Tell that to the poor girl you tried to seduce. Such a sordid, commonplace trick."

A flash of his old spirit returned. "So Demsey went to find scandal, did he?" he said contemptuously. "And you're seizing the chance to ruin an honest man who is only trying to make a living."

"Honest!" I echoed incredulously. "After that trick you employed with the Lindsay girl to discredit Demsey? I saw her at the Concert – a baggage if ever there was one."

"Demsey started it!" Nichols backed further away. "He set those ruffians on me!"

That was true enough; I was on rough ground there. I stepped back and perched upon the end of the organ stool, as if trying for some peace between us. Nichols might retreat all he liked; I was between him and the stair down. He regarded me with that dazed look still, like a man trying to make sense of a world that has gone mad.

"You are not unwronged, sir," I conceded. "But Demsey meant only to scare you, not to kill you."

His face seemed to crumple in fear or as if, perhaps, he meant to cry. Then he caught himself up, said stiffly, "I could not know that."

"No?" I rubbed at my eyes. The fury and the grief returned in full force, flooding through me in a red-hot wave. Demsey lay at death's gate and Nichols was mixed up in it somehow. I would not let him out of this church until he had told me everything he knew. I pushed myself from the organ stool, advanced on him. He backed away, came up against one of the pews. The door of the pew swung open and he ran inside, jumping up on to the seat and vaulting the partition into the next pew. I raced after him but I did not have his suppleness and agility. By the time I scrambled awkwardly over the partition, he was scuttling across the loft to an open door. And another stair down.

I jumped for him as he reached the door. He was fractionally out of my reach but I snagged my fingers round his coat-tails and dragged him back. He stumbled, came down on one knee then struggled up again. I got between him and the door. He ran back. The doors of the pews at this end were locked. He tried to clamber over one of them. I seized him, flung my arm around his chest and pulled him down.

We crashed together against the stone balustrade of the organ loft. I heard bone crack. Nichols screamed out, a strange womanish scream; we were hanging over the balustrade, leaning out over the void of the church, seeing the nave pews far far below.

Then light and pain exploded in my head. The last thing I saw was the patterned floor of the nave swinging below me…

33
AIR

Stone was cold beneath my cheek. My head ached abominably. I pulled myself on to my elbow and the world tilted. Carvings danced crazily around me; shadows leapt and spun. I gasped with pain, fell back. The ribs of the vault curved above me; a thin dusty light strained in through the high windows.

With a great effort, I pushed myself off my back, leant against something hard. The balustrade. I put up my hand to the crown of my head and brought it away sticky with blood. I could hear my own breathing, heavy and ragged, and put my head down between my knees.

At last I looked up. A pew door stood open beside me; I hauled on it to pull myself to my feet. The darkening church swung around me, then steadied. I had a distant recollection of seeing it do so before, a vague memory of half-waking then drifting into sleep again. How long had I been unconscious?

I hung on to the door, listening for someone else in the church. I had arrived here in late morning but the gloomy light percolating into the church suggested it was now dusk. I clung there, trying to banish the headache, trying to work out what had happened. Someone had come up behind me, hit me over the head and rescued Nichols. But who? Nichols surely had few friends, perhaps none except Le Sac. What of his drunken brother? Nichols senior might have come in to practise, seen us, decided to rescue Light-Heels. A drunk man might not think too carefully about how to accomplish such a rescue or know his own strength when striking another man.

I went unsteadily to the stairs leading down. The door was shut and locked. Would a drunk man and a frightened man think sensibly enough to lock the door after them? It seemed unlikely. I heaved myself over the pews to the organ-stool and thence to the door to the second stairs. This too was closed and for a moment I thought I was trapped – but no, the latch lifted and the door creaked open. The stairs were black as coal and I had to feel my way down them; once I stumbled and scraped down three or four steps, jerking myself to a safe halt only with the help of the rope pinned to the wall.

I went out through the arch in the screen into thick twilight, and felt my way down the dark length of the church. The west doors were closed and I lifted the latch with trepidation. But the heavy oak door swung towards me. A voice from the porch said faintly, "Prithee, sir, are you unwell?"

"Who is that?" My own voice sounded unfamiliar, as if it belonged to a sick and feeble stranger.

"Ned Boothby, sir, that died in this porch eighty-eight years ago coming from the church service. I kept the door open for you, sir, knowing you were still in there."

A spirit in the church porch. I had never known such a thing before. The spirits of the dead are usually long disembodied before their coffins come to the church.

"I told them," he said. "Don't lock the door. The gentleman who went in there hasn't left yet."

"Them," I said, almost as faintly, yet suddenly feeling an inclination to laugh. "You saw them leave."

"Several hours since," he agreed. "In a hurry, they were. The gentleman was in a real state."

The *gentleman*. Something in the way he stressed the

word made me pause. "And the other?"

"The lady, sir? She was urging him on all right. *Get yourself together, man. For heaven's sake, don't be such a weakling.* Don't marry one like her, sir, she'll make the very devil of a wife. Ask the gentleman."

The lady. I stood in the chill darkness of the porch. Nichols had no wife. It was not beyond the bounds of possibility that he might have made an assignation with the girl he had used to trap Hugh, but he had not looked like a man awaiting a lover. And the girl was much too short and slight to have hit me. I felt the back of my head again; the wound was too high, the girl could not have inflicted it.

No, only one woman knew of my suspicions of Nichols, knew that I intended to confront him. I myself had told her as we struggled to get Demsey to the surgeon in Gateshead. And I could see so clearly how she might have carried out the attack on Gateshead Fell. She had seen Hugh and me trying to wheedle the name of his killer out of Le Sac, had feared we might be successful; he was after all a spiteful man, who might grasp a chance for revenge. She had shot at us, run off when I chased her, then taken advantage of my fall to find her way to the place where she had previously left her horse. She had been dressed in breeches; I might easily have mistaken her at a distance for a man. Then coolly, brazenly, she had ridden towards us, ready to assume the guise of an innocent passer-by. She had helped to get Demsey to a surgeon, true, but her intention might never have been to kill – merely to prevent our talking to Le Sac. And she had succeeded.

But why, in heaven's name? What game was she playing? Why kill Le Sac, or George? I remembered Lady Anne's hints that Le Sac knew something to Claudius Heron's discredit; could he also have known something about Esther Jerdoun?

I set my head back against the chill wall of the porch. I could not see Esther Jerdoun as a murderer. I did not *want* to see her as a murderer. But I could not deny that she would have had the determination to carry it through.

"Are you all right, sir?" asked the spirit again. "You don't look at all the thing. Why don't you sit down for a moment?"

"No, no," I said, then added more calmly, "Thank you, but no. I really am most grateful for your help."

But I was not, in truth, I was not in the least grateful, as I went out into the cold damp night air to find Esther Jerdoun.

34
RONDEAU

I stood in the street with the spire of St Nicholas towering over me. The stillness of the night, the unwonted quietness of the town, the way the dusk blurred the outlines of roofs and chimneys, all seemed like a dream. I thought for a moment that if I took a single step forward, I would step from my own world into that strange unknown place that haunted me. But I took that step forward and nothing happened, except that I knew the only thing I could do.

I had to go to Caroline Square and see Lady Anne. I did not look forward to her incredulity when I named her cousin as a murderer; but she, if anyone, would know how credible my suspicions were.

I set off towards the square. I had to presume Hugh and I had been shot at to prevent Le Sac naming his murderer; but how could Mrs Jerdoun hope to escape the consequences of her crime that way? Someone else could come along and ask Le Sac for the truth. And why leave the body where his spirit might be found? George's murderer had gone to extraordinary lengths to separate body and spirit; why then neglect to take the same precautions with Le Sac?

Unless – I rubbed my aching brow – unless Le Sac had been attacked upon the moor, lured off the road to some isolated spot. Then the murderer, thinking him already dead, had thrown him into the pond to be found later and labelled a suicide. But life had lingered until after Le Sac had been thrown into the pond; therefore his spirit clung to the water rather than to the place where he had first been attacked. As for Le Sac's horse, that would be hidden somewhere or, more likely, sold to some itinerant vagabond.

I was happier now with the matter of how Le Sac had been killed, though still adrift with regard to the motive. I considered returning to the pond to speak with Le Sac again but, as Lady Anne had said, he was a man of his word. I did not believe he would betray the murderer. A murdered spirit, especially one like Le Sac, might well cling to the only power he had left – the power to torment his killer with the possibility of discovery.

Mist gathered around me, drifting along the street. I stopped on a corner to catch my breath.

And heard footsteps behind me.

The odd quietness and the mist magnified the sound; the steps echoed in the confined street. They stopped.

Silence.

The wraiths of mist swirled around me. I started walking again, more quickly, listening intently. Yes, there were the steps again, at a little distance behind me. I slowed and the footsteps slowed with me. No innocent idler behaved in such a manner.

A thief, it must be a thief. The town could be dangerous at dusk. I turned quickly, and caught a glimpse of a figure moving into a side street. The blur of mist took hold of the figure but it was a man, I saw that much. Yet Esther Jerdoun had been wearing breeches…

There was only one refuge. I quickened my pace. The house in Caroline Square, despite the unnerving things that happened to me there, now seemed sanctuary. I could see it ahead, brightly lit; a footman passed behind a window. I hurried across the square, ignored the mutterings of the spirit. The footsteps echoed behind me, quickening as I did. I imagined I heard my name spoken, and broke into a run.

As I ran, I saw at the last moment a place on the cobbles where the stones themselves seemed to waver. I jolted to a halt but the footsteps behind me were closing in. I heard the spirit in the gardens shout. Just beyond that patch of ground was the safety of Lady Anne's house; there was nothing else to do. I leapt for the door.

But I was already shivering with cold, everything wavering around me. I gasped for breath. Then I was falling, into mud, putting out my hands to save myself. I rolled as I fell…

And found myself sitting in a wet street with rain drenching me, splattering into my face and plastering my hair to my head. My knee grazed a pile of horse dung.

I rose groggily; hands heaved me up. A woman's voice said, "That's what I like. A gent that falls at my feet."

A street woman, gaudy and only half-dressed despite the drizzle. She poked a finger in my shoulder. Her mouth wrinkled archly. "Too much drink, my fine gent. Always lands you in the shit." And she sauntered past me, evidently pleased with her sally.

I stood in that street of tall houses that I had seen before. In the light of the lanterns, neatly dressed tradesmen unlocked doors, motherly women carried empty baskets home with the chink of money sounding from their pockets. Carts rumbled over the cobbles. And no one seemed to think my presence there odd; even the street woman had only believed me to have fallen in the street.

I began to wonder if my presence here was in any way by chance. I had been wondering if Le Sac might had known a secret about Esther Jerdoun. What if this was it? Was my knowledge of this place why she had shot at me? I had after all asked Lady Anne about that strange vision of the room in her presence; I had questioned her about the house on another occasion.

I stood bemused, in the lessening rain, jostled by the passers-by, and heard my name called. I looked round and saw on the doorstep a man frowning at me. The stout red-faced man from the dinner party, the one to whom I had spoken in Lady Anne's house.

"Patterson!" he said again, coming down the steps towards me, looking more and more puzzled. "My dear fellow, you're bleeding! Have you been involved in some accident? Or – never say you have been attacked!"

If this was a part of the mystery, all I could do was to allow myself to be caught up in it, to be carried along and see what came of it. "Yes," I said cautiously, seeing he was waiting for an answer. "Some fellow was following me."

He clapped a hand on my back. "Heavens, man! I shall have the constable's hide for this." He called to his servants, ushered me into his house. I protested for form's sake, but if the answer to this mystery lay anywhere, it lay in or near this house. I was becoming more and more certain of that.

"No, no, man." He overrode my protests. "You cannot wander the streets looking like that! I have a meeting at the Exchange but the servants will take care of you. And I shall speak to the constable before I come home. Devil take it, it is virtually broad daylight!"

And he went off into the gloom, muttering angrily to himself.

In the wake of a servant, I trod upstairs, conscious of the muddy imprints I left upon the stairs. A bath was prepared for me in an elegant bedroom, and I wallowed in hot scented water until it grew cold and my fingers wrinkled. Demsey lay at death's door in a house in Gateshead and I lay idly here, yet I was more and more convinced that here was the solution to all the puzzles and crimes of recent days. If I was patient I would find it.

The servant offered me a dressing robe and a dish of hot chocolate. Clean clothes were laid out upon the bed, and the respectful servant, on the verge of withdrawing, indicated I should ring when I needed help to dress. The curtains were drawn and the candles numerous, in three or four branches placed around the room; the bed covers were brocade and the scent of the bath lingered still. The velvet taste of the chocolate lay upon my tongue.

And a voice whispered, “Master?”

35
LAMENT

I jolted upright, spilling hot chocolate on to my bare knee. "*George?*"

"Master," he sobbed. "Help me, help me, please. I don't know where I am. No one talks to me. I'm so lonely and I don't want to be dead."

I set the chocolate dish carefully down on a small table and looked about the candle-lit room. The shifting shadows made it difficult to see properly but at length I found George, a small dull sheen upon the newel post of the bed.

"There are no spirits in this place, master," he whispered. "And I so wanted to speak to you yesterday but you just shivered and said the room was damned cold, and you wouldn't talk to me. Why wouldn't you talk to me?"

"I wasn't here yesterday, George."

"You were!" he cried. "You brought something for the gent that lives here!" A door slammed open at the far side of the room. "Come and see, master. Come and see!"

I went barefoot across soft rugs into a room that was plainly a gentleman's study. A table shrouded in darkness was piled with books. At George's insistence, I fetched a branch of candles from the bedroom and set it on the table.

"The second book down, master. Look at it."

It was a printed book of music in score in a handsome green binding, with the parts in a pocket at the back.

"Open it, master."

Words stared up at me from the title page.

Seven Concertos in seven parts by Chas *Patterson, Organist, Newcastle upon Tyne.* A dedication page was inscribed to Miss Ord of Fenham. "Look at the first concerto, master."

I turned the pages, read the first printed staves.

"It's the one from the manuscript book Lady Anne gave us," George said excitedly. He started humming but I had already read the tune for myself. "You never said you'd had it printed." He slid closer, lingering upon the silver candlestick. "I won't tell them you didn't really write it."

"George –"

"You brought it yesterday. I saw you. Fresh from the press, you said. And I said, *I didn't know you were having it printed, master.* And you said, *It's cold in here*, and the gent who lives here said, *Damn those children babbling in the street.* I told him it was me but he didn't listen. Master, why didn't you talk to me yesterday?"

I stared at the music; the notes danced and blurred in the uncertain candlelight. George was right; they were the concerti from the book Lady Anne had lent me. And the other book, the one with the unknown Thomas Powell's signature – did that book belong in this place too?

George was insistently demanding my attention. I recalled, at last, that I had not spoken to him since his death and that, unlike Le Sac, he had taken no vow to protect his killer.

"George," I said soothingly. "I'm sorry if I have ignored you – indeed, I did not mean to. I give you my word I was not here yesterday but I cannot explain why I am here today or even where this place is. I need to know everything I can, before I can tell what has happened. I must know, George. How did you die?"

He began to weep, a thin sound in the darkened room. "It wasn't my fault, sir."

"Of course not. I know Mr Heron turned you away from the Fleshmarket."

"He said there was to be no duel and I knew there was!"

"So you tried to go back."

More snivelling. "Yes, sir."

"And this time Mr Demsey intercepted you."

"He said I didn't want to get mixed up with men like Mr Ord and Mr Jenison."

"He was right," I said wholeheartedly. "And Mr Demsey saw you to the door of my house. And then?"

"I waited till he'd gone," he said reluctantly. "Then I went back to Mrs Hill's again."

"With the Vivaldi," I said with resignation, remembering the music clasped in the dead boy's hand.

"It's much better than the Corelli," the boy burst out.

"Never mind that," I said, hurrying on. "How far did you get this time, George?"

"The Bigg Market, sir. That's where the lady picked me up in her carriage."

My heart grew heavy. "Go on."

"She said she was looking for me. She said she wanted me to do something for her again."

"*Again*?"

"I thought she wanted me to take the violin again," he said in a small voice.

"Le Sac's violin!" I said. "*You* sneaked into his rooms while he was ill and took it."

"He never stirred," the spirit said proudly. "Fast asleep he was and snoring. And I knew where he kept it – under the floorboards."

"That's why you were so afraid of Le Sac. You kept thinking he'd find out you'd stolen the violin."

"He deserved it," George said viciously. "I *hated* him."

I shifted the branch of candles and sat down on the edge of the table. "I wonder you wanted to help the lady again, since you were so afraid of the consequences the first time. What did she ask you to do?"

George was a thin pool of light on a chair. "She said Mr Ord and Mr Jenison had stopped the duel this time but she was determined it should go ahead because she wanted to teach Mr Sac a lesson. She said he was arrogant and designing and – and she regretted the day she ever saw him. And she asked me to play the Vivaldi to her – she said she'd give me two guineas. Two guineas, master. Only – only –" His voice shook.

I said gently, "What happened, George?"

He seemed to sniff. "She brought me here, sir, to this house, and took me into a big big room, with a harpsichord in it. And she asked me to play." Another sniff. "I just turned away to get my violin out. And then there was such a pain..." He was crying now. "Such a pain, master, in my throat, and everything was wet and hot. And – and she said, 'Fly away, boy. You're one spirit who will never be found.'"

"In *this* house?" I repeated.

"Well, I knew the house when we got out of her carriage, sir. But when I got in the big room, I felt a bit funny. And when I looked out of the window, when I was getting my violin, I couldn't seem to see the square – just a street with lots of houses instead." The pool of light flickered; he whimpered, "I don't know what happened, sir!"

I was remembering the drunk spirit in the square who never knew where he was, who had insisted I was organist of St Nicholas. I ran my fingers over the title page of the book. Here was the explanation of that puzzle; the drunk spirit had been cast out of this mysterious place into my real world. Might not, then, a spirit from the real world –

George – be cast *into* this place?

And, as George's story seemed to suggest, could the lady come and go between the two places as she pleased? She had certainly used the uncanny connection between them to exile George's spirit and so cover up her crime.

I turned, hearing a noise at the bedroom door. She stood there, smiling in the flickering light of the shadows.

"Alas, Mr Patterson," she said. "You really should have kept out of this affair. You really should."

I saw the candle-light glint on the metal hidden in the folds of her skirt.

"Good evening, Lady Anne," I said.

36
SONG FOR SOLO SOPRANO

She regarded me with amusement. "Confess, sir, did you suspect me before this moment?"

I sighed. "Indeed not, my lady, though I suspected everyone else in turn. Now, of course, I cannot conceive why I omitted you."

How strange, I thought, to be talking in so light-hearted a fashion to a murderess. And she, without a trace of fear, set her head on one side as if curious to hear me out.

"You killed George," I went on, "who trusted you because you had paid him to steal the violin. Then you killed Le Sac, making it look as if he had killed the boy and had done away with himself from remorse. Le Sac of course was your real target."

She inclined her head in acknowledgement.

"But is it not rather an excessive way to be rid of a protégé? Why not merely tell him you refuse to fund him further?"

The flickering candlelight showed a swift spray of emotions across her face. I calculated the distance between us, confident that I could take the knife from her. Once I had heard her explanations.

She laughed softly. "It is not so easy to be rid of a blackmailer."

"A love affair?" I suggested, although I had never imagined Lady Anne susceptible to the softer passions. "An irregularity with money?"

She threw back her head and laughed uproariously. I heard George's spirit whimper in fear. "Mr Patterson, do you not wonder where you are?"

"There have been times I have thought of little else," I confessed. "And of the people in this place. There is a man, particularly, stocky, red-faced –"

"My father."

"I thought him dead, long ago."

She nodded. "In your world, yes. But not in this. Not in *my* world."

I could hear a clock ticking faintly in the bedroom. One of the candles in the branch on the table flared; smoke and a spark drifted from it. The shadows licked at her. I am not a superstitious man, and have only a conventional amount of religion in me, but in that moment I fancied her a devil.

She advanced, and I contemplated putting an end to all this. I was barefoot and wore only a dressing robe but nevertheless... She smiled and shook her head.

"Do not do anything foolish, Mr Patterson. I can come and go as I please. I could kill you and go straight back to your world. It would not trouble me if I never came back here." Did I detect a note of falsity in that statement? No matter, she was continuing. "And once I am back in your world, sir, I will go straight to Gateshead and finish the work I began this morning. In short, sir, if you value your friend the dancing master's life, you will do as I say."

I held her gaze but she did not drop her eyes in shame or confusion. It was clear she meant what she said. I retreated a step or two, putting the table between us, conscious that the wall and curtained window were at my back, preventing me from moving very far. An amused smile played about Lady Anne's lips.

"You have abandoned your pistols, I see," I remarked as coolly as I could. "Too noisy, I suppose. One of them was

Le Sac's, was it not? Stolen from him when you killed him."

She ignored my words. "You need not be afraid yet, Mr Patterson. I do not intend to kill you in this house. You seem to have an ability to step through between worlds and your spirit might exhibit the same trait. I do not want you to escape into your own world and betray me there."

"*Your* world, *my* world?" I said. "I know which is mine. Do you tell me that you originate in this place? That you are not Mrs Jerdoun's cousin?"

She gestured with her hands. "Imagine, sir, a book. Like this music book." She indicated the book I had left open upon the table. "A book has many separate leaves of paper, all stacked neatly one upon another. Imagine that the whole of creation is like this book. Each page is a separate world, each entire unto itself – lying very close to its neighbours, yet with no communication between them. In each of these worlds live sets of people going about their daily concerns with no knowledge of the people in the other worlds, or any contact with them. Yet many have their counterparts in those other worlds. A man like yourself, Mr Patterson, may exist on two worlds, or perhaps more. Or, rather, two men with your name and your characteristics may so exist. Similar, yet different. Two versions of the same man."

She dropped her hands and the knife flashed in the candlelight. Her expression was again one of amusement. "You are a great deal more successful in this world, Mr Patterson. A well-respected concert promoter, a composer much admired even at so young an age, in possession not merely of one organist's post but two, and with dozens of rich pupils pleading for your attention. Oh, certainly you must work hard, but you are recognised as above the average run of musicians, and the patronising speeches of men like my father are tempered by respect."

She leaned forward, her brown hair slipping across her shoulder. "Would you not wish to change places with your other self, Mr Patterson? It would not really be like stepping into another man's shoes. And who knows, *he* might prefer the anonymity of being merely competent and scraping a living."

I was stung by her assessment of me, although I could hardly deny it. But I was more concerned with the implications of what she had said.

"Is that what *you* did?" I asked. "Changed places with your other self in my world?"

She shrugged. "She died young, aged fourteen, an orphan in the care of an aunt and uncle in Norfolk. When I first stepped through to your world I had some considerable work to cover my tracks, to hide the fact that my other self had died. But once I had succeeded in that, I had few difficulties. I inherited her father's money and became a rich heiress. I confess, however, that I was unnerved to discover I had a cousin. Esther does not exist in this world."

She idly turned the printed pages of the music book. I considered disarming her now but the distance between us was too great, and I knew that if she escaped she would do as she threatened and *step through* to my world to kill Demsey. For all I knew she might be able to *step through* in a moment; perhaps she would one second be standing in front of me, the next be a fading shadow. I could not risk that. I would disarm her only when I could be certain of success. If I could distract her …

"That manuscript book I lent you," she mused. "I had it from the original author, of course, to practise a harpsichord lesson from it. It is easy enough to take material objects between the worlds."

"How – how do you *step through* to my world?"

She stared musingly at the rich hangings over the window. "I really do not know, sir. It is a gift I have always had. As a child I used to visit strange worlds in my play, or use them to hide from my father." She smiled. "My governesses always used to remark on my remarkable imagination. I only came to realise that the worlds were real many years later. And there is something about this house." She glanced about her as if seeking something. "It is as if the pages of the book have been stuck together, here, and certain people may step through from one page to another at will. I am not the only person with the ability. Others possess it – the spirit in the garden, for instance, and yourself." She smiled. "Why not ask how *you* do it, sir?"

"I do nothing," I said. "It happens or it does not. A chill, a giddiness and the world shifts like a curtain blowing, then all is still and I am in a different place. I cannot do it at will."

She shrugged. "That skill would no doubt grow."

I did not want it. "And you live two lives? Are you not missed in this world?"

"I am a semi-invalid, sir, so ill that I must keep to my bed all day. I cannot even bear to have a maid with me; such creatures fuss so, you know. I put in an appearance occasionally at the dinner table. My father has lost all patience with me and constantly reminds me how one day my distant cousins in Norfolk will inherit the house and throw me out of it. It is all entailed to a *male* heir, of course."

"And what will you do then?"

"I will thankfully retreat to your world and abandon my prior self altogether," she said mockingly. "I would do so now, except that this world has its uses."

"You prefer my world? Why?"

"My dear Patterson! In your world I am an independent

heiress with no man to tell me what to do or say. Here I am merely a daughter, suffered to have a small allowance and constantly nagged to marry this man or that, who in his turn will tell me where to go and what to do. Which would you prefer?"

I pondered on the matter – not on her reasons, which could not be denied, but on her actions. The curtains were heavy, soft velvet at my back; with my hand behind me I tugged surreptitiously on them, to see how easy they might be to pull down. The curtain rail, unfortunately, seemed good solid oak.

"And Le Sac?"

"Alas, poor Henri. The contact between the worlds cannot be entirely controlled; occasionally the passage opens up of its own accord. Henri was with me on one of those occasions. I involuntarily stepped through, and he came with me. I flatter myself that no one could have reacted more swiftly – I knocked him unconscious, I may say – but unfortunately he did not accept my explanation that he had stumbled and fallen and dreamt the rest."

"You should have killed him then," I said dryly. "It would have saved you a great deal of trouble."

"I was younger," she sighed, "and naively over-confident. I had lived by my wits for ten years or more and believed myself to be able to carry off anything, certainly able to fool any mere man."

"But surely he could not blackmail you over this? Who would believe him?"

"No one," she agreed. "But Henri was always very quick to see the implications of any situation. If I was from this world, I could not be the real Lady Anne from *his* world. He even travelled to the village in Norfolk where my counterpart had lived, to look at the church registers. He found proof of her death. And if she was dead, sir, all the wealth that I had inherited in her stead should have gone to someone else." She smiled, with real malice. "In *that* world, your world, there are no male heirs living, only one female."

"Esther Jerdoun," I said.

"Indeed. Henri had all the evidence he needed to prove I was an impostor." She looked almost admiring as she spoke of Le Sac. "He did not need to prove my origins or explain about a world no one would believe in. He simply needed to threaten to tell Esther that I was not her cousin." She sighed again. "I am afraid I underestimated dear Henri. As, alas, I have underestimated you."

I leaned against the wall, a handful of curtain in one hand behind my back. If I could tempt her across to me, perhaps I could tangle her in it. "I suppose it will not do if I promise to keep your secret?"

"No, it will not," she agreed, raising the knife. "You would never let the boy's murderer go free."

"Nor Le Sac's," I said. "And you were nearly the murderer of Demsey."

"I was aiming for you," she said. "I was always a poor shot. Though, to do myself justice, you escaped the first shot by chance, before he knocked you aside. Mr Patterson, I must ask you to go back into the bedroom and dress."

"Dress?" I echoed incredulously. Certainly, I would feel more at ease with my clothes on, but I could not understand why she insisted upon it. "In heaven's name, why?"

"I explained before," she said impatiently. "I cannot kill you here for fear your spirit will escape to your own world. So I must take you elsewhere. And if I am to walk through the streets with you, you will draw considerable attention bare-footed and in a dressing robe."

Reluctantly, I moved past her into the bedroom. The clothes the servant had laid out for me lay like a dark stain upon the white counterpane. I turned my back on her and began to dress. I could not endanger Hugh, yet I would not go quietly to my own death. I turned back as I buttoned my waistcoat.

"George," I said, "pray go downstairs and tell someone what is going on."

His voice came from the table at the head of the bed. "But they don't listen, master."

Lady Anne laughed. "There are few spirits in this world, Mr Patterson. The dead go straight to whatever realm they inhabit and do not linger in the place of their death. Those few that for some reason do remain – or that we imagine remain – we call *ghosts* and are afraid of them. We certainly do not enjoy a chat with them."

"Go down, George," I said again.

"But they won't hear!"

"Go *down*!" I roared, and I caught a glimpse of his hurried going, upon the bedpost, upon the door handle. Lady Anne, smiling, gestured towards the wall. "We will go this way, sir, by the servants' stair. There is, I am afraid, no escape."

37
MARCH

The servants' stairs were pokey and dark; my candle lit only a step or two and the peeling paint on the walls. Muffled voices echoed distantly; male laughter, a shout, sharp words. I thought of snuffing out the candle and running while Lady Anne was disadvantaged by the darkness, but in a house I did not know I could only fall or lose my way. And that threat to Hugh, always that threat...

At last the dim candlelight showed me a door. "Open it," Lady Anne commanded. I did as she bid; outside, the night air was cold; the moon glimmered fitfully on the cobbles of a back lane.

She reached over my shoulder and plucked the candle from my grasp, setting it upon a small table just inside the door. She pinched the flame, and smoke drifted upwards.

"Go out, Mr Patterson."

I stood my ground. The further I went from this house the greater the danger. I was conscious, too, that I was leaving the only friend I had in this world, since George could not leave the place of his death. But Lady Anne slipped her arm through mine and I felt the prick of the knife below my ribs as she turned a laughing face to me.

"This way, sir. And smile for me. We are a loving couple out for a late stroll."

She pulled me on, laughing for the benefit of the two men who lounged at the street corner, dressed in the rough clothes of miners. As we came up to them, they pushed themselves from the wall and I braced myself for a fight. But to my astonishment, they took one look at Lady Anne, halted in mid-movement and drew back, saluting her respectfully.

She did not speak until we were out of earshot of the men. "I told you, sir, that this world has its uses. Have you ever broken the law, Mr Patterson?"

"Never," I declared. Then, because honesty impelled me, I added, "Leaving aside a few pranks when I was a boy."

She laughed. "I break the law frequently. The only reason more people do not do so is because they fear they will be caught. But when you can escape to another world – why, what is there to stop you?"

We were walking down a hill; I did not recognise the street from my own world but the wisps of smoke that came drifting up to us told me we were heading towards the Key. A gaggle of whores passed us, giggling, three-quarters drunk. They looked once at us and were instantly silent, hurrying past as if they were children trying to get out of the reach of schoolteachers. A hundred yards further on, they burst into giggling again.

"There, sir," said Lady Anne, gazing back at them, "go a considerable source of my income. In return for my protection and organisation, they give me a proportion of their profits. A large proportion, of course. And those gentlemen we passed, who are light-fingered in the extreme, need someone to buy their newly acquired property and dispose of it for them."

I was startled. "But your inheritance –"

"Insufficient, sir. How many gowns do you think it pays for? How many horses? No, I must also have my... *business* interests." She caressed my arm. "In my world I earn money and in your world I spend it. A most excellent arrangement, do you not think?"

I found it impossible to speak. On to a road I knew –

Westgate. I looked up at the houses as we passed and saw windows brightly lit. A cat-fiddle screeched out a jig. I recognised Demsey's school-room.

"The differences between our two worlds fascinate me," Lady Anne mused. "You are uncommonly like your counterpart here, sir, but that is not the case with everyone. Your friend Demsey, for instance, in this world is twenty years older, a fussy and choleric man, not much liked."

I looked up at the house again. Strange to know that a man lived and worked there whom I did and did not know. A man very different from my friend who, for all I knew, lay dead in my world. I opened my mouth to call out but shut it again. Lady Anne murmured, "Most wise," and pushed the knife against my flesh.

"I cannot understand why I co-operate with you," I burst out. "I go peaceably to prevent your injuring me, yet I know full well you intend to kill me in the end."

"Think of Mr Demsey," she recommended.

We walked cautiously on, down the Side, through the pools of light cast by the flaring lanterns. "If you kill me," I said, "my absence will be noted. In my own world."

"I have made provision for that."

"Provision?" I echoed.

"Come, sir," she chided. "Do you not see that I have planned everything from the start?" She was apparently agreeably occupied in studying the windows of the shops. "After our first contretemps in the coffee-house – do you remember that, sir? – it occurred to me that you might be useful. You are known to be violently jealous of Le Sac."

"Am I?" I said with some gloom, reflecting that perhaps I had been quite as obvious and foolish as Demsey had been over Nichols.

"I therefore fomented the argument between you and Le

Sac by arranging the theft of his violin. I had that idea after the loss of the music – or its mislaying, I should say. You know he found the book later at the house of a pupil?"

"I guessed as much."

"I forged your writing on the violin's label to incriminate you, and encouraged poor Henri to think of you as the culprit. You can imagine I was not well pleased when Esther proved more perceptive that I had believed her to be and retrieved the instrument. She does not suspect half the truth, of course. She merely thinks me mixed up in something shady – but that has made her meddling enough!"

I thought back to my encounter with Esther Jerdoun on the bridge. I had thought she was accusing me of stealing the instrument when in fact she had been trying to reassure me that Lady Anne's plottings would not affect me. Her manner, which I had put down to condemnation, must have been a natural embarrassment and anger at the conduct of her cousin.

"Then," Lady Anne continued, "to incite your hatred of Henri, I sent those ruffians to attack you. You are my plan of last resort, sir."

I frowned. "In what respect, my lady?"

"It was possible that Le Sac's 'suicide' would not be convincing. I required an alternative solution to the mystery, in case his death was questioned. In short, sir, I will manufacture evidence which suggests that you killed the boy yourself, out of a belief that he had been conspiring with his old master against you – indeed, a belief that Le Sac never cast off the boy at all but used him as a conspirator to get inside your household. Le Sac found out and confronted you, so you killed him too."

"You will not get Le Sac's spirit to support that story."

"Come, come, sir. You spoke to him yourself. He will do anything to torment me. I have simply to persuade him it is to my disadvantage that he keeps quiet and he will do it. Bear in mind, sir, that you will disappear, which will itself suggest your guilt. It will be assumed you fled for fear of being discovered."

"Demsey knows what happened," I pointed out.

She laughed softly. "The dancing master may not survive, sir. And as for my cousin..."

With fear squeezing my heart, I stopped. "What of her?"

"You must see, sir, that I must be rid of her. In a little while, when it will not look too suspicious."

I fell silent. We walked on, on to the Key. Torches burned outside the shops and brothels, and on the low keels at rest along the wharves. I smelt the acrid dryness of the high piles of coal and heard a dog barking. And I knew now that only I stood between Lady Anne and the success of her ruthless plans. Only I could save Hugh and Esther. And I could only save them if I first saved myself.

We walked on. High on the hill across the river, a light flickered around St Mary's church in Gateshead. Ahead, I saw the bulk of the building that in my world was Thomas Saint's printing office. In this world, it stood empty and derelict, a shell with rafters gaping. Around the ruined walls lay a great litter of slates and laths, fragments of stone and brick. A dog sniffed and pawed at the rubble.

The pressure of Lady Anne's arm on mine halted me. We stood looking across to the trees and hidden buildings on Gateshead Bank. Overhead, stars swam in a thin stream of smoke; below, water slapped gently against the wharves. The tide was at its highest, perhaps beginning to ebb. Lady Anne glanced back along the torchlit Key and I saw that the nearest bystanders were some distance off. Whores, by the look of it.

I shifted uneasily, but Lady Anne was already pulling away from me. The dog was pattering towards us in idle curiosity.

"I have a problem, Mr Patterson."

"Indeed?" I said dryly.

"Oh, indeed." She laughed. "Think of it. Mr Charles Patterson, the respected organist and composer, is called upon to examine a body which looks uncannily like his own. So alike indeed that it might be a twin. I do not want to avoid a scandal in one world to create another in a second."

"You seem to be making life difficult for yourself in both," I said.

She shook her head. "A momentary difficulty. Simply, Mr Patterson, I need to ensure that your body is never found."

Instinctively, I knew her plans and, without thinking, protested. "The river – no!"

"The tide is just turning, and will carry your body out to sea."

The memory of the spirits weeping and wailing in the billows of smoke rose up before me. Not that, I thought in panic, and took a step back. The dog hesitated, then padded on.

"Remember what I told you," Lady Anne said. "There are few spirits in this world. Perhaps you will follow the general custom here and go straight to some heavenly paradise." I caught the glint of amusement in her eyes. "Or perhaps, like the boy, you will find yourself alone and unheard." She lifted her hand, the light gleaming on the knife.

The dog barked.

Startled, Lady Anne cast the dog a quick glance. In that instant I brought up my arm violently, knocking her hand away. The knife clattered to the ground. I threw myself against her, and my weight sent us crashing to the cobbles. The fall knocked the breath out of me, and as the dog skittered away in alarm I gasped for air.

In the flare of the lanterns I saw Lady Anne, on hands and knees, scrabbling for the knife. I struggled up, threw myself at her again. But she had the knife in her hand and swung her arm wildly. I staggered back out of reach.

I needed a weapon. My eyes set on the litter surrounding the derelict printing office. The dog was standing, legs braced, barking its loudest. Gasping still, I ran towards the building. Behind me, I heard Lady Anne swear.

Nothing. No weapon. Just a clutter of roof slates and tumbled stone. I swung round the corner of the printing office – into darkness. No lamps, only the glimmer of the river in the thin moonlight. I saw enigmatic humps of debris, rotting coils of rope, a haphazard pile – of baskets? I heard Lady Anne swear again. I flattened myself against the wall in a deep shadow and tried to still my breathing. The dog must have run off; I heard its barking in the distance.

Lady Anne lingered at the corner. Was she conscious that the outline of her body was visible against the faint moonlit shimmer of the river? She moved against the wall, into darkness. She was coming towards me. I strained to see her, to catch the glint of the knife…

Metal flashed in the moonlight. I flung out an arm to fend off the blow, felt pain, the warmth of blood. I stumbled, twisting away from her second lunge. My foot caught in something – a twist of rope? An unravelled basket? I staggered, threw out my arms to keep my balance, heard her laugh. Then I went down, landing upon my injured arm and crying out.

Rolling over, I tried to crawl away, knocked against

something, heard boxes clatter down. My foot was caught fast and when I tried to pull away, pain near blinded me. Lady Anne lunged, stabbing down like a bird from a great darkness. Her ragged breath was loud in my ears...

Out of the darkness a second figure loomed above me. I felt a rush of air and over my head swung a thick plank of wood. The sharp ends of nails glinted in the moonlight. The plank struck Lady Anne in the stomach; a rib crunched and she screamed, flinging up her hands. The knife clattered on to stone as she staggered backwards, doubled over, screaming. And the plank swung again, crashing into her shoulder as she tried to turn away from the blow, then again upon her back as she went down in a crumpled heap.

Over her, vengeful hate flaring in his wild face, stood Claudius Heron.

38
FINALE

He leaned down to help me up. I grasped a hand that was cold and dry, and left it stained with the blood that ran down my own arm. He steadied me, said urgently, "Patterson? Are you hurt?"

I was in no mood to be polite. "How the devil did you come here?"

"That boy of yours. His spirit told me the woman was taking you out of the servants' door and I managed to catch sight of you as you walked off." The wildness was dying out of his face but there was a darkness in his eyes still, an anger that burned deep. "I would have reached you sooner but I was accosted upon the Side by a man who claimed he knew me, and kept talking of people I had never heard of. Patterson, where in heaven's name is this place?"

"How did you reach it?"

His lean cheeks reddened. "I have been following you, whenever I could, since the boy's inquest. I was close behind you in the square and somehow… Damn it, will you believe *now* that you are in danger!"

His hand was upon my shoulder and his cool voice quite returned. "We must get you to a surgeon." He tore off his cravat and wrapped it around the wound in my arm. "I could have prevented this."

A cool voice and cool hands, yet the vengeful look upon his face as he hit out at Lady Anne haunted me. I had not imagined he could feel so strongly. What had caused that rage?

But at that moment I glimpsed movement behind him,

shouted, pulled myself from his hands. Lady Anne had dragged herself up and was stumbling round the corner of the derelict building, back to the Key. I ran after her, heart thumping, head reeling, arm aching abominably. Behind me, Heron cried out.

Round the corner of the printing office I was suddenly in the middle of a gaggle of women, a crowd of whores in ragged gowns with bared breasts and hooked-up skirts showing grimy legs. They pawed at me, dragged at my clothes, tugged at my hair. I yelled, tried to pull away, swung my fist and connected with the face of one of the women. Her head snapped sideways; she crumpled, dragging down her neighbour. I hooked a foot under a dirty ankle and uptipped another, who went down in a flurry of skirts and curses. Heron was close behind me, swinging wildly so that the whores scattered in alarm and we were free and running.

But Lady Anne was nowhere to be seen. Her whores had protected their protectress.

"The house," I yelled as we raced along the Key. "We must get back to the house." That house, and that house alone, could afford us passage back to our own world. If we did not catch Lady Anne, and she *stepped through* to our world, Demsey and Esther Jerdoun were at her mercy.

I came to the Sandhill, glimpsed a movement, glanced up the hill into Butcher Bank. A woman was loading up a cart. I ran up to the cart, snatched up the reins and urged the horse into action. The woman shrieked and the horse damn near bolted. But I got the cart turned and back on to the Sandhill where Heron was waiting. He leapt for the box and clambered up. The cart was filled with offal and stank of blood and urine; livers, hearts and guts spilled from a great pile and hung down behind us.

Pain throbbed in my arm as the horse galloped on; we raced across the Sandhill, scattering a group of drunken sailors. On to the Side, where I flogged the labouring horse mercilessly up the steep road. At St Nicholas's Church, the horse got a second wind and galloped off again. The cart bumped and jolted, throwing us from side to side so that Heron gripped tight hold of the seat.

"We must stop Lady Anne getting back to our world," I shouted. "She will kill Demsey and Mrs Jerdoun."

"I understand none of this!" Heron shouted back. "But I trust your judgment, Patterson."

I hoped he was right to do so. We turned up a new street and only then did I recognise our surroundings. A slow-moving brewer's dray blocked the street halfway down; I vaulted from the cart and ran for the house.

As I came up to the front door, it opened and a gentleman came out. Young, well-dressed, self-assured, laughing at something. Meeting on the doorstep we stared at one another – and I saw my own face, astonished and startled, perhaps even fearful…

Heron seized my arm and pulled me past him, up the steps. We barged into the house, stumbled to a halt in the hallway with servants hurrying forward to intercept us. I raised my voice. "George!"

A distant cry. "The attic, master!"

We ran for the stairs. The servants caught at us. "Get rid of them!" I cried to Heron. He tripped one footman, shouldered another as they seized him. One caught at the skirts of my coat; I swung a fist, pulled free.

I took the stairs two at a time, leaping round the angles in the flights, slipping on the blood that was dripping from my arm, trying to work out where the servants' stair was – for this public stair would certainly not go up to the attics.

Below, I heard shouting and a call for the watch. Had Heron been overcome? I ran on.

George's voice, close by, said, "The second door, master." An elegant sitting room. "Under the picture of the lady." I flung open a door on to the shabby servants' stair.

As I scrambled up the wooden steps, I could hear movement above. George's voice urged me on. "Quick, master, quick!" Up ever narrower stairs. Surely Lady Anne must have gone by now? Why should she delay? A last flight; giddy and exhausted, I fell into a large room, scattered with low beds...

Lady Anne was crouched over a bucket on the floor, spewing out vomit mixed with blood. She stared at me with lips stained scarlet and hands clutching at her stomach. I stumbled to a halt. Claudius Heron had done more damage than he had anticipated, with the nails in that plank he had wielded.

She screeched at me in a spray of blood. "I'll kill you, damn you!"

I glimpsed metal in her hand. That damned knife again. As she lunged at me I snatched at the blanket on the nearest bed, swung it through the air. The knife sliced into it, her hand tangling in the folds. She screamed as I seized her wrist, felt the flesh chill and bloodless, took hold of her other hand to restrain her...

I saw a light in her eyes, an expression in her face. She seemed to dim, to become momentarily translucent. In astonishment, I almost let her go. *She was stepping through.* And then I saw my own hand, stained with blood, begin also to become thin and transparent. I heard George cry out, and Heron too from just behind me, and felt a great dizziness...

I came to myself upon cold damp cobbles. A thin drizzle

dampened my face. Raising myself, I saw with relief the familiar shape of Caroline Square around me, the darkness-shrouded gardens, a thin curve of moon behind the leaves.

Above, on the open door of the house, I saw a sheen of light. George, excitedly calling to the servants within for help.

Upon the doorstep, Claudius Heron sat and stared out into the night.

39
TRIO AFTER THE CONCERT

The clamour of the coffee-house folded around us. Heron sat back in his chair, one arm stretched out to the dish upon the table, his eyes fixed upon the design. He wore still the neat sober clothes he had worn for the inquest when he had sat in charge of the inquiry into the death of Lady Anne, whose fatal injuries he had himself inflicted.

He had looked upon his own handiwork with, as far as I could judge, no emotion, either of horror or remorse. The eight jurymen had heard how Mrs Jerdoun had heard her cousin call out and hurried upstairs to find her dead of... Of what? Claudius Heron had listened to the evidence, persuaded the jury it would be immodest to look upon the body of Lady Anne, informed them there were no visible wounds, suggested to the few witnesses – the cousin, the surgeon, the servants – the word *apoplexy*. And the eight reputable and honest tradesmen had decided that the lady had been struck down by the hand of God.

So the matter was ended. There was nothing to connect Lady Anne's death to the murder of George and the suicide of Le Sac, nor to the attack on Demsey and myself on Gateshead Fell. That had no doubt been the work of unknown criminals, perhaps those who had robbed the postboy, and everyone marvelled at Demsey's luck in surviving so vicious an attack. Lady Anne's death had been bloody, but most of that blood had been shed in that strange other world, and Mrs Jerdoun's discreet maid had dealt with the little that had stained our own world. And if no one knew exactly what had happened to Light-Heels

Nichols after he was seen walking through Amen Corner with Lady Anne – well, there were more important things to be concerned about than the whereabouts of a mere dancing-master, particularly one so universally disliked.

In the clamour of the coffee house, I was still pondering another meeting I had had, only an hour or two earlier, with Mrs Jerdoun. She had drawn me aside after the inquest and to my astonishment, had apologised to me. "I knew my cousin was a scheming woman..."

"You tried to warn me, madam."

"That was not enough," she said. She was dressed in black, as custom demanded on the death of her cousin, but the colour did not suit her; it made her skin seem sallow and her gleaming hair dull.

"I knew," she went on, "or suspected at least, that she had a hand in Le Sac's death. That was why I was at the pond, to see if I could persuade him to talk. And I had some suspicions that she received money from sources she was not willing to reveal, which could only be discreditable." Her eyes met mine steadily. "I could make the excuse, sir, that I had no evidence against her, but in truth I acted from pride, not wishing our family name to be dragged in the mud. And more than that – I have always been a woman to take care of my own business."

"I cannot blame you for keeping silent, madam," I said. "No one would have believed accusations against your cousin."

"Nevertheless," she said, "I should have made the attempt. If I had, Mr Demsey would not have been injured, and – more importantly – your life would not have been endangered."

More importantly? My breath caught in my throat. And we stood looking at each other for a moment in a stillness so complete, so excluding the rest of the world, that I could hardly breathe.

Mrs Jerdoun smiled faintly. "I trust you forgive me, sir?"

I hardly knew what I was saying. "Indeed, madam, I –" I took my courage in both hands. "And I trust, madam, that this wretched business will not give you a distaste for my company?"

She laughed softly. "Oh, no, sir. You may count on that. You will see me again." And she turned and walked away into the last of the crowds dawdling from the inquest.

In the coffee-house I looked at Claudius Heron beside me, still silent, still preoccupied. I said, "I have not yet properly thanked you for your help."

He made a dismissive gesture. "I was singularly inept. I was not there when you were attacked on the fell, nor when the woman trapped you in that house –"

"You were, I think," I interrupted diplomatically, "always suspicious of Lady Anne's activities?"

He flicked a glance at me with his pale eyes. "I knew suicide was a unlikely route for Le Sac to take. When he clashed with Jenison and Ord over that duel, he tried to enlist my help against them. Seeing I was not amenable to flattery, he threatened to invent and spread rumours about the conduct of my financial affairs." He hesitated, added, "And other matters." A glance at me. "I am a widower, Patterson. You understand my meaning."

I nodded. His gaze lingered on me a little longer, with something in it I could not fathom. He looked away, went on. "Le Sac spoke like a man accustomed to blackmail. Moreover, he hinted he could count upon Lady Anne's support, and I had the impression he had some hold over her. Who then was more likely to have a reason to dispose of him? It was obvious that the boy's death was merely a preliminary, the prelude to the real play, so to speak."

"Poor George," I said. At least he was back in his own world again.

Heron shifted uneasily in his chair. "But there was no proof!" he said in some frustration. "And I knew you to be in danger too, particularly after those ruffians attacked you. Lady Anne had plainly used you in her schemings against Le Sac and I suspected she intended somehow to blame you for his death. After the boy's inquest I knew you would be her next target." He flushed. "At least I was able to prevent her killing you. I had no notion, however, of what I would discover in Caroline Square. Or, rather, *out* of it."

We kept silence. Outside the window, the sunshine was flecked with smoke and fragments of soot, and a lady walked past with a kerchief held to her face.

"Patterson." Heron's voice was very still and level. "Are we mad or sane? Did we merely dream?"

I eased my arm within its sleeve, feeling the weight of the bandage upon it.

"No dream, sir. But a great mystery."

"One I hope not to face again," he said. "This *stepping through* she spoke of. Will it happen again, do you think?"

"I think –"

But what did I think? Looking back over the past few hours, it did all indeed begin to seem a dream. Yesterday I stood on the verge of a river in another world, staring at death. Today I sat comfortably in a coffee-house with an agreement to direct the Concerts at the next season, the promise of a higher wage for it and a volume of concerti praised by all knowledgeable lovers of music. (*My* music, attested to by my signature, yet not my own.) Today too I had the smiling half-promise of Esther Jerdoun, and the patronage of Claudius Heron.

"I think," I said, "I shall keep clear of the house in Caroline Square."

New for 2007:

CRÈME DE LA CRIME PERIOD PIECES

GRIPPING DEBUT CRIME FICTION FROM DAYS GONE BY

A new strand from the UK's most innovative crime publisher.

TRUTH DARE KILL

Gordon Ferris

The war's over – but no medals for Danny McRae. Just amnesia and blackouts: twin handicaps for a private investigator with an upper-class client on the hook for murder.

Newspaper headlines about a Soho psychopath stir grisly memories in Danny's fractured mind. As the two bloody sagas collide and interweave, Danny finds himself running for his life across the bomb-ravaged city.

Will his past catch up with him before his enemies? And which would be worse?

Fast-paced post-war noir, with a grimly accurate London setting.

Published May 2007
Price £7.99
ISBN: 978-0-9551589-4-0

THE CRIMSON CAVALIER

Mary Andrea Clarke

Regency London: a dangerous place for an independent, outspoken young woman – especially one with an unusual taste in hobbies.

A prominent unpopular citizen is murdered, apparently by an infamous highwayman known as the Crimson Cavalier. To the chagrin of her self-righteous brother, Georgiana Grey sets out to track down the real culprit.

But her quest for the truth is obstructed on all sides, and soon her own life is at stake.

Published August 2007
Price £7.99
ISBN: 978-0-9551589-5-7

NEW TITLES FOR 2007 FROM OUR BESTSELLING AUTHORS

From ADRIAN MAGSON: a fourth rollercoaster adventure for Riley Gavin and Frank Palmer.

NO TEARS FOR THE LOST

A society wedding…
A crumbling mansion…
A severed finger…

For once, Riley Gavin and Frank Palmer are singing from different hymn books. As bodyguard to former diplomat Sir Kenneth Melrose, it's Frank's job to keep journos like Riley at bay.

But Sir Kenneth's dubious South American past is catching up with him. When he receives a grisly death threat involving his estranged son, the partners-in-crimebusting stop pulling against each other.

Helped by former intelligence officer Jacob Worth, they discover Sir Kenneth has more secrets than the Borgias, and his crumbling country house is shored up by a powder which doesn't come in Blue Circle Cement bags.

Published July 2007
Price £7.99
ISBN: 978-0-9551589-7-1

From MAUREEN CARTER: Birmingham's feistiest detective is finding things tough again.

HARD TIME

An abandoned baby…

A kidnapped five-year-old…

A dead police officer…

And Detective Sergeant Bev Morriss thinks she's having a hard time!

Bev doesn't do fragile and vulnerable, and struggling to cope with the aftermath of a vicious attack, she is desperate not to reveal the lurking self-doubt.

But her lover has decided it's time to move on and the guv is losing patience. And her new partner has the empathy of a house brick. But she can scarcely trust her own judgement, so what's left to rely on?

Just when things can't get any worse, another police officer dies.

And the ransom note arrives.

And hard doesn't begin to cover it.

Published June 2007
Price £7.99
ISBN: 978-0-9551589-6-4

From LINDA REGAN: a sparkling follow-up to *BEHIND YOU!* (ISBN 978-0-95515892-2-6), the sell-out debut from a popular actress turned crime writer.

DI Banham and DS Grainger take a walk on the seedy side of Soho in

PASSION KILLERS

A convicted murderer has recently come out of prison, to the horror of six women who were involved in his crime.

Twenty years ago they were all strippers in a seedy nightclub.

Now some of them have a lot to lose.

Two of the women are found dead – murdered, and each with a red g-string stuffed in her mouth.

Enter D I Paul Banham, ace detective but not so hot when it comes to women. He focuses his enquiries on the surviving women, and finds that no one has a cast-iron alibi.

Everyone is a suspect and everyone is a potential victim.

And Banham is falling in love…

Published September 2007
Price £7.99
ISBN: 978-0-9551589-8-8

MORE TOP TITLES FROM CRÈME DE LA CRIME - AVAILABLE FROM A BOOKSHOP NEAR YOU

From Adrian Magson:

No Peace for the Wicked

Old gangsters never die – they simply get rubbed out. But who is ordering the hits? And why?

Hard-nosed female investigative reporter Riley Gavin is tasked to find out. Her assignment follows a bloody trail from the south coast to the Costa Del Crime as she and ex-military cop Frank Palmer uncover a web of vendettas and double-crosses in an underworld at war with itself.

Suddenly facing a deadline takes on a whole new meaning…

ISBN: 978-0-9547634-2-8 £7.99

No Help for the Dying

Runaway kids are dying on the streets of London. Investigative reporter Riley Gavin and ex military cop Frank Palmer want to know why. They uncover a sub-culture involving a shadowy church, a grieving father and a brutal framework for blackmail, reaching not only into the highest echelons of society, but also into Riley's own past.

ISBN: 978-0-9547634-7-3 £7.99

No Sleep for the Dead

Riley has problems. Her occasional partner-in-crimebusting Frank Palmer has disappeared after a disturbing chance encounter, and she's being followed by a mysterious dreadlocked man.

Frank's determination to pursue justice for an old friend puts him and Riley in deadly danger from art thieves, black gangstas, British Intelligence – and a bitter old woman out for revenge.

ISBN: 978-0-9551589-1-9 £7.99

Gritty and fast-paced detecting of the traditional kind, with a welcome injection of realism. - Maxim Jakubowski, The Guardian

From Maureen Carter:

Working Girls

Fifteen years old, brutalised and dumped, schoolgirl prostitute Michelle Lucas died in agony and terror. The sight breaks the heart of Detective Sergeant Bev Morriss of West Midlands Police, and she struggles to infiltrate the deadly jungle of hookers, pimps and johns who inhabit Birmingham's vice-land. When a second victim dies, she has to take the most dangerous gamble of her life – out on the streets.

ISBN: 978-0-9547634-1-1 £7.99

Dead Old

Elderly women are being attacked by a gang of thugs. When retired doctor Sophia Carrington is murdered, it's assumed she is the gang's latest victim. But Detective Sergeant Bev Morriss is sure the victim's past holds the key to her violent death.

Her new boss won't listen, but when the killer moves uncomfortably close, it's time for Bev to rebel.

ISBN: 978-0-9547634-6-6 £7.99

Baby Love

Rape, baby-snatching, murder: all in a day's work for Birmingham's finest. But she's just moved house, her lover's attention is elsewhere and her last case left her unpopular in the squad room; it's sure to end in tears. Bev Morriss meets trouble when she takes her eye off the ball.

ISBN: 978-0-9551589-0-2 £7.99

Many writers would sell their first born for the ability to create such a distinctive voice in a main character.

- Sharon Wheeler, Reviewing the Evidence

From Penny Deacon: two dark, stunningly original futurecrime chillers

A Kind of Puritan

Would anyone care if a killer was murdering people with no status, no worth to society? Boat-dweller Humility – a low-tech person in a mid-21st century hi-tech world – cares a lot. When she finds a body in the harbour, she is determined to track down the killer. But it puts her in the gravest peril. Soon enmeshed in a deadly maze of sabotage, arson and missing identities, she's struggling to stay alive.

ISBN: 978-0-9547634-1-1 £7.99

A subtle, clever thriller...

- Daily Mail

A Thankless Child

Life gets more dangerous for loner Humility. Her boat is damaged, her niece has run away from the commune, and the man who blames her for his brother's death wants her to investigate a suicide. She's faced with corporate intrigue and girl gangs, and most terrifying of all, she's expected to enjoy the festivities to celebrate the opening of the upmarket new Midway marina complex. Things can only get worse.

ISBN: 978-0-9547634-8-0 £7.99

...moves at a fast, slick pace... a lot of colourful, oddball characters... a page-turner...

- newbooksMag

MORE EXCITING DEBUT CRIME FICTION

IF IT BLEEDS **BERNIE CROSTHWAITE**

Chilling murder mystery with authentic newspaper background.
Pacy, eventful... an excellent debut. -Mystery Women

ISBN: 978-0-9547634-3-5 £7.99

A CERTAIN MALICE **FELICITY YOUNG**

Taut and creepy crime novel with authentic Australian setting.
a beautifully written book... draws you into the life in Australia... you may not want to leave. -Natasha Boyce, bookseller

ISBN: 978-0-9547634-4-2 £7.99

PERSONAL PROTECTION **TRACEY SHELLITO**

Erotic lesbian thriller set in the charged atmosphere of a lapdancing club.
a powerful, edgy story... I didn't want to put down... -Reviewing the Evidence

ISBN: 978-0-9547634-5-9 £7.99

SINS OF THE FATHER **DAVID HARRISON**

Blackmail, revenge, murder and a major insurance scam on the south coast.
... replete with a rich cast of characters and edge-of-the-seat situations where no one is safe... -Mike Howard, Brighton Argus

ISBN: 978-0-9547634-9-7 7.99